PAYBACK

PAYBACK

JONNIE JACOBS

FIVE STAR
A part of Gale, Cengage Learning

GALE
CENGAGE Learning·

Farmington Hills, Mich • San Francisco • New York • Waterville, Maine
Meriden, Conn • Mason, Ohio • Chicago

GALE
CENGAGE Learning

LIBRARY OF CONGRESS CATALOGING-IN-PUBLICATION DATA

Jacobs, Jonnie.
    Payback / Jonnie Jacobs. — First edition.
      pages ; cm
    ISBN 978-1-4328-3112-7 (hardcover) — ISBN 1-4328-3112-7 (hardcover)
      1. Married women—Fiction. 2. Adultery—Fiction. 3. Man-woman relationships—Fiction. 4. Stalkers—Fiction. I. Title.
    PS3560.A2543P39 2015
    813'.54—dc23   2015008360

First Edition. First Printing: September 2015
Find us on Facebook– https://www.facebook.com/FiveStarCengage
Visit our website– http://www.gale.cengage.com/fivestar/
Contact Five Star™ Publishing at FiveStar@cengage.com

Printed in the United States of America
1 2 3 4 5 6 7 19 18 17 16 15

ACKNOWLEDGMENTS

My heartfelt thanks to Rita Lakin, Margaret Lucke, and Camille Minichino for their feedback and suggestions in the writing of this book. They are not only a wonderful critique group, but great friends and a lot of fun.

CHAPTER 1

Marta knew her presentation was going to be a disaster the moment she stepped to the front of the conference room. Right off the bat she stumbled, and her subsequent attempts at wit fell like lead weights on crystal. It became increasingly clear that the bleary-eyed corporate drones she was addressing didn't share her vision for their project, or her sense of humor. She forced herself to speak slowly, fighting her natural inclination to rush her words. The proposal was well organized and understandable, yet she sensed herself treading water against a tide of disinterest. And she had no idea how to turn it around.

Marketing wasn't her usual role. Marta was the nuts-and-bolts side of the partnership. It was Carol who was the saleswoman and rainmaker. Carol was naturally gregarious. She connected with people in a way Marta envied but had never mastered. It was Carol who'd prepared the presentation. Carol who was supposed to be making the pitch. But she'd woken the morning of the trip with a one-hundred-and-three-degree temperature and a stomach that would tolerate nothing but small sips of water. Dropping the presentation in Marta's lap at the last minute was hardly her fault. Nonetheless, as Marta concluded her remarks and opened the floor to questions, she couldn't help feeling annoyed.

The silence that filled the room was deafening. Marta forced a brave smile. She hadn't dared focus on individual faces during her talk for fear of losing what little confidence she had left, but

7

now she let her gaze sweep over the small group seated before her. A ruddy-faced man in the second row was whispering to the woman on his left, but most of the audience had already turned to scanning messages on their cell phones. Marta was vaguely aware of an attractive man at the back of the room who watched her with a smile. She could only conclude it was a smile of pity.

She gathered her notes. "Thank you for giving me the opportunity to lay out the benefits of choosing C&M Advantage for your public relations and communications needs. If you have further questions, please don't hesitate to call us."

Further questions indeed. There hadn't been a flicker of interest the entire time. Marta made her way to the exit, grateful that no one tried to engage her in conversation along the way. In the hall, she picked up her pace, mentally shaking off the bored and disdainful expressions that had sucked the air from her lungs for the past half-hour.

Thank God it was over.

The hotel elevator took an eternity to arrive, and Marta then endured half a dozen stops before finally reaching her own floor. When she slid her key card into the slot on the door and the lock failed to flash green, she cursed under her breath. She felt like screaming and kicking the door as hard as she could.

All in all, it had been a bad day.

A terrible, horrible, very bad day, to quote from the book that had been one of her daughter's childhood favorites.

What a way to spend her fortieth birthday!

Farther down the hallway, two younger women exited a room. They were wearing exercise clothes that fit their athletic bodies like a second skin, and they walked jauntily past Marta, ponytails bouncing, without so much as a glance in her direction.

Just wait, Marta admonished them silently. *This isn't the life I envisioned twenty years ago, either.*

Marta sighed and neither kicked nor screamed—drama was decidedly not part of her makeup. Instead, she set her briefcase and purse carefully at her feet and tried the card a second time, sliding it in and out of the slot with the care of a lock pick. The light switched to green, and Marta dragged herself into the stuffy, overly warm room. If the windows had been operable, she'd have thrown them open and let in the cold evening air. But the windows were sealed, like the entire hotel. Like, it sometimes seemed to Marta, her own life.

She kicked off her shoes and sat on the edge of the king-size bed. It was her birthday, dammit. And here she was stuck in a bland hotel room, a thousand miles from home. For what? Had she and Carol actually thought they might have a chance to land the Century Solar account? Or any national account?

The sad part was, they had.

Sure, the companies at the conference represented a stretch for them, but they were confident they could deliver. Weren't the Pollyanna pundits of personal growth always advising people to dream big and believe in yourself?

What a crock. What she needed was a magic wand.

And she had lost hers a long time ago. She wanted to dig a hole, crawl in, and stay there forever. Or better yet, set sail for some uninhabited tropical island. At the very least, she wanted to expunge the entire day—the entire year really—from memory.

She flopped back onto the bed, where the soft comforter cushioned her like a fluffy white cloud, and closed her eyes. Feeling sorry for herself wasn't going to change anything. Besides, she thought, mimicking her mother's stern tone, she had responsibilities.

For better or worse, her mother's words had shaped Marta's life. Level-headed and dependable, conscientious and sensible—not traits she necessarily aspired to, but she was who she was.

Wife, mother, and struggling entrepreneur. Someone who could be counted on to steer a safe course whatever the waters.

The ping of her cell phone announced a new text. She rolled over to read it.

Happy Birthday. The evening is young—kick up your heels and have some fun.

Love you,

Cassie

At least her sister was sober enough this year to remember her birthday. And a text from Cassie was often more gratifying than a phone call. Actual conversations between the two of them had a way of going downhill fast.

Marta checked the time. It was already six o'clock in Georgia. Jamie should have been home from school an hour or so ago, but she hadn't yet called, as she was supposed to. Now that her daughter was driving, Marta worried more than ever, especially when she was out of town and unable to monitor Jamie's comings and goings. What if she'd had car trouble? Or an accident? Or, God forbid, done something really stupid, as teenagers were apt to do?

The wise course would be to hold off calling. Give Jamie a chance to call and check in, as they'd agreed. But a niggle of worry had already lodged itself in Marta's chest. After a day that left her feeling wounded and raw, she needed a touch of the familiar. She wanted to hear her daughter's voice, and to know that she was safe.

Jamie answered on the fifth ring, just before the call rolled into voice mail. "Hi, Mom." She sounded breathless.

"Hi, honey. Where are you?"

"Home. Where'd you think I'd be?"

"Home."

"Then why'd you ask?"

Because the phone rang five times before you answered and you

10

sound out of breath. Because even though I shouldn't, I worry. But Marta bit her tongue. "How was your day?"

"Okay. How was yours?

"Pretty lousy, actually."

"That sucks. Do you know we're out of toilet paper?"

Had she actually expected sympathy? Or a happy birthday? At least she'd scored big time with the touch of familiar. "No, I didn't know, but I left money for groceries and stuff."

"I haven't really had time."

"Maybe you could get your dad to go. Is he home?"

"In the garage, where else?"

Gordon was refurbishing a 1967 Mustang—an undertaking he approached with an inexplicable determination, given that he wasn't at all mechanical. Marta suspected the appeal lay largely in the fact that it was an excuse to retreat, alone, to the garage.

"You want me to get him?" Jamie asked.

Remembering the argument they'd had the morning she left, Marta thought it better not to disturb him. "Just tell him I called, will you?"

"Yeah, sure."

"Is Alyssa still coming to spend the night?"

"Not really."

"Not really?"

"She got invited to a party."

And Jamie obviously hadn't. "It must have been last minute. Maybe you'll still get invited, too."

"You're clueless, Mom."

"I'm—"

"I know, you're the best mother I have." It was an old joke but Jamie no longer laughed at it the way she used to. "I gotta go. See you tomorrow."

★ ★ ★ ★ ★

Despite having skipped lunch, Marta wasn't hungry, but she could most certainly use a glass of wine. Or two. She eyed the room's minibar, then decided to take Cassie's words to heart. Fun was out of the question, and she couldn't remember the last time she'd kicked up her heels, but she deserved more than a plastic water glass of cheap wine in a dreary hotel room.

No way, though, was she going to take the chance of running into someone from today's fiasco. Rather than head for the hotel bar downstairs, she bundled up and walked two blocks to the Sheraton.

The bitter night air stung her face, and already the predicted snow had begun to fall, not softly like in a Currier and Ives painting, but with the sharpness of icy needles. Marta crossed her arms, lowered her head, and pushed on against a fierce wind. She was not going to spend her fortieth birthday feeling sorry for herself!

The bar in the Sheraton was hopping with activity, and Marta thought about abandoning her plan until she spotted an empty booth toward the back. She made a beeline to grab it before someone else did. She scanned the wine-by-the-glass list, then contemplated the menu of specialty drinks propped on the table in front of her.

Wine was such a predictable choice for her. Chardonnay or Zinfandel, depending on the time of day and her mood. A pleasant enough routine, but a rut all the same. She was turning into her mother, Marta thought with sudden horror. Habit as a substitute for living. Before she knew it she'd be wearing her glasses on a chain around her neck and making orange Jell-O with marshmallows, calling it salad.

Marta pushed the wine list aside and ordered a Pink Moose instead. She had no idea what it was, but the name appealed to her and it was made with rum, which she liked. Her phone buzzed in her purse. She checked caller ID, hoping it was Gordon, coming out of his mechanic's lair long enough to ask about her day and wish her a happy birthday. But it was Carol.

"How'd it go?" she asked.

"We're not going to get the Century Solar contact. Or anything else."

"I should have been there. I feel bad foisting it off on you at the last minute."

"There'll be other opportunities. How are you feeling?"

"The worst of it is over, I think. I hope you don't catch it. What a birthday present that would be. Happy B-day, by the way. I'm sorry you have to spend it on the road."

"I doubt it would be champagne and cake even if I was home."

"Why do you say that?"

"Gordon is miffed at me for suggesting he attend a neighborhood cocktail party without me. We'd already accepted, and it was a farewell for a couple who are moving. But you know Gordon. I had to practically twist his arm to get him to agree to go in the first place, and then when I wasn't going to be there—"

"My fault. I'm really sorry."

"Don't worry, Carol. It's not a big deal. Gordon would thank you, in fact." Always a bit reserved, her husband had pulled even further into his shell since losing his job at Tufts a year and a half ago.

Being let go was not the same as being fired, Marta had reminded him more than once. Especially for an untenured professor. But they both knew that the sexual harassment allegations Gordon faced were the real reason he'd lost his job.

"It's the bigger things that are important in a marriage anyway," Carol reminded her. "And Gordon is a good man."

"You're right, he is." It was just that lately good didn't feel like enough. Marta sometimes wondered how the attractive, fun-loving guy she'd married eighteen years ago had morphed into a humorless wet noodle.

The waitress brought Marta's Pink Moose—a tall, frothy drink with a spear of pineapple. Marta considered moose and pineapple an odd pairing. Shouldn't a drink with pineapple be called a Pink Palm or a Hawaiian Sunset? But then, what would go with moose? The more she thought about it, the more certain she became that it was a question better left unanswered.

"You ever heard of a Pink Moose?" Marta asked Carol.

"A dessert or the kind with antlers?"

"It's a bar drink. And I just ordered one."

"You? I thought you were a wine kind of girl."

"I am. Or I was until tonight." Marta swizzled the pineapple spear and discovered a maraschino cherry at the bottom of the glass. "I should let you go. Talk to you when I get home."

Two-thirds of the way through her drink, she became aware of someone standing nearby. She looked up and into the eyes of a tall, athletically built man, considerably younger than her, dressed in dark slacks and a light blue shirt, open at the collar.

"This place is packed, isn't it?" he noted wryly.

Marta nodded. He had the most amazing blue eyes she'd ever seen. They were almost teal with flecks of amber, and set off with laugh lines at the corners.

He nodded at the largely empty booth. "Would it be okay if I joined you?"

"I . . . I, um . . ." She felt an inexplicable flutter in her chest. "I'm not very good company, I'm afraid."

"Your company has got to be preferable to spending time with myself." He slid into booth across from her, signaled for the waitress, and ordered a double scotch for himself. "And she'll have another of whatever that is."

"A Pink Moose," Marta told him.

"Never heard of it."

Marta laughed. "Me either. I think it's a house specialty."
"Any good?"

"Yeah, actually it is. I usually stick to wine but this is . . . tasty. Want to try it?"

The words were out of Marta's mouth before she realized it. What was she doing offering a sip of her drink to a total stranger? It must have been a much stiffer drink than she'd imagined.

The man raised his eyebrows and smiled. And then took a slow sip of her Pink Moose.

"I'm Todd," he said, extending a hand.

She returned the smile and tried to ignore the roller-coaster sensation in her stomach. "Marta."

CHAPTER 2

Jamie hadn't been totally honest with her mother. She'd been careful not to tell an outright lie. And she wasn't doing anything really sneaky, either. She intended to tell her dad where she was going, and she'd make sure to be home by curfew. Her dad wouldn't press for details like her mom would, and his mouth wouldn't get all tight with disapproval when she said she was going to the movies with Harmony Shaw. Her dad wouldn't care, but her mom didn't like Harmony.

Jamie didn't actually like Harmony either. It was hard to like someone so stuck on herself. But Harmony was pretty and popular and way cooler than anyone else Jamie knew. Being around Harmony was an adventure. Not that Jamie had much opportunity to hang out with her. In fact, if they hadn't both gone to the same dopey summer camp last year, Harmony wouldn't even know Jamie's name. She'd actually been surprised when Harmony called. All her real friends must have been busy. Whatever the reason, Jamie was excited.

She tried on four pairs of pants before settling on the blue cargo pants that camouflaged the extra weight she'd been fighting for as long as she could remember.

"You've got curves," her mother always told her. But Jamie knew better. She had flab.

The place she wasn't curvy was up top, where she actually wanted to be. She chose a yellow blouse with smocking along the neckline that made her breasts look fuller than they were.

She took one last look in the mirror, grabbed her purse, and went to the garage to tell her father she was going out.

"I thought Alyssa was coming here for the night," he said, his voice muffled from under the old Mustang.

"She couldn't make it, so I'm going to the movies with another friend."

He scooted out from under the car and gave her his all-purpose smile. "Have fun, Toots."

Jamie hated the nickname, but complaining just made him use it more often. He thought he was being funny.

Jamie drove the short distance to Harmony's house, parked in front, and waited for her friend to show. After five minutes she texted, "I'm here."

A few minutes later, Harmony bounded down the stairs, her sleek blond hair swinging around her shoulders. Her mother stood at the door and waved to Jamie, as though she and Harmony were best friends.

"Let's go," Harmony announced.

As soon as they rounded the corner, Harmony unbuckled her seat belt and pulled her sweatshirt over her head. Underneath, she was wearing a low cut and very tight pink T-shirt with rhinestone trim. Next, she reached for her backpack, pulled out a pair of stretchy black pants, and unzipped her jeans.

"What are you doing?" Jamie squealed. "Buckle your seat belt."

"I'm changing clothes. It won't take long. Just don't hit anything."

Jamie had already slowed down. She was terrified of being in a car without her seat belt buckled. Her parents had drilled that into her head from as far back as she could remember. And she was equally terrified of driving a car with an unbuckled passenger.

"Turn here," Harmony said suddenly.

17

"That's not the way. The theater is downtown."

"The movie was just an excuse."

"An excuse?"

"I needed cover to get out of the house. My parents are like in major crackdown mode. And TJ is totally off limits right now."

It took Jamie a few seconds to process Harmony's words, and another few to ponder their meaning. "Who's TJ?" she asked finally.

"He graduated our freshman year. You probably don't remember him. We hooked up a few months ago."

Jamie was slowly getting the picture. "So we're not going to the movies? We're meeting TJ instead?" She wasn't sure if she was disappointed or just nervous. She hoped TJ was bringing along a friend for her.

Harmony laughed. "Not us, silly. Me. You can just drop me off at his place. If my mom calls be sure to act like I'm with you though. Okay?"

"Wait. What about me?"

Harmony brushed the air with her hand. "Go to the movie, if you want. You can fill me in later. It's probably better if we can talk about it like we've seen it. But you need to pick me up before eleven. Parental crackdown mode includes clocking in by eleven."

Jamie was speechless. Finally, she asked, "Can't TJ drive you home?"

"He doesn't have a car. Besides, my parents think I'm with you."

"So I'm just your chauffeur?"

"You're my cover story." She turned toward Jamie and gave her a pleading look. "You're the only one I can count on."

"I—"

"And my mother likes you."

18

"Your mother doesn't even know me."

"She's met you." Harmony crammed her jeans into her backpack and tossed it into the back seat. "Pull over there on the right. That green apartment house."

Jamie had barely slowed to a stop when Harmony opened the car door. "Before eleven," she reminded Jamie. "I'll text you." She jumped out of the car and turned to close the door. "By the way, lose those pants. They make you look like a hippo."

Jamie couldn't believe what had just happened. A slap in the face would have been less painful. She was used to being snubbed, but never so obviously. She wanted to go home, hide in her room, and let Harmony deal with the fallout. But she knew in the end, that would be worse. She wasn't sure how, but Harmony would find a way to make sure it was.

Far better to have Harmony as a friend than an enemy.

But what to do now? No way was Jamie going to the movie by herself. There was no fun in that, and she didn't care about the stupid movie, anyway. What she'd been looking forward to was hanging out with Harmony. Besides, she'd die if she ran into someone from school. She could just imagine the talk— poor, fat Jamie, so pathetic she has to go to movies alone. The movie was not an option. Instead, Jamie headed for the big Barnes and Noble in the mall. It was one of her favorite places to spend time. And she certainly wouldn't run into anyone from school there on a Friday night.

CHAPTER 3

Marta awoke to the heat of bare flesh and the contours of an unfamiliar body next to hers. An arm that was definitely not her husband's was draped casually across her middle. The gray light of early morning was beginning to seep around the curtains and into the room, also unfamiliar. Outside, it was snowing.

In a flash, the dreamy warmth of half-sleep was shattered by the stark reality of where she was and what she'd done. Marta was appalled.

What had she been thinking?

Next to her, Todd—that was his name, wasn't it?—stirred in his sleep and nuzzled closer. Marta struggled against a suffocating tide of shame and guilt, a torrent that grew stronger as her memory of the night unfolded in her mind. The easy conversation, the laughter, the tantalizing brush of a hand across the back of her neck. The sense that right then, right there, the world was a perfect fit.

One drink had led to another, and then to a light dinner of bar appetizers, more drinks, and caresses that strayed below her neck. The path of events that had landed her in Todd's hotel room, in his bed, was less clear, but she had no trouble remembering what had happened once they were there. In spite of her shame, Marta experienced a pleasurable rush at the memory. She allowed herself a brief, voyeuristic replay—Todd's taut body pressed against hers, his hot breath in her ear, the caresses of his fingers on her belly, the urgency of unbridled passion.

A terrible mistake, but a guilty pleasure, too.

She stole a look at him as he slept. One last look, before she fled.

God, he was good-looking. More so this morning, in fact, wrapped as he was in the vulnerability of slumber. She would have loved to touch him, to brush her fingers across his lips, cementing their softness to tactile memory. But she didn't dare, and not only because she was afraid of waking him. She was afraid, too, of her own reaction.

Carefully, so as not to disturb him, she pulled away and slid to her side of the bed. She needed to leave now, before he woke up. Before they faced "the morning after."

She had just folded back the sheet, ever so slightly, when Todd reached for her, traced a finger down her hip, and pulled her close.

"Don't," she said, then softened the remark because in truth, she had no reason to be angry with anyone but herself. "I can't. I have a plane to catch."

"Can't you reschedule?"

Marta shook her head. "I need to get home."

"Nobody has to be anywhere on a Saturday."

"I do."

Todd propped himself up on one arm, shaking his head to clear it. "I'll drive you to the airport, then."

"It will be easier if you don't. I have to shower, pack, check out of my hotel." She kissed his cheek lightly, the way she might an old uncle. "Really, it's better this way."

Todd rolled onto his back, arms under the pillow at his head. He watched as Marta gathered her clothes from the floor where she'd tossed them last night. In the bathroom, she rinsed her mouth with the mouthwash she found in the hotel vanity tray

21

and dressed quickly. She prayed she wouldn't run into anyone from yesterday's meeting before she was safely back in her own hotel room.

"I wish you wouldn't run off," he said when she emerged fully clothed, if rumpled. "Speaking for myself, I found last night pretty fantastic."

It had been, but Marta kept that thought to herself.

"It's not you," she explained, standing at the foot of the bed where Todd was watching with a smile on his lips. "It's me. Last night was a mistake. I don't do things like this."

The smile deepened. "You just did."

Marta took a cab back to her hotel, keenly aware of the knowing smirk on the driver's face. A disheveled woman leaving one hotel in the early morning hours to go to another. Did he think she was a call girl or just some needy woman desperate for a good time?

Back in her own room, Marta quickly showered and packed her bag, then remembered to check her cell phone for messages. Nothing from Gordon. No messages at all.

On her way to the airport, thankfully with a different cab driver, she watched the snow come down in big, thick flakes and tried to eradicate the memory of the previous night from her mind. She would simply pretend it hadn't happened. If she could make herself believe that, then maybe everything would be okay.

The line at the check-in counter was long and moved slowly. Marta joined the column of travelers snaking their way to the front. Finally, the ticket agent checked her bag.

"Your flight is delayed because of the weather," he announced.

"Delayed?" Marta experienced a swell of panic. "For how long?"

"A couple of hours at least. Be sure to watch the monitor for updates."

"But—"

"Mother Nature at work. There's nothing we can do about it."

Boarding pass in hand, Marta turned and began walking aimlessly toward the gate, almost colliding with a man rushing toward her.

"Good. I got here in time," Todd said. His face glowed with undisguised pleasure.

Recognition hit Marta like a fist to her chest. "What are you doing here?"

"I looked online and saw that your plane was delayed. I should have checked before you ran off this morning. There was no need for you to rush, after all."

No need maybe, but Marta knew it was better that she had. "How'd you know what plane I'd be on?"

"Morning flight to Atlanta. There are a limited number of options." The corners of his blue eyes crinkled as he reached for her carry-on. "You had breakfast yet?"

CHAPTER 4

"You need more than coffee," Todd announced after they'd settled at a table in the small Starbucks outside of security. "Remember, they don't feed you on planes anymore."

"Coffee's fine." Marta had reluctantly agreed to this much after brushing aside his suggestion that she forget the flight altogether and spend the day with him. She figured she owed Todd an explanation. And she did have several hours to kill.

He broke off half his scone and offered it to her.

She shook her head, shaken by how attractive she found him. Her whole body felt electrified.

"You're not one of those women who's always dieting, are you?"

"Hardly."

"Good. You're beautiful and sexy just the way you are."

No doubt a line he used at every opportunity. Even so, she felt another feather-like tickle in her chest.

"There's something I need to tell you," she said, and took a deep breath. Say it, she told herself. Right now, before things go any further.

She looked up. "I'm married."

"I guessed as much."

It wasn't the reaction she expected. "You did?"

His blue eyes crinkled. "You're wearing a wedding ring."

Marta quickly tucked her left hand into her lap. The ring was so much a part of her she'd forgotten she wore it.

"So you can see that last night was a mistake," she said. "A huge mistake on my part."

Todd sucked on his cheek a moment. "There's married, and then there's married," he said.

He looked her in the eye, waiting to see if she'd clarify what was true in her case.

But Marta was no longer sure.

Until last night, she'd have responded without a second thought. She was married, end of story. But did a truly committed wife succumb to temptation as easily as she had? Did a loving wife melt around another man?

Todd smiled. He had a gorgeous smile that lit up his whole face. "It's complicated, isn't it?"

She wasn't about to discuss Gordon or her marriage. She'd betrayed both enough already. "What about you?"

"Not married. Never have been."

"A confirmed bachelor, then?" It came out like she was teasing him, which hadn't been her intention.

"Not at all. I've just never met the right woman."

"There's plenty of time still. How old are you? Thirty?"

"Thirty-seven."

"No way." He looked much younger. "Still, I've got several years on you."

"Hard to believe. You look fantastic."

Marta felt herself blush.

"Really, you do." His blue eyes found hers. "I find most younger women uninteresting anyway."

Another line. He was good at them. "Why did you come to the airport this morning?" she asked.

Todd thought about it before answering. "Last night was . . . it was amazing," he said finally. "I know it sounds hokey, but it was. I've never met anyone like you. Funny, irreverent, and yet sweet, too." He winked. "And really good in bed."

He was a smooth talker, and full of bullshit. But Marta's skin tingled all the same.

"What does your husband do?" Todd asked.

"He teaches at Howell College. American history."

"Impressive."

Marta couldn't tell if he was being sarcastic or serious. Howell was hardly a world-class institution.

"Tell me about your daughter," Todd said, leaning forward.

"How did you know I have a daughter?"

"You mentioned her last night."

"I did?"

He nodded. "Jamie, right? Any other kids?"

Marta actually remembered very little about last night. She wondered what else she'd told him.

"No other children." The personal questions made her uncomfortable. She turned the focus back on Todd. "Do you travel a lot on business?"

"More than I'd like. But that's the nature of consulting."

He told her about his job, which he enjoyed despite the travel, about his sister in Portland who raised Great Danes, his apartment in Chicago overlooking Lake Michigan that was still mostly unfurnished even after two years. The conversation flowed easily, as did the laughter. Marta nibbled on Todd's scone and then finished it off.

Finally, she realized that nearly two hours had passed and she still needed to get through security.

Todd walked her to the end of the long line of passengers waiting to be screened.

Marta held out her hand. "Good-bye, then."

"I'll call you."

"No. Please don't. It's been an experience I won't forget. A very nice one, I'll admit. But it can't go any further."

Taking her hand, he pulled her toward him. Marta turned

26

her head for a peck on the cheek, but Todd found her mouth. The kiss was long and deep, and left Marta both breathless and embarrassed.

"Have a safe trip," he said, and gave her a playful pat on the rump.

The plane was taxiing down the runway for takeoff when Marta was hit with a frightening thought. What if Todd was a terrorist or a drug runner and had managed to slip contraband into her bag? It was a ridiculous notion and she laughed at the absurdity of it. Was she so unaccustomed to male attention that she could only surmise there must be an ulterior motive?

Once the plane was airborne, she adjusted her seat, reclining it back just a little so as not to intrude on the passenger behind her, and drifted into a dreamy half-sleep. Miles above the earth, with Todd safely in her past, she allowed herself to indulge in one last memory of her Cinderella moment.

When the plane touched down in Atlanta, Marta shook her mind clear and slipped into the familiar role of wife, mother, and businesswoman.

Turning on her phone, she was instantly greeted with the ding of incoming texts. Three of them. All from Todd.

Miss you already.

Miss you still.

Miss you even more.

It wasn't until half an hour later, waiting at the carousel for her bag, that she thought to wonder how Todd had known her number.

Jamie wasn't an early riser, especially on weekends, but this morning she found it harder than usual to pull herself from her bed. The humiliation of being used by Harmony last night was bound to be worse in the glare of morning. Hopefully, Harmony wouldn't blab about it to her friends.

She clomped downstairs as noisily as possible. Somehow that made her feel a little better. She stopped short when she saw the bouquet of balloons in the kitchen.

"What's this?" she asked her dad, half afraid he'd found out what had happened and was trying to cheer her up.

"Your mom's coming home today. It's her birthday."

"Her birthday was yesterday." A fact that Jamie had overlooked in her eagerness to see Harmony. She felt bad about it, but her mom wasn't a kid anymore so it wasn't exactly a big deal.

Her dad looked confused, like he was making a mental calculation in his head. "Well, she's home today so we'll celebrate today."

Jamie noticed that her father had bought flowers, too. Carnations, which her mother hated. Her dad has never been good with details.

"I didn't get her anything," Jamie said.

"Make her a card, why don't you. It's the thought that counts."

Even if the thought is a day late? Again, she felt a stab of guilt. But she toasted a bagel and dutifully returned to her bedroom to make a card.

If only she'd known her father was planning a celebration, but he probably hadn't planned it. He rarely planned anything. Once he got a bee in his bonnet about something, though, he jumped right in.

It had been years since Jamie made either parent a card, and she felt silly doing so now. What was there to say besides Happy Birthday? Or more accurately, Happy Belated Birthday.

She wished she'd thought to do something earlier when she would have had time to get her mom a present. She considered dashing out right now but she had no idea what to buy. Simpler to just make the stupid card.

CHAPTER 5

The closer Marta got to home, the more slowly she drove. But there was only so long she could avoid the inevitable necessity of facing Gordon and confronting the life she'd left behind three days earlier. There was no logic to the hesitation she felt. It wasn't as though she had a scarlet *A* emblazoned on her chest, after all. And not a single paparazzi camera had flashed in her face the entire time she had been in Minneapolis. So why was she feeling so exposed?

She took a deep breath when she finally pulled into the driveway. With luck, she'd slip seamlessly back into her old, heretofore comfortable, skin, and that would be the end of it.

Gordon greeted her with a kiss. "Welcome back," he said. "How was the trip? You must have gone nuts waiting in the airport for what, three hours?"

"It wasn't so bad," Marta mumbled. "There were lots of us in the same predicament."

"But a major snowstorm this late in April . . . nobody expects that."

Jamie shuffled down the stairs. "Hey, you're home."

"And very glad of it," Marta said and laughed. So far, so good. This was a scenario that had played out countless times before. Maybe she could handle this homecoming thing, after all.

But when she entered the kitchen and saw a large, airborne bouquet of colorful balloons she knew it wouldn't be easy.

In the center of the table sat a sparkling glass vase filled with red carnations. Not flowers she was particularly fond of and not a color she liked, but flowers all the same.

"Happy birthday," Gordon said jauntily. "I got a cake, too."

"Yeah, happy birthday, Mom. Even if it is a day late. I'm sorry I forgot yesterday."

Guilt rolled over Marta, sucking the air from her lungs. What would they think if they knew what she'd done?

Jamie handed her a birthday card. It was homemade, with glitter and sparkles, and the message was carefully penned in assorted bright colors.

Happy Birthday to the best mother I have (or could ever have).

Marta felt her eyes grow moist. "This is wonderful. Thank you so much."

She was sure God was toying with her.

Later in the evening, as they were getting ready for bed, Gordon circled an arm around her. "I'm glad you're home," he said.

"I'm glad too."

"I'm sorry your presentation didn't go well."

"It couldn't have gone much worse."

"You hardly had any time to prepare," he reminded her. He rubbed her back, tracing a circle between her shoulder blades.

"It wasn't that. I'm just no good at speaking in front of a group. And I hate it." To Marta's surprise, her voice choked with emotion and she felt her throat grow tight. She was an emotional time bomb, but she was fairly sure it wasn't the presentation that had her on edge.

"Speaking of large groups, I may be giving my paper on the economics of American Colonialism at the History and Humanities conference this summer. I just got word yesterday." He was beaming.

"That's wonderful." It had been a long time since Marta had seen him this animated. She gave him a celebratory kiss. "Congratulations."

"The paper needs revising and I'll have to work up a talk around it, but it's a great opportunity."

Marta was relieved to move the focus of their conversation away from her trip. The less said about her time in Minneapolis, the better. And she was truly happy for Gordon. The loss of his job and the precipitating sexual harassment talk had been a huge blow to his self-esteem.

A female undergraduate had accused Gordon of making lewd and suggestive remarks about her appearance and, on two occasions, touching her breasts. Gordon adamantly denied it, countering that she'd propositioned him in an effort to raise her grade from a C to an A.

The university had procedures for handling this sort of thing, and probably nothing more would have come of it if the girl's father had not been an alumnus and major donor to the school. When a second woman came forward with a similar story, the department took the easy way out and declined to renew his appointment. The fact that the two accusing women were close friends didn't sway them.

Marta had doubted her husband only for the briefest of moments. Gordon might well have said something the woman found insulting, if only because he was so socially clueless, but she couldn't imagine him being forward enough to touch her, even if he'd wanted to. Her belief in him hadn't been enough, however, to keep him from feeling like a failure.

He'd hoped to move to a more prestigious college than Howell. But after an exhaustive and disappointing job search, he claimed to be relieved to be at a school where he could concentrate on teaching without as much pressure to publish. After the vote last fall to put his tenure on hold, however, he'd become increasingly withdrawn.

"It's not only a great opportunity," she said, "it's a real feather in your cap. I'm proud of you."

Gordon climbed under the covers and patted Marta's side of the bed. "It was lonely without you here," he said.

Marta froze.

Gordon was a kind and caring husband. And while he might have annoying idiosyncrasies, she was sure she loved him.

But she wasn't in the mood for sex.

"I'm tired," she said, slipping between the sheets with her back toward her husband. "I really just want to sleep."

He kissed her neck. "You sure I can't change your mind?"

"Not tonight. I'm sorry."

She would have liked to snuggle closer for warmth and comfort, but it wasn't fair to send a mixed message, which was how Gordon would see it. She hoped he might sense her need, but he didn't. He sighed and turned his back on her.

"See you in the morning," he said.

Marta wanted to sleep, but she couldn't. Less than twenty-four hours ago she'd been in bed with a man who wasn't her husband. A man she barely knew. She was disgusted with herself, and at the same time, her skin tingled at the memory. She wondered what might have happened if she hadn't been married, or if she was the type of woman for whom marriage made no difference. She let her mind drift for awhile, following a fantasy of romance and adventure with Todd, a dream-vision of soul-mate fulfillment.

Gordon's snores reached a fevered pitch. Marta turned onto her back and poked him lightly in the ribs. The snores subsided.

There had been a time when Marta fantasized about Gordon, too.

They'd met when he was a graduate student and she a mere sophomore. He had substituted one day for the regular T.A.

who led her discussion group, and Marta was immediately smitten. The vision of his lean body, his quirky smile, the lock of unruly hair that fell over his dark eyes was seared into her brain. He was all she could think about. When she ran into him in the library several weeks later and he actually remembered her, she had already conducted such a torrid romance with him in her mind that she was tongue-tied. Even after they'd been dating long enough to be considered "in a relationship," the sight of Gordon striding across campus in her direction sent her heart into orbit.

She couldn't remember when he'd ceased to fuel her romantic fantasies. She was sure, though, that what had happened in Minneapolis was less about Gordon than about her.

Sunday morning Marta made a family breakfast, something she hadn't done in months. Thick, hickory-smoked bacon, a mushroom and cheese omelet, and blueberry pancakes. While she was waiting for the coffee to finish dripping, she checked her phone for messages. Nothing more from Todd. She felt oddly let down.

Slipping her phone back into her pocket, Marta finished setting the table, which looked festive with the vase of birthday flowers at the center, even if they were red carnations.

"The flowers make the table look cheerful," she told Gordon, touched by his effort to celebrate her birthday.

He looked up from the morning paper. "Glad you like them."

When Jamie bounced downstairs moments later, he set the newspaper aside and filled his plate, as did Jamie. Marta took a small serving of omelet. She wasn't at all hungry.

"So what did you two do while I was away? Anything exciting?"

Gordon looked up from the comics page, which he'd been pretending to ignore while they ate. "Nothing exciting for me.

34

Jamie went out with a friend Friday night."

"Really?" It was good to hear that Jamie's social circle was larger than just Alyssa. Marta turned to her daughter. "Who'd you go with?"

"Harmony Shaw." Jamie's voice was so soft Marta could barely hear her.

"That's nice." Marta tried to keep her response neutral. "I didn't know you and Harmony were such good friends."

"We're not really. We just went to a movie."

Harmony was the kind of girl Marta's mother used to call fast. The kind of girl who today might be called a skank. That was Marta's opinion, and not one shared by Jamie.

But today especially, she wasn't in a position to criticize. "What movie did you see?"

"The new Ryan Gosling movie."

"How was it?"

Jamie shrugged. "Okay."

Marta hadn't seen the movie, but she'd read the reviews, which were all over the map. "What did you think of the ending? Isn't there some big twist?"

It was Jamie's hesitation and the flicker of nervousness in her expression that made Marta think there was more to the evening than just the movie. She felt the familiar clench of maternal fear. Jamie was hiding something.

But really, could Jamie have done anything worse than what she herself had done? Marta was in no position to be judgmental.

CHAPTER 6

Marta was at her desk Monday morning when Carol swept into the tiny offices of C&M Advantage, bearing two takeout cups from The Daily Joe across the street. She set her briefcase on her own desk and handed Marta a steaming grande latte.

"Thank you." Marta took a sip, then set the cup on her desk before it could burn her fingers. "Boy, do I need this today."

"Rough morning?"

"Rough couple of days. But more importantly, how are you feeling?"

"Much better. Just guilty about sending you off to Minneapolis at the last minute."

"You shouldn't feel guilty, but it was a wasted trip."

Carol rolled her chair closer to Marta's and popped the lid on her own cup—straight and black. Carol subsisted on little more than black coffee, carrot sticks, and expensive wine. Her husband, Mark, was a wine snob as well as the sort of successful physician who could afford to keep their wine cellar well stocked with quality stuff.

"I could make a follow-up call," Carol offered. "Show the Solar Century folks we're seriously interested in their business."

"They know that."

"It can't hurt to remind them."

"Believe me, it won't make any difference." Marta ventured another sip, then licked the foam from her lips.

"You don't know that for sure. If we want to—"

"The trip was a disaster, so forget it, okay?" Marta's sharp tone surprised even herself.

Carol arched an eyebrow. "Whoa. What's the problem?"

"What do you mean?" But Marta knew full well what Carol meant. She wasn't usually this testy, even in the morning before coffee.

Her friend's expression softened. "Is something wrong?"

"Nothing's wrong." Nothing that Marta wanted to discuss. "My presentation sucked. Period. End of story. We need to forget about the Solar Century account."

"Okay, if you say so." Carol conceded the point but she clearly wasn't convinced. "Is it all right if I contact some of the other companies at the conference?"

Marta heard the sarcasm in Carol's tone, but the remark was accompanied by the familiar smile. Tall and slender, with the sleek, chin-length hair of a fashion model, Carol had initially struck Marta as standoffish. But her good humor and inviting smile had convinced Marta otherwise.

"Of course you can," she said. "I'm sorry I snapped at you just now. I guess I'm still a little jet lagged, as well as bummed about the trip."

"Don't beat yourself up over the presentation. We both knew it was a long shot. If we're going to fight our way into the big leagues, there are bound to be setbacks."

They'd started C&M Advantage a year ago, propelled by a mutual need to sink their teeth into something more meaning-ful than grocery shopping and errands. Both had recently moved to Sterling because of their husband's jobs—Mark's as an anesthesiologist, Gordon's at Howell College. And both women had left careers they loved. Marta had been a reporter with the *Boston Globe;* Carol, a public relations specialist at a multi-national company in New York.

Their early clients were local, but the list had gradually grown to include regional interests as well. The Solar Century account would have been a golden opportunity to prove themselves on a national level.

"I feel like I'm holding you back," Marta lamented. "My background is nowhere near as impressive as yours."

Carol shook her head. "Don't be ridiculous. And don't you dare even think about leaving me."

There was a knock on the partition that separated their office space from what they jokingly referred to as the lobby—the small area that housed the printer, a large work table, and, they hoped someday, an office manager.

A young man in a brown delivery uniform cleared his throat. "Marta Crawford?"

Marta stood. "Yes."

"Delivery for you, ma'am." He handed her a vase burgeoning with long-stemmed yellow roses and baby's breath.

"For me?"

"What gorgeous flowers," Carol exclaimed.

"There must be a mistake." Sending flowers was the sort of thing Carol's husband did on occasion, but not anyone Marta knew.

"Maybe you made a better impression on the Solar Century people than you thought," Carol observed.

"No way."

"Gordon then. Friday was your birthday, after all."

"He already bought me flowers." Red carnations, which were nowhere near as lovely as the roses.

Marta pulled the card from the envelope with caution. She sensed a joke, or a mistake. She couldn't decide which would be more humiliating.

She read the card silently.

"Missing you. Todd."

Carol was squirming impatiently in her chair. "So who are

they from?"

"Nobody you know." Marta closed her fingers around the card. Her heart was beating wildly and she could feel her face turning several shades of pink.

Playfully, Carol reached for the card. She read it and looked up. "Who's Todd?"

A slide show of memories flooded Marta's mind. Todd's aqua blue eyes looking at her intently, his sleep-tousled hair, the electrifying touch of his fingers on her neck. She felt light-headed and fluttery. "My brother-in-law," she said without thinking.

"You don't have a brother-in-law."

Marta snatched the card away from Carol. "He's just some guy," she said impatiently.

"Some guy?"

"Someone I met." Marta's pulse was racing. Breathing had become an effort.

"Met when?"

"Really, it's nothing."

"Two dozen roses are nothing?"

"It's not like—"

"Oh my God." Carol's eyes widened. "This past weekend? In Minneapolis? Is that where you met him?"

"What does it matter?"

Carol cocked her head. "Who is he?"

Marta wanted her friend to stop with the questions. She didn't want to make what happened any more real than it was already by talking about it.

"Nobody important," she said.

"But he sent you flowers."

Marta nodded numbly. The flowers, the note, the renewed shock of what she'd done—raw emotion overtook her. She covered her face with her hands. "It's nothing. Forget it, okay."

Carol touched Marta's wrist. "You're really upset, aren't you?"

Tears spilled from Marta's eyes and she wiped them with the back of her hand.

"What's wrong?"

"I did something really stupid."

"You? You're the last person in the world to do anything stupid."

"Not true. Besides, this was really, really stupid."

"What did you do?"

Marta didn't want to talk about it, didn't want anyone knowing what a fool she'd been. "It's too embarrassing."

"We've all done embarrassing things, Marta. Are you sure you're not getting yourself worked up over nothing?"

Marta bit her lip. The genie was half out of the bottle already and Carol was her best friend. "Remember when I was drinking the Pink Moose?"

"Yeah, it was your birthday."

"I let myself get picked up." Marta reached for a tissue and blew her nose.

"By this Todd guy?"

Marta nodded.

"So you had a drink, big deal."

"Several drinks."

"Okay, several drinks. What did you do? Dance on the tables? Strip naked? Throw up on him?"

"Not that I remember."

"You aren't the first woman to get drunk and make a fool of yourself in public."

Marta looked at the floor and tried, unsuccessfully, to choke back tears.

Carol stared at her, then seemed to suddenly understand.

Her eyes opened wider. "Picked up," she repeated, "as in hook-up?"

Marta nodded silently.

"You actually slept with him?" Carol's tone was more disbelief than disapproval. "What were you thinking?"

"Obviously I wasn't thinking."

"He wasn't one of our potential clients, was he?"

"God, no." At least Marta hoped not. Although, come to think of it, Todd had looked somewhat familiar. Could he have been in the room during her disastrous presentation?

"Well, that's something, I suppose," Carol offered.

"I don't know what got into me. I was just feeling so down. Upset about the Solar Century presentation, worried about Jamie, miffed at Gordon. It was my birthday and he didn't even call."

Spoken aloud, Marta's excuses sounded hollow. Since she couldn't understand herself why she'd done it, she couldn't really expect anyone else to understand.

"It is rather out of character," Carol admitted. "Were you really drunk? Did he slip you a roofie or whatever they're called?"

Date rape would let her off the hook morally, but it wasn't the truth. Marta blew her nose. "I'd been drinking but I wasn't drunk. There's no excuse for what I did."

"Do you want to see him again?"

Marta shook her head vehemently. "No."

"He was that bad?"

She shook her head again. "Actually, what I said about not wanting to see him isn't exactly true. Even though I feel terrible about what happened, guilty and ashamed and filled with self-loathing, there's a part of me that still savors the experience. How awful is that?"

"I'd say it's probably normal."

"Normal? You'd do something like that?"

"No. At least I think not. But I'm not you. Mark isn't Gordon."

"This isn't about Gordon."

"It isn't?"

"It really isn't. It was my weakness. Something totally separate from Gordon."

"That makes no sense."

"I love my husband. It's not like I want to be with Todd instead."

Carol eyed the vase of roses. "I don't think Todd sees it that way."

The scent of the flowers was making Marta sick. "Get them out of here," she said. "I don't want to see them."

"Shall I put them in the lobby?"

"How about the trash?"

"They're gorgeous, Marta. I'm not going to simply toss them."

"You take them then. No wait, Mark will ask where they came from. Take them to the hospital or a nursing home. Just get them out of here." Marta hugged herself in despair. "God, Carol. What am I going to do?"

"Well, don't thank him for the flowers, that's for sure." She stood up and reached for the vase. "If you ignore him, he'll lose interest."

Marta nodded. "I hope so."

For a brief moment the thought saddened her.

CHAPTER 7

Out of the corner of her eye, Jamie could see Oliver Glick staring at her from his locker across the hallway. Okay, not staring really, but he kept sneaking looks in her direction, and he wasn't at all subtle about it. Oliver wasn't subtle about anything. With his pointy nose, thick glasses, and his stupid save-the-dinosaurs T-shirts, you'd think he'd lay low, but Oliver acted like he didn't care what people thought. He sat behind her in English and waved his hand every time the teacher asked a question. That put Jamie right in Mr. Darby's line of vision, so he sometimes called on her, even when she didn't have her hand up.

Oliver was making Jamie uncomfortable with his eye game. She decided to put on a mean face and stare right back. She made a production out of it—none of Oliver's sidelong and furtive glances. She folded her arms and faced him squarely.

Big mistake. He smiled at her.

God, he was such a loser.

She grabbed her algebra book and headed to class.

"Hey," Oliver said, falling into step beside her.

Jamie picked up her pace and ignored him.

"I wish I'd known you were going to be at Barnes and Noble Friday night," he offered.

She stopped in her tracks. "What?"

"My mom saw you there, deep into a book. She said you were there for hours."

"Your mom? I don't even know your mom."

43

"Sure you do. She works there. You've talked to her before."

"And she knows me?"

"Yeah, of course. I mean you're there a lot and we go to the same school and stuff."

"What's she look like?" In the future, Jamie would avoid this woman at all costs. Or maybe she would stay clear of the bookstore altogether.

"Tall with curly gray hair. She's always got a pair of glasses hanging around her neck."

Jamie knew exactly who Oliver was talking about. She was like the store supervisor or something, and she was often in the stacks, talking to customers. "That's your mom?"

"Yeah."

Jamie hadn't counted on there being spies in the store. She thought fast. "I was meeting this guy I've been seeing, but not until ten because he had to work. I figured I'd read while I was waiting."

It didn't exactly make sense but Oliver didn't seem to notice. Or get the part about meeting some guy.

"I like hanging out in that store, too," he said. "It's better than the library even, although sometimes the library is better if you need to do a lot of research."

"Yeah, well . . ." Jamie managed her best dismissive huff. "I've got to get to class." She hoped he'd keep his mouth shut about where she'd been Friday night, although it might not matter much because his circle of friends was even smaller than hers.

She'd had a lot of friends when they'd lived in Boston. She got invited to birthday parties and sleepovers, and there had been a whole group of them in the neighborhood who hung out after school. If she'd stayed, she'd still have more than just her one friend, Alyssa.

Jamie hated Georgia, and she hated her parents for dragging

her here. Even if, as her parents told her over and over, it meant having a roof over her head and food on the table, which wouldn't have been the case in Boston. So what if her dad lost his job? Her mom worked. And Tufts wasn't the only school in the state. She didn't understand why they'd had to move to Sterling, Georgia, of all places.

"We can't afford the mortgage on my salary," her mom explained.

"Teaching jobs are tight these days," her dad added.

They both agreed that "Life involves making hard choices."

Her parents made being an adult sound so complicated, when it really wasn't. When you were an adult you were in charge of your own life. You could do whatever you wanted.

Jamie couldn't wait until she was eighteen.

Because they didn't have any morning classes together, Jamie didn't get a chance to talk to Alyssa until lunch.

"Greetings BFF," Alyssa said, dropping into the empty chair at their usual table in the corner of the lunchroom.

"Hi yourself."

"Halfway through Monday, and already I can't wait for the week to be over."

"The weekend isn't much better."

"No school, though." Alyssa pulled a bag of chips from her backpack.

Alyssa was a brainiac so it wasn't the work part of school she minded, but the social side, the who's friends with whom stuff that was what other kids cared about most. Jamie cared too, but Alyssa didn't often hold it against her.

Alyssa had what adults sometimes referred to as an "athletic build," although she was the least athletic person Jamie knew. She wasn't chubby in the way that Jamie was, but she was broad-shouldered and solidly muscular. She had straight, dark hair that Jamie envied like crazy.

"Be glad you weren't at Jake's party Saturday night," Alyssa groaned.

"Just rub my nose in the fact that I wasn't invited, why don't you."

"Come on, don't be like that. You know that's not what I meant."

"You did stand me up at the last minute."

"I'm sorry, okay? Really. My mom made me go. I would have had a lot more fun with you." Alyssa tore the chip bag wide open and set it between them. "Take as many as you want."

"You trying to buy my forgiveness?"

"Absolutely. I've got a granola bar, too, if you're going to drive a hard bargain."

Jamie took a fistful of chips and laughed.

"I don't know why I was even invited to the party. I think it was my mother's doing. She and Jake's mom are on the library committee together."

"She arranged a playdate for you?" Jamie asked, incredulous.

"Pretty much."

"How embarrassing."

"Yeah. It was horrible, too. No one even talked to me. And there was alcohol, not that anyone offered me any. I felt like a skunk at the pet parade."

Jamie was secretly pleased, but she knew that was mean-spirited so she tried to ignore the feeling. Alyssa was her best friend, her only friend in fact. It wasn't that she wanted Alyssa to be miserable, because she didn't. She just wanted the both of them to be happy together.

"I forgive you for dumping me," Jamie told her, "but I'm not going to feel sorry for you. You did go to a party, after all."

"How was your weekend?"

Jamie shrugged. Harmony's dismissive treatment still stung.

She'd been thrilled when Harmony suggested a movie, hoping the invitation might mean an eventual entree into the popular crowd. What had happened was too humiliating even to share with Alyssa.

"My mom came home," Jamie said dryly, "and we had cake for her birthday."

"Wow. Our lives really do suck."

Just then Harmony sauntered by, flanked by two of her friends. Jamie looked up and smiled. "Hi."

Harmony looked right through her and walked on without so much as a nod.

She hadn't expected Harmony to greet her like a close friend, but after what Jamie had done for her, she might at least have said hello.

"Why'd you even bother talking to her?" Alyssa asked. "She's such a stuck-up snob."

Jamie took a fistful of chips. "Yeah, she is. But I'm trying something new. Smother your enemies with kindness."

"Harmony wouldn't recognize kindness if it bit her in the rear."

"Probably true." Which made Jamie bristle even more.

She tried to convince herself that Harmony didn't matter, but she did. Not Harmony herself, because Alyssa was right about her. What mattered was what Harmony represented. She was cool and popular. Jamie was not. Even Alyssa had gotten invited to a party, no matter that her mother had arranged it.

Oliver, Jamie thought sadly, wasn't the only one who was a total loser.

CHAPTER 8

Marta pushed her grocery cart through the aisles of the supermarket on autopilot. Her hands reached for items out of habit while her mind grappled with bigger things.

She'd meant what she told Carol. She did love Gordon and she had no desire to leave him.

So why had she so readily jumped into bed with Todd? And why, despite the panic she'd felt at receiving the flowers, did she still savor the memory of that night?

Her family meant everything to her. As did her marriage.

Marta had discovered she was pregnant while she and Gordon were still dating, and she'd been terrified to tell him. But Gordon hadn't run. He hadn't even missed a beat. They'd get married, of course. It was only a matter of time in any case, he explained. Now it would happen sooner rather than later.

And instead of feeling the burden of impending parenthood, which, to be honest, weighed heavily on Marta, Gordon embraced it. He painted the walk-in closet that was to become a nursery, researched car seats and cribs (although it didn't much matter since they could only afford what was available secondhand), and added *What to Expect When You're Expecting* to his evening reading.

Through the sleepless nights with a colicky baby and the lean years of their early marriage, through a string of professional disappointments, their marriage remained strong, even when they weren't exactly happy.

But not anymore.

In Marta's mind, a sharp chasm separated past and present, although she couldn't recall when the first cracks had appeared, or what caused them.

The loss of Gordon's job had certainly been a factor, but Marta's own disappointment played a role as well. She had loved her job at the *Boston Globe,* and she resented being dragged off to a hick town in Georgia. Although she had dutifully attended parent events at Jamie's school, she'd never connected with the other mothers, most of whom had known one another since their children were in kindergarten. She joined a quilting group, which looked askance at the art quilts she favored, and a book club whose taste in books favored inspirational tales, often with a religious message. This was so different from her own, admittedly eclectic, interest in literature that she found the gatherings painful.

Then she'd met Carol and her life began to take shape again. Gordon, too, seemed to settle into his position at Howell. She had hoped their marriage was on the mend.

But the roses from Todd upset her in ways she didn't fully understand. They filled her with trepidation and dread, but also triggered a sharp quickness inside her, like the exhilarating drop of a roller coaster. And that scared her more than anything.

"Smells good," Gordon said, taking his seat at the table.

Marta had made beef stew. It was an old family recipe she didn't make often because it took a lot of work. At the store, she'd loaded up on the ingredients, determined to rekindle her faltering marriage.

As was often the case, Jamie came to the table plugged into her iPod.

"Not during dinner," Marta reminded her. "You know the rule."

Jamie didn't respond.

Marta tapped her hand, motioned to the earbuds, and mouthed "off." With a huff of disgust, Jamie reluctantly removed the earbuds and clicked off the iPod.

"I don't see what difference it makes," she grumbled. "It's not like we ever talk about anything interesting."

"What would you like to talk about?"

When Jamie rolled her eyes and said nothing, Marta asked, "How was your day?" It was a stupid question, and one she instantly regretted, but she'd felt the need to break the silence.

"It sucked. What else is new. Why do you even bother to ask?"

"Maybe because we keep thinking it might be different."

"It won't be," Jamie said.

Marta looked to Gordon, hoping he'd jump in. No earbuds for him, but he might as well have had them for all he contributed to the conversation. As usual, he was content to eat in silence unless he was asked a specific question.

"Well, then," Marta suggested, "tell us what was so bad about it."

Jamie put her fork down. "You don't get it, do you? It's not like it's one specific thing, it's . . . it's everything."

Gordon jumped to life. "Don't use that tone with your mother, young lady."

Marta cringed. This wasn't the kind of involvement she'd been hoping for.

She leaned forward, toward Jamie. "Honey, we're trying to understand. We'd like to help."

"You can't help, Mom. Nobody can."

Marta's cell phone rang in the kitchen. She would have let it go to voice mail but Jamie, looking for reprieve from Marta's questioning, raced to retrieve it from the counter. "It's Aunt Cassie," she said, handing the phone over.

Marta sighed. Conversations with her sister took more energy than she had right then.

"Hi, Cassie," she said. "Can I call you back in a bit? We're right in the middle of dinner."

"I guess."

"It's not an emergency, is it?" With Cassie, Marta never knew what to expect. She could be calling from jail. Or some rich man's yacht. Or simply to complain.

"Nothing you'd consider an emergency."

"Good." Marta tried to sound upbeat. "I'll give you a call later this evening."

No sooner had she flipped the phone off than it rang again. She answered, no longer able to keep the irritation from her voice. "I told you I'd call you back and I will."

Silence.

"Cassie?"

Another stretch of silence, then, "It's Todd. Did I get you at a bad time?"

Marta's heart thudded to a stop. She felt exposed, as if he were right there at the table with them.

She needed to think fast. "Like I said," she explained, carefully articulating each word, "I'll call you later."

She hung up and turned off the phone. Her hand shook as she slipped it into her pocket.

"Is Aunt Cassie in trouble again?" Jamie asked.

"I don't know. We didn't get a chance to talk."

"Then why did she call you back?"

Marta's throat was dry. She felt as if her skin were flayed and her mind was on full display. "She didn't mean to. She hit the wrong button on her phone."

"This is good stew," Gordon said. Marta wasn't sure if he was trying to help her out or simply commenting on the dinner, but she was grateful.

"I know you like it."

"I thought it was too much trouble. You usually—"

"I decided we deserved a treat."

"Oh pu-leeze," Jamie said. "See why I prefer to listen to music?" She shoveled the last of her dinner into her mouth and pushed away from the table. "I've got homework to do."

Marta watched her daughter's retreating back and sighed. "Remember when dinner time used to be fun? When we all wanted to share our day with each other. Funny stories, complaints, questions. The point was we talked to each other."

Gordon shrugged. "She's not a little girl anymore."

Pause. "I wasn't referring just to Jamie."

Gordon put down his fork. "And we're not newlyweds anymore."

"I know that." Marta struggled to explain. "It's just . . . sometimes it feels more like we're roommates than family. Like you and I have drifted apart."

Gordon's eyes narrowed. "I'm trying, Marta. You think I like being a failure?"

"You're not a failure. And I wasn't blaming you."

"It sure sounded like you were."

"I was simply making an observation."

"I know it's my fault we're stuck here in Sterling. It's not like I had a choice."

"Gordon, this isn't about work. It's about us. I feel like we're stick figures sometimes. Or the Tin Man. We go through the motions of living but we're not." *And the motions of loving,* she added silently.

"I'm not sure what your point is," Gordon said after a moment.

How do you explain a violet sunset to someone who was color blind?

"Forget it."

They cleared the table in silence.

"You want to watch a movie?" Marta asked as she put away the leftovers. "We got a new envelope from Netflix today."

"I don't think so. You go ahead and watch it if you want, I'll watch it another time."

"I didn't mean right this minute. We can start it later."

He shook his head. "I've got work to do."

When the dishwasher was loaded and Marta was alone in the kitchen, she turned on her phone again.

Another text message from Todd. *Call me, I miss you.*

Ignoring him, she returned her sister's call.

Cassie was a recovering alcoholic with good intentions but frequent relapses. She was so exasperating, Marta sometimes wanted to throttle her, but she also had a big heart and a puppy-like naiveté that made it impossible to stay angry. Marta loved her younger sister, and hadn't given up hope that she would eventually find her footing.

"Hi, Cassie. What's up?"

"I needed an excuse to call you?"

"No, of course not." But Cassie never called without a reason. Marta was the one who initiated calls just to touch base.

"I wanted to hear about your trip."

"What trip?"

"To Minneapolis. Wasn't there a business thing you had there?"

"Right." Why did everything have to remind her of Todd? "Thanks for the birthday text, by the way."

"So did you take my advice and have some fun?"

"It was cold and snowy, and boring as hell."

"You didn't do *anything*?"

"Nothing exciting." Nothing Marta would admit to.

Cassie hesitated. "Sorry to hear that."

"Yeah. So how are you?"

"I've been better."

"What's the matter? Are you ill?" Marta worried that someday Cassie would call with truly bad news, the way their mother had only a few years earlier when she'd announced she had stage four cancer.

"I was sick but I'm better now."

"Was it the flu?"

"Probably. I felt like shit." Cassie paused for the telltale inhalation of a cigarette. "I missed a few days of work."

"But you're better now, right?"

"Yeah, but the thing is, the fuckers fired me. I mean, can I help it if I get sick?"

In Cassie's case, she probably could. Besides, if Marta had to guess, she'd say Cassie's illness, whatever it had been, somehow involved alcohol.

"So you're out of a job?" Marta bit her tongue and didn't add *again*. "What are you going to do?"

"I'm too bummed to even think about it yet. I was hoping you could spare a little cash, you know, just to tide me over for a bit."

Déjà vu all over again, Marta thought. "What about unemployment insurance?"

"It wasn't that kind of job!"

No, of course not. "How much do you need?"

"A thousand would do, I think."

"A thousand?" This was déjà vu doubled. In the past Marta had sometimes given her sister a month's rent, or maybe a couple of hundred bucks for groceries. "I don't have a thousand dollars to spare. Why so much this time?"

"I've got expenses. The power company is threatening to turn off my service if I don't pay up."

Marta's irritation boiled to the surface. "You were working until recently. Why didn't you pay your utilities?"

"Don't go getting all high and mighty with me. It's not my fault things don't work out. You always get lucky. Me, it's like I've got a black cloud over my head."

How many times had they had this argument? Marta's head hurt just thinking about it. She'd tried to make Cassie understand that people made their own luck. She'd tried to help her see that her lifestyle and life choices weren't conducive to success. But it was a losing battle.

"You've got a husband, a job, a nice house," Cassie whined. "You've got it made. I don't see why you can't help me out a little." Another drag on the cigarette. "Besides, you got Momma's money."

"I've told you, there isn't any money. What little there was, I spent on her medical bills."

"You can't have spent it all."

"Well I did. And then some."

"Then you shouldn't have. It wasn't yours, it belonged to both of us."

Marta had had enough. "It didn't belong to either of us. It was Momma's money."

"What am I going to do?" Cassie sounded suddenly so broken and discouraged that Marta's anger faded.

"You need to get your life in order, Cassie. You need a job and you need to keep it. You need a budget. And maybe you need to start going to AA meetings again."

"Maybe what I need is a sister who doesn't think she's so perfect!"

Marta relented. "I'll try to send you something." But Cassie had already hung up.

Marta stared at her phone feeling worn down and unappreciated. She was tempted to return Todd's call, but she resisted. Unlike her sister, Marta tried to do the right thing. Or had, until the trip to Minneapolis.

She sent Todd a text instead.

Thank you for the flowers, but this needs to stop. Please don't contact me again.

She hesitated, then closed her heart to regret and hit send.

CHAPTER 9

Marta was at her desk Wednesday morning, working on a mailer for one of her favorite clients, the Sterling Humane Society. She loved animals and was friends with the woman who ran the shelter, so it should have been a job she could put her heart into. But she was having a tough time focusing.

After the uneasy homecoming, things had been fairly smooth at home. Jamie kept her eye-rolling and theatric huffing to a minimum. Gordon was upbeat about working on the revisions for his paper.

And there hadn't been a single text or email or phone call from Todd.

That was good, wasn't it? Of course it was. Now she could relax and put the whole episode of Minneapolis behind her.

So why did she feel so lost?

Marta stared at the computer screen for another fifteen minutes, then finally gave up and logged off. She had a meeting in Macon that afternoon with Youth In Transition, a new client. It was important she be clear-headed.

"I'm going to head out," she told Carol. "I'll stop by the printer and pick up the flyers for Mountain Camp on the way to my meeting."

"Great. I know Dan is eager to get going."

"I'm still skeptical about a winter outdoor camp in Vermont."

Carol chuckled. "It's not for the likes of us."

"That's for sure. I'm glad we convinced Dan of that." He'd

been eager for them to experience a week in the wilderness firsthand in order to better present the camp to would-be participants. They'd convinced him the adventure would not enthrall them the way he hoped.

Marta grabbed her coat and the folder with her notes for the upcoming meeting, then headed out. She was almost to her car when out of the corner of her eye, she caught sight of a familiar-looking man across the green.

Todd?

She turned for a closer look. He was too far away for her to be sure, but he did have the same lean build and sandy brown hair. And he was about the right age, but a lot of men fit that description. Besides, what would Todd be doing in Sterling?

Marta had only seconds to study him further before the man turned the corner and was gone. No, she decided, not Todd. Just another case of her overactive imagination. Like yesterday when she'd thought she'd seen him in the grocery parking lot, only to discover, on closer inspection, that the man she saw had a darker complexion and was a bit heavier.

Was it wishful thinking? Had she regressed to the level of a lovesick teenager, seeing Todd everywhere she looked? Such silliness. She didn't even want to see him. Really, she didn't. Yes, there was a hollow space inside her, but it wasn't a hollow Todd could fill.

She had to get her head straight. She had to stop thinking about him. But the brief glimpse of the man who might have been Todd had unsettled her. She trudged across the street to The Daily Joe for coffee to drink in the car.

The shop was small, with a counter by the window and two tiny tables. More a place to grab an order to go than to hang out. Marta missed the bustling and packed coffee shops she'd known in Boston.

Donna, the barista, greeted her warmly. "Your usual latte?"

"Yes, thanks." Marta eyed the pastries but for once, her better sense prevailed. "How's your family?"

"Good. All except my brother, of course. With him, it never is."

"I know the feeling. My sister lost her job again."

Donna shook her head. "Siblings. You can't turn them away even when you want to."

"How true." Marta still hadn't told Gordon about the money she'd sent Cassie. It was less than her sister had asked for, but in the end, sending her something was easier than not doing so. And she worried about Cassie.

"Now that daughter of yours," Donna said. "She's another story."

"Jamie tries my patience at times, too."

"But she's got spunk. She's not like those other girls who come in here, all giggles and no brain." Donna handed Marta her coffee. "You don't have to worry about Jamie."

Marta laughed. "I'll try to remember that."

Marta's discussion with the Youth In Transition board went well, and she left the meeting with a smile on her face. They'd been unanimous in their support for the approach Marta outlined, as well as the specifics she'd suggested in terms of outreach. She was always nervous with new clients, but they were such an enthusiastic group she'd actually enjoyed herself.

In preparing, she'd talked to teens in foster care—kids who'd never known a real family and who had no private resources—and she'd seen firsthand what happened the day they turned eighteen. The existing support system, such as it was, vanished, and they were thrown out into the world to fend for themselves. How could you find a place to live without first and last months' rent? How could you support yourself, no matter how hard you worked, starting from nothing? Youth In Transition was working to provide transitional support for those teens who had aged out of the traditional system. They needed sponsors and landlords and businesses willing to work with them. That's where C&M Advantage came in. She and Carol could help them tell their story in a way that would elicit support.

Marta was still going over a few of the finer points in her mind as she walked the block and a half to her car. She'd opened the door and set the project file on the back seat when she heard someone come up behind her.

She straightened, hitting her head on the car roof, and yelped. Turning around, she found herself face to face with Todd.

He smiled apologetically. "Sorry. I didn't mean to startle you."

"How could I not be startled with you sneaking up on me like that?"

"I wasn't sneaking up. I saw you walking down the street and I wanted to say hello."

Marta's heart raced. She couldn't tell if it was the mere fact of being surprised, or because it was Todd who'd surprised her. "What are you doing here?"

"I'm here on business. What about you?"

"Business also."

"Serendipity." He rubbed his hands together against the chill in the air. "Come on, it's cold out here. Let's grab a cup of coffee and catch up."

Catch up? What could they possibly have to catch up with? They had nothing in common but a one-night stand.

"I need to get back to the office," she said, not as convincingly as she intended. Could it really be coincidence?

"Can't you spare half an hour? It's so great running into you."

Todd was smiling his trademark slightly off-center smile. He looked good, better than she remembered. The familiar scent of his aftershave triggered a memory of their night together that nearly rocked Marta off her feet.

"There's a place only a block from here," he said. "Local, not one of those cookie-cutter chains."

She shouldn't. Absolutely not. What she should do is get into her car and drive away as quickly as possible.

But Todd had a way of fixing his eyes on her that made him hard to resist. And what was one cup of coffee in the middle of the afternoon?

As if reading her mind, he added, "It's just coffee."

She glanced up the street to check that no one from the meeting was watching, then relented. "Okay. But I can't stay long."

"Great." He put a hand on her elbow and nodded to the right. "It's just around the corner and up the street a bit."

Todd did most of the talking as they walked, keeping up a steady monologue about Macon's historic homes and tidbits of the area's history.

"You come here often, then?" Marta asked.

"Often enough." He took her elbow again to guide her. "Here we are. Why don't you grab a table while I get our order. What would you like?"

"Just coffee," she said. "Black." She found an empty table and sat down.

The coffeehouse was warm and cozy, and smelled deliciously of rich, freshly roasted coffee and buttery pastries. Like the coffeehouses she'd loved in Boston. Also like Boston, the place was crowded, and most of the patrons tapped away at laptops and notebooks.

Todd returned with two steaming mugs and a plate laden with a scone, assorted nut breads, a very large cinnamon roll, and a lemon tart.

"I wasn't sure what you'd want," he said, sliding into the chair next to hers.

"What did you do, get one of everything?"

He grinned. "Not quite, but close."

Marta couldn't have eaten, even if she'd been hungry. She'd expected Todd to sit across the table from her, not so close that his thigh brushed hers.

"Here's to us," Todd said, raising his mug in a toast.

Marta gripped her mug and kept it firmly on the table. "There is no us."

"You and me, we're here having coffee, aren't we? The two of us." He took a slow sip, regarding her over the rim of his mug. "Did you like the flowers?"

"Yes. I mean no, no I didn't." Marta shook her head and leaned away. "I don't want you sending me flowers."

"Why?"

"Why?" Her voice rose, causing the man at a nearby table to look their direction. She dropped the volume. The last thing she wanted was someone eavesdropping. "Because I'm married," she explained, dropping her voice further on the last word. "Why can't you understand that what happened was an aberration?"

"Did you ever stop to think that maybe it's your life that's the aberration, and that the woman in Minneapolis was the real you?"

She shook her head. "The real me is a wife and mother who happens, also, to have at least several years on you."

Todd leaned back in his chair and turned, studying her. "You're an amazing woman, you know that? No, of course you don't. You have no idea. Maybe that's part of what I find so attractive about you."

Marta felt a galvanizing tingle down her spine. Amazing? When was the last time anyone had called her amazing? Ever? "Please," she said. "I told you—"

"I know what you told me, but I haven't been able to get you out of my mind."

"I'm sorry if I misled you. That wasn't my intention."

"I understand that." He rocked forward again and began tracing circles on the tabletop with his fingers. "I guess maybe I misled you, too."

"How so? Don't tell me you're married?"

"No." He paused. "My wife died three years ago."

"I'm so sorry." Marta felt a rush of sympathy. "How did she die? Or would you prefer not to talk about it?"

"It's painful."

"Of course it is. I didn't mean to pry."

"No, I want you to understand."

Marta waited for him to continue.

"She was murdered," Todd said finally. "Right in front of me." His voice caught and he grew still. "We'd gone out to dinner and were walking back to the car. I heard what sounded like an explosion, and when I turned to look at her, she was already crumpled on the ground. At first I thought maybe she'd tripped and fallen, but then I saw the blood. Just a little at first, hard to see in the dark. And then, suddenly, lots of it. Her neck, her chest—"

"Oh, my God!"

"She died in my arms. I wasn't able to save her."

Marta felt the heat of Todd's grief. "How terrible. Did they find who did it?"

"A lowlife punk. It was part of a gang dispute. A case of mistaken identity."

"They thought your wife was someone else?"

He dropped his head to his hands. "They thought I was someone else. They were aiming for me."

"Oh, Todd. What a tragedy."

He nodded and his chin quivered. "It was awful. I've been dead inside ever since. People said to give it time, that I'd be able to move on at some point, but I knew they were wrong. My life was over. I was an empty shell."

Marta felt her throat tighten. "I can only imagine how terrible it was for you."

He took a breath and looked up. "Then I met you. You were fresh and funny. You made me feel alive again."

"I what?" An amazing woman. And now, fresh and funny. Heady stuff. But oddly disquieting, too.

"I know it sounds crazy," he added, "but I'm already falling in love with you."

"You don't even know me," she told him softly.

"I know enough to know I want to know more."

"You're a terrific guy, Todd. Good-looking, kind, smart. There must be lots of women who would welcome your attention."

"But they aren't you."

"This is—"

"I can't lose you, Marta."

What had she done? "I'm not yours to lose," she said. "I'm married. Why is that so hard for you to understand?"

He touched her hand. "I heard how you talked about your husband. You can't honestly prefer him to me."

Marta pulled her hand away and sat back. "What? I hardly mentioned him."

Todd smiled. "I'm sure he's a nice guy and all, but come on, you can't really love him."

"I do." The vehemence in her voice caught her by surprise.

"I don't believe that. I know what you were like with me the other night."

"That was . . . it was a mistake."

"It didn't feel like a mistake."

"Todd, this is silly. Gordon and I have been together a long time. We have a history together. A daughter."

"That's a reason to batten down the hatches and stop living?

You only get one chance at life. Don't you want more than what you've got now?"

Marta was feeling increasingly uncomfortable. The qualities that were so tantalizing about him now also unnerved her.

She reached for her purse. "I'm sorry, Todd. I shouldn't have agreed to have coffee with you. There's no point. This has got to stop."

"Don't toy with me, Marta. I'm not a thing."

"I'm not toying. I'm trying to make you understand. There was never an us and there never will be. There can't be."

He seemed both hurt and angry. "You should think about it."

"I have."

"I mean really think about it." He leaned closer and whispered in her ear. "Call me, okay? I'll be waiting."

Marta slung her purse over her shoulder and headed for the door, walking as quickly as she could. She was half-afraid Todd would come after her, but she heard no footsteps behind her. When she reached the door she looked back and saw him still sitting at the table, watching her.

CHAPTER 10

Gordon hated mornings.

His limbs simply refused to move. No matter how much he intended to get up, he found himself lying there, staring at the ceiling. The day that stretched before him—hell, the weeks and years—seemed to demand far more than he could give.

On rare occasions, he was eager to spring from the prison of his dreams, only to be confronted moments later by his own sorry image in the bathroom mirror, and the dreariness of the day that awaited him.

Either way, mornings were hell.

It hadn't always been like this. He used to welcome the promise in each new day. In his life. He welcomed what lay ahead.

How had his existence become so bleak? Oh, he understood his step-by-step descent into the wasteland of his current nontenured position at a second-rate school, but on a deeper, cosmic level, it made no sense at all.

Marta didn't get it, even though she claimed she did. She would listen sympathetically when he tried to explain, then proceed to list all the reasons he had to be thankful. As if he'd never considered the matter himself. He had his own list, longer than Marta's, but it wasn't enough to banish the gloom from his soul.

This morning he'd already tried to will himself out of bed twice, only to fall back into a hazy sort of half sleep. Now, he opened his eyes again, glanced again at the bedside clock, and groaned. Gloom or no, he had to get up or he'd be late for his class.

As he turned onto his side, it dawned on him that maybe his funk wasn't as all-encompassing as he imagined if he still cared enough to get to class on time. Or maybe it was just easier to go through the motions.

Howell College frowned on professors—strike that, assistant professors—who didn't show up for their own classes. The students wouldn't care whether he was there or not. They didn't pay much attention even when they were physically present, and there were always a distressing number of them who were not.

Finally, Gordon propelled himself from the cocoon of his bed and into the bathroom, where he realized he had time for a shower or a shave but not both. He chose the shower.

The air was still moist from Marta's shower earlier that morning, and smelled of the apricot-scented body wash he used to find so tantalizing. Now it was nothing more than a familiar household scent, like the lemon dishwashing soap or the slightly musty smell of the front hallway where their winter jackets hung. He wondered, briefly, where all the joy had gone.

Marta had been in a hurry this morning, up early and scurrying about like a squirrel gathering nuts. Lately, it seemed she was always in a hurry. Unless she wanted to talk. Then she had all the time in the world. She would raise whatever was on her mind obliquely, then become agitated when Gordon failed to grasp what she was trying to say.

Most recently, it had been his failings as a husband, although she hadn't spelled it out in so many words.

"It feels like we're drifting apart," she'd told him over dinner last week. "We used to have so much to say to each other."

"We've been married a long time," he'd explained. "We don't need to be always talking."

"That's not what I mean." And although she'd tried to explain, Gordon knew she was really pointing out the ways in which he fell short.

He wanted to be a better husband. He really did. But he wasn't sure how to make that happen. He sometimes felt like he was encased in a suit of armor. It wasn't a symbol of valor, but a shell. Somewhere inside, he was alive. But stuck in his shell, he was stiff and awkward. And he couldn't find the words to explain this to Marta.

Thankfully she had come home the following night from some meeting in Macon all fired up about eighteen-year-old kids aging out of foster care, and Gordon was no longer in the crosshairs. Even then he'd wondered if Marta had been subtly reminding him that there were people with bigger troubles than his own.

Of course there were. Gordon got that. But it didn't make his own troubles any less pressing. There was enough grief out there for both him and the hapless foster kids.

Only one student showed up for afternoon office hours. Dimitri Dibinski, a foreign exchange student whose intensity unnerved Gordon. When Dimitri finally left, Gordon checked the hallway. Office hours weren't over for another forty minutes, but when he saw no one waiting, he locked up and called it a day.

On the way home he stopped by the grocery store. Marta had left him a note that morning.

I may be late this evening, she'd written. *Will you pick up romaine and a tomato for salad, and put the casserole in the oven? It should cook at 350.*

P.S. It's in the orange pot on the second shelf of the fridge.

Although he wouldn't admit it, Gordon enjoyed grocery shopping. As long as he had instructions, the task was simple and straightforward, something he could accomplish, usually successfully. It made him feel useful and needed.

Jamie wasn't yet home so he put the groceries away, changed into his sweats, and went out to the garage. His 1967 Mustang needed a lot of work to reach classic car status. Work and money. Gordon didn't mind the work, but unless he won the lottery, he'd never be able to afford the kind of restoration he would have liked.

He'd started the project when his professional life in Boston had gone to hell. The injustice of a groundless accusation legitimized by political correctness and big money had come close to sending him off the deep end, but he'd been saved by a chance encounter with a neighbor selling an old Mustang—a car Gordon had lusted after since he was a teen. Buying it made no sense at all, but Gordon's life right then made no sense either. Better to buy an old car that needed work than to go around smashing windows or screaming from rooftops.

Although Gordon knew nothing about cars, he'd taken to the task of rebuilding the Mustang with an enthusiasm he didn't know he had. The work took his mind off his troubles and gave him an excuse to shut himself away where no one would bother him. It had been a surprisingly satisfying decision.

Now, he worked intently, installing pistons and new rings until his head began to hurt from the fumes. He opened the garage door to air the place out, then went back to work.

A male voice called "Hi," and Gordon looked up to see a man walking up the driveway toward him. The man was nicely dressed in dark slacks and a black leather jacket. He was younger than Gordon, and carried himself with the sort of casual self-confidence Gordon never seemed able to master.

"You live here?" the man asked.

Gordon nodded. Not a salesman, he hoped.

"How's the neighborhood?"

"The neighborhood?"

"Sorry, let me back up. I sometimes jump to the point a little too quickly." The man offered Gordon an abashed grin. "I was looking at that house down the street, the one that's for sale. I'm wondering what you think of the neighborhood."

Gordon hadn't actually given the question much thought. In the two years since they'd moved here, he'd met only a handful of neighbors. They were nice enough but he didn't really know them well. That was why he hadn't wanted to go to the party last week when Marta was out of town.

"It seems fine," he said. "I'm probably not the best person to ask, though. My wife and daughter are the social members of the family."

"You've raised a family here then? How are the schools?"

"We just moved in a couple of years ago, but the high school seems good. How old are your kids?"

The man chuckled. "I don't have any yet. I'm working on finding a wife first."

The guy wasn't married but he was concerned about the neighborhood and schools? Gordon imagined he had a bit of a control issue. Or maybe he was simply concerned with property values.

"Hey," the man said, "that's an awesome car. What is it, a '70?"

Gordon brightened. "A '67. It needs a lot of work still."

"It's great you can do it yourself. I've always dreamed about rebuilding a car but I don't have the know-how."

"I didn't either when I started. It's kind of learn-as-you-go for me. You want to see the engine?"

Gordon wasn't sure how long they talked. It was mostly about cars. The man asked intelligent questions and actually listened to Gordon's responses. Gordon was enjoying himself for the first time in a long time.

"Say," he said finally. "Why don't you come in and have a

beer. I need to put some stuff in the oven. My wife will be home soon and you can ask her about the neighbors."

"Sure, if I'm not imposing."

Gordon wiped his hands on the rag he kept handy, then led his new friend into the kitchen. Jamie had come home without his noticing and was standing in front of the fridge with the door open.

"Hi, Dad," she said without taking her eyes off the contents of the fridge.

"Hi, honey. I brought a friend. This fellow is thinking about buying the house down the street that's for sale." He went to the sink to wash his hands. "This is my daughter, Jamie," he explained over his shoulder. "I'm Gordon, by the way."

"Hi, Jamie." The stranger gave her a friendly nod. "I'm Todd."

CHAPTER 11

Marta pulled into the driveway, happy to finally be home from work. It had been a long, hectic day, and she was exhausted. The lights were on inside the house, which gave her hope that Gordon had remembered to put dinner in the oven. She was looking forward to doing nothing but changing out of her work clothes, pouring herself a glass of wine, and vegging out for the evening.

The welcoming aroma of cooking food greeted her as she entered the house, along with the low buzz of conversation from the kitchen. A neighbor? One of Gordon's colleagues? Maybe a friend of Jamie's, although Marta thought it unlikely that Jamie and her friend would be hanging out in the kitchen with Gordon. Damn! She was in no mood to play hostess.

As she hung up her coat, she thought about bypassing the kitchen and heading directly upstairs, but curiosity and conscience won out. She headed toward the kitchen.

As she neared the door, she heard Gordon announce, "Ah, here she is now."

At first she thought she was looking at a heartwarming scene. Father, daughter, and visitor seated around the kitchen table, having a friendly conversation. Each of the adults had a bottle of beer in front of him, her daughter, a soda.

But it took her only an instant longer to recognize the visitor at the table, schmoozing so easily with Gordon and Jamie, was none other than Todd.

The picture was so wrong all she could do was stare.

Gordon made the introductions but Marta wasn't listening. Her head was spinning.

"This guy knows his cars," Gordon said.

"How nice." Marta's skin prickled, and anger simmered inside her. Had he told Gordon about their night in Minneapolis? Would he? Why else was he here?

"Todd is interested in buying the house down the street," Gordon said. "He was asking about the neighborhood."

Marta forced herself to breathe. "Is that so?" She was amazed her voice sounded so normal. "It's actually not a very nice house. The layout is odd and it needs a ton of work."

Gordon shot her a critical look. "That's for him to decide, isn't it?"

"Are you from around here?" Marta asked Todd. It was as close as she could come to "Why are you here?" without sounding like an idiot.

Todd shook his head. "I'm thinking of relocating."

"It's a sucky town. I'd think twice if I were you."

Gordon gave up with the nasty looks and jumped in. "It's not so bad. I thought you—"

"Yes it is," Jamie volunteered. "I hate living here."

Todd chuckled, turning his amused blue eyes toward Marta. "Your daughter has been giving me an earful for the past half-hour or so."

Marta fought the urge to find the nearest heavy object and bash him with it. "Nice to have met you," she said icily. "Tom, is it?"

Gordon corrected her before Todd had a chance.

"In any case, please excuse me, I have things to take care of. Gordon, why don't you show your guest out while I change."

"Oh, that's not necessary," Gordon said. "He's staying for dinner."

Marta had turned to head upstairs. Now she abruptly turned back. "He's what?"

"I invited him. There's plenty of food. And I thought that would give you a chance to answer some of his questions about the town."

Marta was dumbfounded. Gordon was one of the least outgoing people she knew. That he'd invite a practical stranger to stay for dinner was beyond belief.

"I'm awfully tired tonight," she protested. "Maybe another time."

Gordon started to argue, but Todd raised his palms in acquiescence. "I understand perfectly. I didn't mean to intrude on your evening. Your husband and I were talking and then your delightful daughter joined us, and I lost track of time."

"Please stay," Gordon said. "I apologize for my—"

"I appreciate the invitation but I need to be going anyway."

"I'll walk you to the door," Marta offered. "That way I can answer any questions you have. About the 'neighborhood.' "

Todd shook Gordon's hand. "Thanks for the beer." He took Jamie's hand next and leaned in closer. "I loved the incident with your history teacher. You've got a real gift for storytelling."

Jamie blushed. It was all Marta could do to keep from kicking Todd right then and there. She followed him out onto the porch and closed the door behind her.

"What the hell are you doing?"

"What do you think I'm doing?"

Marta crossed her arms. "Don't you dare come here again. You need to leave me alone. Leave my family alone. Do you hear me? You've crossed the line, Todd."

"I love the way you get so fired up about things."

"This isn't funny."

His fingertips grazed the back of her neck. "I wasn't trying to be funny. I'm deadly serious."

"About what? Invading my life and harassing me?"

"You won't answer my texts. You won't take my calls. I didn't know how else to reach you."

Marta drew in a breath. "I don't want you to reach me," she said emphatically.

"Why won't you give me a chance?"

"A chance to destroy my family? What are you doing?"

"I wanted to see you. I want to know all about you."

My God, what had she done? "This has got to stop!"

He brushed his thumb across her lips. "See you soon," he said, and whistled his way down the stairs.

Marta stood on the porch, shaking with anger until he'd driven away. Then she took a deep breath to calm herself.

When she got back inside, Gordon was steaming. "What's gotten into you, Marta? You were downright rude."

"I've had a long day. I'm tired. I don't feel like sharing my evening with a stranger."

"This is my house, too, you know. If I invite a friend for dinner, the least you can do is be civil."

"A friend? You just met the guy."

"Yeah, and we hit it off. Besides, he just might be our neighbor someday."

Jamie was still at the table, listening in. "Way to go, Mom. You're always telling Dad he needs to be more outgoing, and then you chase his friend out of here."

"I didn't chase—"

"You did too. You were like . . . like a mad dog."

Marta heard the reproach in her daughter's voice and mentally stepped back. Finding Todd in her house terrified her, but they were right. She had been rude. Intentionally and desperately rude. Todd was the last person in the world she wanted mixing with her family.

But they knew nothing of what brought her to that point, and she hoped they never would.

"I'm sorry. I wasn't very nice. I guess my day was even more stressful than I'd thought." She gave Gordon a kiss on the cheek. "If he ends up buying the house down the street, we'll invite him for dinner and I'll be on my best behavior. I promise."

The next morning Marta tried to redeem herself in the eyes of her family. Slowing her usual pace, she fixed a breakfast of bacon, eggs, and toast. She counted on the aroma of cooking bacon to get Gordon out of bed in time to eat it.

"What's this?" he asked, shuffling into the kitchen. "A peace offering?"

"You might say that."

Gordon laughed. It was a wonderful sound Marta hadn't heard from her husband in a long time.

"Can I hold out for orange juice, too?"

"We don't have any. I guess I could run to the store."

"No, this is fine. Very nice, in fact." He patted her shoulder, then piled his plate with eggs and two strips of bacon.

Jamie was less enthusiastic. "No fair," she said.

"What's not fair?"

"You tell me I need to lose weight and then you make bacon?"

"I never said you needed to lose weight."

"You hint at it often enough."

"I do not."

"Yes, you do."

Marta was appalled. Was she not only a bad wife, but a bad mother, too? "Breakfast is good for you. All the diet gurus agree on that."

"But not bacon," Jamie grumbled. She broke off half a piece anyway, and when she'd finished that, went back for another slice.

By the time Marta left the house that morning, family order

was more or less restored. But her inner equilibrium was still in turmoil. Where would Todd turn up next?

At the office, Marta made a conscious effort to put her personal problems aside, and dug into drafting a brochure for the Youth In Transition outreach project. Thankfully, Carol was out of the office for the morning, so Marta was spared the temptation of conversation and further self-recrimination.

Lucy Summers, the director of the humane society, called just before noon to remind her of the upcoming Adopt a Friend Fair.

"You've got the photographer lined up?" she asked.

"Right." A local man she and Carol had used for many of their publicity shots.

"And you'll be there?" Lucy asked.

"Absolutely." Adoption events were held regularly at various locations in town, but the fair was a big deal and the main kickoff for their annual fundraiser. There would be food, activities, and a clown and balloons for the kids. And members of the media. At least Marta hoped they would be there. She'd done her best to hype the event.

"I hope the weather cooperates. The paper this morning mentioned the possibility of rain."

"We'll keep our fingers crossed," Marta said. There were some things beyond even the control of the most careful planning.

She found a few minutes late in the afternoon to call her sister. The check had been cashed but she'd not heard a word of thanks. It was part peevishness that made her call, but also a small niggle of worry. There was no shortage of ways for Cassie to get into trouble.

But her sister didn't answer, so Marta got neither thanks nor reassurance.

She was putting her phone back in her purse when she heard the familiar ping of an incoming message.

She clicked and saw a text from Todd.

I'm crazy about you! Let's talk soon.

He'd signed it with a red valentine heart.

CHAPTER 12

Jamie liked math, and algebra was one of her favorite classes, but today she found her thoughts drifting to the man her dad had been talking to last night.

Todd. Each time she silently said his name, she got a warm feeling in her belly. He was movie-star cute, like a young Leonardo DiCaprio. Clearly a man rather than a boy, but not a real grown-up like her dad, either. More like an older brother sort of grown-up. He was funny and nice, and he'd looked right at her when they were talking. He seemed to really listen because he asked thoughtful questions, not the sort of dumb, canned responses she got from most older people. He'd said she had a knack for storytelling. Nobody had ever said she had a knack for anything before. Maybe she'd be a writer someday, or a journalist. It was probably a more interesting life than anything involving math.

Mr. Vaughn's voice broke through her thoughts. "Jamie, can you tell us the first step in solving this problem."

Which problem? Jamie wasn't sure where they were. The blackboard had filled up with a lot of numbers and arrows since she'd last looked.

"I . . . uh . . . I'm not sure."

"Number five," Oliver whispered from behind her.

Five. Jamie looked down at her book. It was one of those train questions but her mind was blank. She felt her face grow pink.

"Perhaps," Mr. Vaughn said, "you'd like to take a stab at the answer?"

"Let me," Oliver pleaded. "You haven't called on me yet."

Mr. Vaughn gave Jamie a pointed look, then sighed. "Very well, Oliver."

Oliver gave a concise recitation of the correct solution. He liked math even more than Jamie did.

"Thanks for helping me out," Jamie told him after class as they wove their way through the crowded hallway. "I think my mind was somewhere else."

"That was pretty obvious."

"I know. It was embarrassing."

"I thought you liked Mr. Vaughn's class."

"I do. It's just . . . don't you sometimes find yourself daydreaming without even realizing you're doing it?"

Oliver peered at her through his thick glasses. "Not really. What were you daydreaming about."

"Nothing important."

"That boy you said you were meeting Friday night at the bookstore?" He poked her playfully in the ribs. "I bet that's it. You're sweet on him, aren't you?"

Sweet? Who used that expression these days? Obviously people like Oliver. She picked up her pace. "I've got to get to English."

"Me too," he said, matching her stride. "We're in the same class, remember?"

Jamie tried to stay focused during the rest of her classes. It was easy in English because they had a test, but not easy at all in civics, where Mr. Brand droned on and on about the constitutional limits of executive power. At least she didn't have to worry about being asked a question. Mr. Brand was in love with the sound of his own voice.

She was relieved when the dismissal bell finally rang.

Fridays, Jamie usually got a ride home with Alyssa. But Alyssa had an orthodontist appointment after school today, so Jamie was stuck either taking the bus or walking. She wasn't looking forward to walking. The day was overcast and cold. Not as cold as it got in Boston, but in Boston you expected it to be cold, and dressed for it. In Sterling, the trees were already in bloom.

Still, she preferred the cold to taking the bus. That made her feel like she was in grade school. Hardly anyone took the bus unless they had to. Except Oliver. He didn't see the point in wasting his time walking when he had better things to do. But he lived pretty far out on the edge of town.

"Hey." Harmony caught up with Jamie as she was shutting her locker. "I didn't see you at lunch."

"I was there."

"Really? Guess I missed you."

Jamie didn't believe that Harmony had given her a moment's thought during lunch. She had barely acknowledged her at all for the past week.

"Hey," Harmony said again, lowering her voice to barely above a whisper. "Maybe we can go to the movies again this weekend."

"The movies?"

"Like before."

Jamie wanted to tell Harmony off, to come back with some scathing, hurtful remark that would take her down a peg. But standing up to Harmony wasn't easy, and besides, Jamie couldn't think of anything to say.

Harmony took Jamie's elbow and steered her to the side of the crowded hallway, where they wouldn't be overheard. "Look, I'm sorry about misleading you last time. I was desperate, and my mom likes you."

"How can she? She doesn't know me."

81

"She knows you're one of the 'good' kids." Harmony managed to make "good" sound suspect. "I knew she'd let me go with you."

"Pretend to go with me, you mean," Jamie shot back. "You used me so you could spend time with your boyfriend, what's-his-name. And now you want to do it again. Are you nuts? You think I like killing a whole evening by myself?"

Harmony looked more irritated than ashamed. "It's not like you have plans, do you?"

"I might."

"Both Friday and Saturday nights?"

"I'm not sure."

"Please, Jamie. I—"

"Could I bring a friend?"

Jamie and Alyssa usually just hung out on the weekends. Would it really matter if they picked up Harmony first? Assuming Jamie could convince Alyssa to go along with the plan.

"I'm not really interested in going a double date," Harmony said with a flick of her long, blond hair. "T.J. and I get so little time alone."

"Let me check my social calendar," Jamie said sarcastically. "I'll get back to you." She turned to go.

Harmony grabbed her arm. "I can make it worth your while. What do you want?"

"What do I want?"

"Money? Pot? Alcohol?"

A life, Jamie thought, pulling away. *That's what I want.* But even Harmony couldn't give her that. "I said I'd let you know."

Jamie slammed her locker shut, turned up her coat collar, and headed outside. Why hadn't she stood her ground and told Harmony no? She hated herself for being so wishy-washy, so eager for a crumb of friendship from someone like Harmony. But the truth was, she was also envious. It wasn't fair that some people had all the luck while others had none.

A blast of north wind hit her in the face as she headed up the hill in the direction of her neighborhood. It cut through her thin jacket and whipped loose strands of hair into her eyes. She probably should have taken the bus, after all.

She'd only gone a couple of blocks when a car slowed beside her and the horn tooted. She looked over warily.

"Hey," the driver called out. "Remember me?"

She squinted to see through the window. Todd! The relief of finding a friendly face paled in comparison to the thrill of seeing him. Her heart started beating faster.

"You want a ride?" he asked. "It's cold out there."

Was she dreaming or was this really happening? "Thanks." She climbed into the car. "I was already half frozen. What are you doing here, anyway?"

"Just passing by."

"How did you recognize me?"

Todd laughed. "You're not the sort of girl one forgets. Do you walk home every day?"

Jamie shook her head. "Sometimes I get a ride with my friend, Alyssa. Her parents let her have the car a couple times a week. Sometimes I get to use our car, but not very often." And sometimes her dad picked her up, but Jamie wasn't about to mention that because it made her sound like a little kid. "I don't mind walking, really, except for the cold."

"I'm with you there. I'm a warm-weather kind of guy." Todd gave her an impish smile, and Jamie drank it in like melted chocolate.

"Your dad said you lived in Boston before moving to Sterling. Did you like it there?"

Jamie shrugged. "Better than living here." She didn't want to get into the reasons she disliked Sterling. Then he'd know how unpopular she was. "Where are you from?"

"Just about everywhere. I grew up in the Midwest, but I've moved around a lot since then. At the moment I'm living in Chicago."

"Where was your favorite place to live?"

"Tuscany."

"Italy?"

"Right. You ever been?"

Jamie scoffed. "Hardly. My family doesn't travel much."

"Why's that?"

"I dunno. It's expensive, I guess. And I don't think my dad's much interested."

"Your mom's the more adventurous one?"

Her mom was certainly more lively than her dad. "I think so."

They'd arrived at Jamie's house and Todd pulled to the curb.

"I'm sorry about the way she acted last night," Jamie said.

"Not a problem."

"She's not usually so rude."

Todd smiled again. "She couldn't be, given that she's got a daughter with so much sparkle."

Jamie felt herself blush. "Thanks for the ride." She got out of the car quickly, before she said something stupid. At the front door she turned. Todd was still at the curb. He waved, and she waved back. She felt a flutter in her chest like she'd been brushed by butterfly wings.

CHAPTER 13

"Pretty good turnout for a pet adoption event," Carol noted with a nod toward the crowd. The park was dotted with food booths and activity stations, all teaming with interested participants.

Marta nodded. "We lucked out with the weather. And I think Friday night's television news coverage helped."

"You can bet the channel wouldn't have even mentioned the fair if you hadn't hounded them. No pun intended."

"I didn't hound them," Marta protested.

Carol grinned. "Call it what you want. You did good. I just wish we had bigger fish to fry than dogs and cats."

Marta winced at the image. "Not the best idiom, but I get the point."

Carol was pushing for bigger challenges and richer clients. Marta wasn't against the idea, but she wasn't consumed by it either. She preferred working for causes she believed in.

"Don't get your hopes up," Carol said, "but I spoke with a potential new client the other day. It's something that might give us a prominent national platform."

"A commercial business?" Marta had reservations about taking on clients solely because they paid well.

"No, it's a charitable foundation, but I got the impression they're big. Tim Whitaker, the man who contacted me, is a scout for them."

"A scout?"

"A go-between. He's making inquiries into a handful of public relations agencies the organization is interested in."

"Did you look them up online?"

"He wouldn't give me the name of the organization. They want to remain anonymous at this point."

A national nonprofit. That would be the best of both worlds—work Marta found valuable and more money. "Very mysterious," she said.

"I don't think it's that so much as wanting to protect their privacy."

"I'll keep my fingers crossed."

A woman walked by with two teenage boys following close behind.

"Three?" One of the boys asked her. "How did we end up with three cats?"

"Well, I liked one and your mom liked another."

"That's two," the second boy pointed out.

"I'm glad to know your math skills are still sharp."

The first boy drilled down. "So where's the third cat come in?"

"The cat your mom chose has a sister," the woman explained, somewhat sheepishly. "The two cats have lived together their whole lives."

The boys looked at one another and groaned. "We wanted a dog," the first boy said.

"Your mom and I agree. Dogs are too much work."

"And three cats aren't?"

"Don't you love it?" Carol whispered when they'd passed.

"Cats trumping dogs?"

"No, the two moms thing. Not that I'm against it or anything, but it always takes me by surprise. Especially in Sterling of all places."

"There could be another explanation," Marta offered.

"Like what?"

"Sisters?"

Carol shook her head. "I don't think that's it." She glanced at her watch. "Anyway, I've got to get going. Looks like everything is under control here. Once again, you did great."

Marta wandered past the puppy pen, where a litter of black labs had attracted quite a crowd. She would have loved a dog but Gordon was allergic. He claimed that even the supposedly allergy-free dogs set him off. When Jamie was younger and had been begging for a dog, she'd tried to convince Gordon to visit an allergist and see if something couldn't be done. But he resisted and she finally gave up.

Further on, she stooped to pet a shaggy brown dog whose tail was thumping like a nonstop metronome. He nosed her hand and looked at her with big, sad eyes.

"Oh, you're a cutie," she said, tickling his head behind the ears.

The volunteer holding the leash agreed. "This is Chester. I'm surprised he hasn't been adopted by now. Maybe today will be his lucky day."

By afternoon, the fair was winding down. Marta made another sweep of the grounds, talking with volunteers, families looking for a pet, and the many casual attendees who came for face-painting, games, or simply a chance to see the animals. From her perspective, the day had been a success. She didn't know the exact number of animals who'd been adopted but she bet it was sizable. Just as important, the event had given the humane society, and their funding campaign, lots of publicity. The pledge board's oversized thermometer of donations had risen considerably.

Feeling pleased, Marta decided to pay another visit to her shaggy friend with the big eyes. She hoped that today had indeed been his lucky day.

A man in a blue sweater was hunched down next to the dog, and the dog was showering him with the same gleeful wags and whimpers he'd shown Marta. The man's back was to her, but as she approached, he stood and turned.

She stopped in her tracks. Todd.

He caught her eye and waved. "What a cute guy, huh? His name is Chester."

"What are you doing here?" There was nothing friendly about her tone.

"Same thing I imagine most folks are doing, enjoying the dogs and the music."

His jovial tone set her nerves on edge. "You're interested in adopting a dog?"

"I'd love to but I'm afraid it's not in the cards at the moment. I did make a contribution to the humane society, however." He pointed to the "I-heart-paws-and-claws" sticker on his sweater.

Marta hadn't heard from him in several days. She'd hoped that was the end of it.

"Why are you in town at all?" she demanded. "Don't you have a job?"

Chester didn't appreciate being ignored. He barked and wagged harder. Todd gave him a final pat on the rump and joined Marta.

"I was hoping I might run into you here," he said.

"What made you think I'd be here?"

"The humane society is a client of yours, right? I played a hunch and won."

"How did you know that?" She couldn't remember mentioning it, although she might have.

"You're important to me, Marta. Like I said the other day, I want to learn everything I can about you."

"And like I said the other day, you need to leave me alone."

"I can't."

"Why not?"

"Come on, Marta, you know why." He stepped closer and took her hands in his. "I had to see you. I can't get you out of my mind."

Marta pulled her hands free and glanced around to see if anyone had noticed. She feared the intensity of Todd's gaze and the low, hushed tone of his words might garner attention. "You have to stop this. It can't go on."

"That's where you're wrong. I'm not taking no for an answer."

As a wave of panic exploded inside her, Lucy Summers, the humane society director, walked over to them. She was short and plump and a bundle of energy. "Thanks so much, Marta. You did a great job getting the word out."

Standing possessively close to her side, Todd said, "She did, didn't she? But then, that's not surprising. Marta's a pretty amazing woman."

Lucy offered her hand. "Hi, I'm Lucy Summers. I don't believe we've met."

"Todd Wilson, an old friend of Marta's."

"Pleasure to meet you, Todd. I hope you'll be a friend of our shelter as well. We need all the friends and support we can get."

"I'm with you," he said.

When Lucy moved on, he took Marta's elbow. "Let's go someplace where we can talk."

She pulled away. "There's nothing to talk about."

"Oh, but there is."

A group of volunteers passed by, calling out a greeting. Marta had no interest in talking to Todd, but neither did she want their disagreement to play out in public. "Okay, let's take a walk," she said.

He led her to a path along the creek. They walked in silence for a while, Todd whistling lightly under his breath. The cool air was tempered by a clear sky and bright sunshine. Marta could feel the hint of real warmth from the sun's rays on her back.

"What a gorgeous day," he said finally, echoing her own thoughts. "Don't you just love the first signs of spring?"

"Todd, what's going on? You know I'm married. You know I'm not interested in any sort of relationship with you. I'm sorry if I misled you. I really am. I know you've had a rough life recently, with . . . with losing your wife and all. But I'm not the answer to your problems."

"I think you are."

"But if I'm not interested—"

"You haven't given me a chance, Marta."

God, he was exasperating. How could you convince someone who didn't listen? "You must have friends," she said. "There have to be plenty of women who would jump at the chance to know you better."

"Not really. I sort of cut myself off from people after what happened."

"Then go out and find people who share your interests. Go meet new women." She sounded like Dear Abby. "It makes absolutely no sense to keep coming after me."

Todd stopped and turned to face her. He picked up her hand and lightly tickled the flesh of her palm with his fingers. Marta tried to pull away, but he wouldn't let go.

"Why are you so afraid to be yourself?" he asked. "To listen to your heart?"

Marta shook her head. "You've got it all wrong. Seriously wrong."

Todd leaned closer and kissed her, softly at first, then more passionately. She struggled to push him away. Todd put his hand on her chin and looked her in the eyes. "There's a woman inside you, Marta. A wild, passionate, wonderful woman, and

I'm in love with her."

A cloud passed in front of the sun, and Marta felt a shiver. Or maybe it was the L-word that got to her. "No, Todd," she said. "You can't be. You don't even know her."

"Neither," he said, "do you."

CHAPTER 14

Gordon was on his way to the library when Alan Warner, the history department chairman, hailed him.

"Hold up," he called out from his office. "I'll walk with you."

Gordon stopped and hovered self-consciously in the hallway while Alan grabbed a jacket and locked his office door. He was in his mid-fifties, balding with a bit of a paunch. Gordon liked him well enough, although they had little in common and rarely talked outside of department meetings. The postponement of Gordon's tenure vote had further strained what was already a rather tenuous relationship.

"I'm on my way to the library," Gordon volunteered, because he felt the need to say something congenial.

"Good, good. I won't keep you."

"I didn't mean I was in a hurry."

"No, of course not." Alan punched the button to summon the elevator even though they were only on the second floor. Gordon usually took the stairs. "Say, any word on that paper you submitted for presentation at the History and Humanities conference?"

"As a matter of fact, yes. It looks encouraging."

"That's wonderful. I heard some favorable feedback on it indirectly."

Gordon would have liked to press Alan for details but suspected that would be bad form. "That's good to hear."

"It would certainly be another check on the plus side when

your tenure vote comes up," Alan noted.

They stepped outside. Alan pulled a pair of sunglasses from his pocket and slipped them on. Gordon, who hadn't yet replaced the pair he'd broken several weeks ago, squinted into the bright sunshine.

A voice called out from his left. "Hey, Gordon! I was just thinking about you."

Shielding his eyes from the glare, Gordon glanced in the direction of the voice. "Todd," he said in surprise. He was pleased to have a chance to atone for Marta's rudeness the other night. "I never expected to see you here."

"I won't keep you," Alan said. He headed off to the parking garage but not without a farewell pat on Gordon's back. "Good luck with that paper. I'll keep my fingers crossed for you."

"Thanks."

"You're writing a paper?" Todd asked.

"It's one I've finished. Now I'm revising and waiting to see if it's accepted. What are you doing on campus?"

"Just thought I'd check it out. You know, part of getting to know the community. Plus, I've always liked college campuses. I once even envisioned myself as a professor."

"Why didn't you follow through?"

"Too much work. And to tell the truth, I don't think I'm smart enough. You, on the other hand, must have the smarts as well as the drive."

In Gordon's case, the decision to teach had more to do with inertia than drive, but he didn't bother to elaborate.

"Want to grab a bite to eat?" Todd asked. "It's almost lunch time."

Gordon usually brought lunch from home and ate at his desk, to save both money and the aggravation of small talk. In fact, there was a soggy tuna sandwich waiting for him in a desk drawer. It was suddenly entirely unappealing.

"Sure, there's a food court across the quad." Gordon led the way, dodging the steady flow of students on bikes and skateboards, as well as those lost in their cell phones. "So what was your field?"

"Field?"

"You said you'd once envisioned academic life."

"I majored in sociology, but minored in partying. Or maybe it was the other way around." Todd laughed. "Not a good combination in any case. The academic idea was mostly a fantasy. You know, only a couple hours of work a day, long summer vacations, an occasional sabbatical. Not to mention all those cute coeds hanging on your every word."

"That's a fantasy, all right." Gordon couldn't tell if Todd was joking.

"It's not like that?"

"Not at all. More like low pay, long hours, and no respect from the students."

"Guess I lucked out then." Todd pumped his hand in the air and grinned. "You don't sound happy. Why not try something else?"

"I'm not sure what I'd do." Gordon had, on occasion, considered leaving academia, but it was mostly an idle thought. He had no idea what he'd do instead, or where to start. There wasn't much call for history majors in the business or tech worlds. And to tell the truth, the idea scared him. Academia was the only world he knew.

"How about you?" he asked. "What do you do for a living?" Gordon realized they hadn't covered much personal territory the other day.

"Consulting mostly. We're headquartered in Chicago but I'm on the road as much as I'm there."

"What kind of consulting?"

"Oh, you know, financial matters."

Gordon didn't have any idea what that meant. It was one of the reasons he knew he wasn't cut out for a career in business. "So why are you looking to move to Sterling?"

"It seems like a nice town and I'm getting fed up with the snow and cold." They'd reached the food court and Todd was studying the options for lunch. "What's good?" he asked.

Gordon laughed. "Nothing, really. The burgers aren't too bad but they're heavy. The pizza's not bad, either."

They opted to share a pepperoni pizza, and Todd insisted on paying for them both. "Low pay and long hours, remember?"

Gordon tried to protest. He'd been making a point, not pleading poverty. But Todd brushed his concerns aside. "I'll put it on the expense account."

Expense account. Wouldn't that be something? Gordon had a fleeting vision of working in a job where he'd have a similar perk. But it would never happen. If he wasn't in academics, he'd probably be stuck in a cubicle working for the big guys who did have expense accounts.

"Thanks," he said

The pizza was worse than Gordon remembered, but Todd didn't seem to mind. He devoured two pieces while they talked sports, movies, weather, and about Todd's love of sailing and Gordon's fear of the water. The conversation flowed easily, which surprised Gordon since he'd always had trouble making small talk.

As they were finishing up, Todd suggested they take in a ball game sometime. "You a Braves fan? I think I can get tickets for the game this Sunday."

Gordon wasn't much of a baseball enthusiast, but he enjoyed Todd's company. And Marta would be pleased. Wasn't she always encouraging him to be more outgoing?

"That sounds like fun," he said. "I'll have to check with my wife, though."

"Why's that?"

The question surprised Gordon. He shrugged to cover his embarrassment. "Uh, to see if we have plans for the day."

Todd nodded. "Hope you can make it."

When Gordon arrived home that evening, Marta was in the kitchen rinsing lettuce for the salad. It wasn't often that she beat him home, but Gordon had been so energized by his lunch with Todd that he'd dug into the rewrite of his conference paper with an enthusiasm he hadn't felt in a long time. All in all, he was in an upbeat mood.

He greeted Marta with a kiss, which landed slightly askew because she turned to pat the salad greens dry with a paper towel just as he planted the kiss. She smiled at him over her shoulder.

"How was your day?" he asked.

Marta shrugged. "I spent most of it on the Youth In Transition mailing. How was yours?"

"Pretty good. Alan Warner said he'd heard some positive scuttlebutt about that paper I submitted for the History and Humanities conference."

"That's wonderful!"

"Final decision is riding on the rewrite though." Gordon reached for a cherry tomato from the salad bowl and popped it into his mouth. "It will certainly help my chances for tenure if it's accepted for presentation."

Marta dried her hands on her apron. "It'll work out, Gordon. I'm sure it will. I know this past year has been hard on you, but the department's decision was a financial one. It wasn't directed at you personally."

Gordon didn't share his wife's confidence, but it was nice to hear her voice support. Some days he wasn't so sure she had much faith in him anymore.

"You'll never guess who I ran into on campus today," he said. "Todd Wilson. The guy who is interested in buying the house down the street."

Something in Marta's expression shifted. It was a subtle shift but notable because it seemed so incongruous. "What was he doing on campus?" she asked, sounding annoyed.

"I don't know. Getting a feel for the town, I guess. We had lunch."

"You what?"

The remark had the sting of a slap. Reflexively, Gordon recoiled. "Lunch. We had lunch. It wasn't anything fancy. We went to the food court on campus."

"I thought you took your lunch. I made your sandwich this morning."

So that's what this was about? "I wasn't planning on running into him. I'm sorry about the sandwich."

Marta took a breath. "No, that's okay. It was just tuna, nothing special." She turned her back to him and continued tearing lettuce. "How was lunch?"

"Fine. He's an easy guy to talk to. In fact, he invited me to the Braves game this Sunday."

Marta's hands stilled. She stood still as stone. "Why would he do that?"

"I guess maybe he's trying to be neighborly."

"Neighborly?" Her voice echoed with the how-stupid-can-you-be tone that always made him wonder what he'd done wrong. She swung around to face him again. "He's not really serious about the house down the street," she noted icily. "He hasn't even looked at it."

"How do you know?" And why did it matter? Gordon didn't understand what had Marta so ticked off.

She brushed his question aside. "There's something not right about that man."

"What do you—"

"This whole act, showing up in our garage, running into you on campus . . . it makes no sense."

"Act?"

"Right."

Gordon was having trouble following her. "What are you suggesting? That Todd is a serial killer or government agent or something?"

He expected her to laugh. But she didn't.

"I don't know, Gordon. I just have a bad feeling about him."

"You've made that clear from the start." He generally trusted Marta's instincts about people, but this was crazy.

"You didn't agree to go to the game with him, did you?"

"In fact, I did."

Marta stared at him. Her face grew pale. "You can't," she said finally.

"Can't?" Where did she get off telling him what he could and couldn't do?

"You don't even like baseball."

"I don't dislike it. And I happen to enjoy the guy's company."

"You—"

"Do we have other plans?"

She looked at him blankly.

"Or do you simply not want me to go to the game?"

"I . . . I . . ." Marta stared at the floor. She was breathing rapidly.

Gordon was thoroughly perplexed. "I thought you'd be happy," he said after a moment. "Aren't you always on my case to be more outgoing?"

Marta put her hands on her chest. "Please don't go, Gordon." She looked ill. "I can't explain it. But I don't trust the man."

Gordon didn't get it. Was she threatened by the idea of Gordon having a friend? He sensed she was saying more than he understood.

"Am I missing something? What's the big deal?"

Marta looked as though she might be on the verge of tears. Or maybe something more. She shook her head. "Please. As a favor to me."

"Let's talk about it another time," he said, thoroughly baffled.

If it meant that much to her, he wouldn't go. In some ways it would be a relief since he wasn't sure he could keep up his end of a full day's conversation with Todd anyway.

All the same, he didn't like being told what he could and couldn't do, who he could and couldn't be friends with. He was used to Marta's complaints but this was over the top.

And it was perplexing as hell.

CHAPTER 15

Marta was livid. What in the hell was Todd up to? He had no right worming his way into her life. No right cozying up to Gordon and pretending to be a friend.

She worried, too. Would he tell Gordon about their one-night stand? Did he intend to blackmail her? What the hell was she going to do?

She had tried kindness. And she'd tried reason. She'd explained that she was happily married and told him to leave her alone. And he'd ignored her. Whatever game he was playing, it was dangerous.

Her stomach churned. She'd have to be firmer, she decided. Forget the niceties. Just lay it out in no uncertain terms. Make him understand.

But right now, she needed to smooth things over with Gordon.

During dinner, she tried to calm down. None of this was Gordon's fault. He didn't see Todd the way she did. He didn't know what she knew. Her earlier outburst had clearly confused and angered him.

But her attempts to make nice were met with silence. Gordon said little, and what he did say was addressed to Jamie. As a result, Marta's remarks, too, were addressed largely to Jamie, who appeared uncharacteristically upbeat. Although everyone was civil, the meal was tense and unpleasant. Marta couldn't wait for it to end.

As soon as dinner was done, Gordon retired to his study and Jamie to her room. Marta grabbed her cell phone and withdrew to a quiet corner of the living room with the intention of sending Todd a strong, clear message he wouldn't be able to ignore.

For a full five minutes, she stared at the phone, trying to figure out how to do that. *Leave me alone* sounded adolescent. *This has got to stop* came off as melodramatic. Both seemed to invite a response, and neither was particularly strong.

She finally concluded no written message could sound angry or definitive enough to get through to him. As much as she hated the idea, she'd have to tell him directly.

She started to punch in Todd's number but chickened out. Instead, she called Carol.

"What's up?" Carol asked. Laughter and conversation buzzed in the background. It sounded as if she was out at some social event.

"Have I got you at a bad time?"

"It's okay. I've got a minute. Is something wrong?"

"I have a crisis," Marta said.

"One of our accounts?"

"It's personal." Marta lowered her voice. "It concerns that little, uh, issue I have."

"Todd?"

"Right. He was on campus today and just 'happened' to run into Gordon."

"You're kidding!"

"No. They had lunch together."

"My God. Did he tell Gordon what happened between you two?"

"I don't think so. Not yet anyway."

"But you're worried he might?"

"Why else is he doing this? I'm sure it wasn't a coincidence that he ran into Gordon. Just like it wasn't by coincidence that he met Gordon in the first place. Pretending to be interested in buying the house down the street was just a ruse."

"There's a chance it was legitimate."

"It's not. Believe me. I don't trust him. I don't know exactly what he's up to, but it's not good."

"What are you going to do?"

"I was hoping you'd have some advice. I don't think a text message or email will be enough. I need to talk to him. Should I call him? Meet him face to face?"

"He hasn't taken *no* for an answer so far," Carol pointed out.

"That's what worries me."

"Listen, Marta, this is too complicated to think through right now. Just don't do anything rash tonight. We'll talk tomorrow, okay?"

Although she longed to get rid of Todd once and for all, she wasn't eager to talk to him. With luck, maybe something would come to her in her sleep. "Thanks," she said. "Enjoy your evening."

Gordon was in bed and already asleep by the time Marta joined him. He rolled onto his side, facing away from her, and began snoring lightly. She slid in next to him and cuddled close, craving the warmth and comfort of his presence. Together, just the two of them wrapped in the cloak of night, she felt safe. Todd couldn't touch them.

She pressed her face against Gordon's back and silently apologized for bringing Todd into their life. And cursed herself again for being so stupid.

She slept fitfully and awoke exhausted. Despite a seemingly endless stream of dreams, the solution to her problem was no clearer by morning than it had been the night before. And Gordon was only marginally less distant. He kept his nose in the paper over breakfast and left for campus early.

Carol's was the first truly friendly greeting Marta received all morning. But Carol hadn't come up with any simple answers, either. In fact, Marta wasn't sure she understood how serious the situation was.

"Maybe you haven't been clear enough with him," Carol suggested as they brainstormed over coffee and scones.

"I've tried." But how hard had she really tried? She might wear her indignation on her sleeve, but had she made her point with conviction? When she was honest with herself, she had to admit that on some level she'd been flattered by Todd's attention.

Until he'd insinuated himself with Gordon, that is. That had knocked her right out of her fantasy world.

"Whatever you've told him," Carol said, sipping her coffee, "he's not wanting to hear it. He's been through a lot, remember."

"About his wife being murdered, you mean?"

Carol nodded. "That would be enough to make anyone a little neurotic."

Marta agreed. That's why she'd made an effort to be *nice*. "I feel bad about rejecting him, especially now that he again has . . . feelings for someone. I feel bad about the whole sorry mess. Nonetheless, creepy is creepy."

"Creepy? I thought you said he was cute."

"He is, but he's acting creepy. It's like he's stalking me."

Carol laughed. "Oh, come on. That's a bit extreme."

"Is it?"

"He's probably just lonely and misguided."

"And unwilling to take *no* for an answer." Marta sighed. "Which brings us back to the situation at hand. How am I going to convince him to let go?"

"Better not to script these things out ahead of time. Just remember, be clear and forceful."

"Easy to say."

"You can do it."

Marta took one last sip of coffee, then stepped outside for privacy. With a pounding heart, she placed the call. Todd's phone rang five times before rolling over to voice mail. She hung up without leaving a message.

Damn. Having worked herself up for the call, she wanted to get it over with.

Just then, her phone rang. But it was her sister Cassie, not Todd.

"Where have you been?" Marta asked, and then cringed at the sharpness of her tone. "I called and called. I was getting concerned."

"Sorry. There was a problem with my phone service."

"What happened?"

"I forgot to pay my bill."

Typical Cassie. "How could you forget something like that?"

"I'm not as organized as you, okay? But I got it fixed. Everything's cool now."

"Glad to hear it," Marta said tersely.

"What's your problem? You got ants in your pants or something?"

"I'm at work. I've got things to do."

"Don't be mad, Marta."

"So why'd you call?"

"I wanted to say hello and see how things were going."

"Maybe you could throw in a *thank you* as well. I know you got the check I sent because you cashed it."

"And I wrote you a thank-you note."

"Funny, I never got it."

"Well, the post office isn't perfect. Or maybe I forgot to put a stamp on it. Anyway, how are you doing? Anything new with Gordon's job?"

"We're all good. Nothing new really." Marta was relieved to hear from Cassie but she wasn't about to discuss the current state of her marriage. And she certainly wasn't going to mention Todd.

"And how's my favorite niece?"

"Jamie seems happier these days. I'm keeping my fingers crossed it continues."

"She's a great kid," Cassie said. "Don't forget, neither one of us was exactly bouncing with happiness when we were her age. She's going to be just fine."

Marta found it ironic that Cassie, who had never been able to get her own life in order, was confident that Jamie would. She was forever cautioning Marta to step back and let Jamie be her own person.

"So how are you doing?" Marta asked.

"Great. I think I might have a job."

"That's wonderful! Tell me more."

"Well, I met this guy who's going to be looking for a receptionist soon."

"Soon?" Marta's initial elation gave way to caution.

"He needs to finalize the lease."

"But he's actually found office space?"

"Yeah. It needs some work, though."

Which could entail months. "What kind of business is it?"

"You know, general business. I think they sell plumbing or something. All I have to do is answer the phone and take messages and stuff."

Marta cringed, thinking about the sort of messages Cassie might take. Her sister was not good with details. "But the job," she asked, "it's a real job? With a paycheck?"

"Of course it is. Why do you always doubt me?"

Maybe because history proved Marta right more often than not. Still, she hated that she so often sounded critical. "Sorry. I didn't mean that the way it sounded. I'm just a little frazzled at the moment. Can we talk later?"

"Sure. Anytime." Cassie's tone was short. "Give me a call."

Marta closed her eyes and pressed her fingers to her temples. Another person she'd managed to tick off. She should probably call Cassie back right now and apologize. She never intended to give her sister a hard time, but it always seemed to happen. She really had to learn to lighten up.

She was caught up in mentally chastising herself when the phone rang again.

"You called?" Todd said without preamble.

"Yes, I . . . I want to tell you something." Marta took a breath to fortify herself.

"Great," he replied. "I'm right outside. Come on out and we'll talk."

"I'm not interested in *talking*, Todd. I just want to tell you that—"

"I'll be waiting." He disconnected before she could say another word.

Marta's heart pounded. *You can do this,* she told herself. *Clear and forceful. No hemming and hawing. No empathy. No smiles.*

She headed for the door before she could lose her nerve.

He was parked on the street, half a block from her office, leaning casually against his car. His face lit up when he saw her. "Come on, get in," he said.

Marta shook her head. "I'm not here to socialize, Todd. I'm here to say you need to stop this . . . this obsession of yours. I am not interested in you or any kind of relationship with you. My husband is not your friend."

She was speaking rapidly and her voice sounded tight. She made an effort to slow down. *Clear and forceful,* she reminded herself. "No way do I think you just *happened* to run into Gor-

don on campus any more than you *happened* to strike up a
conversation with him in our garage. You need to stay away
from me, and stay away from my husband."

"I *need* to, do I?" Todd smiled.

"Yes, you do." Somehow the words didn't sound as forceful
as she intended.

"You can't fool me, Marta. You say one thing, but I know
you're attracted to me. I know that deep down you want to be
with me."

"No, Todd, I don't."

He traced the line of her chin lightly with his thumb. "Marta.
Sweetheart."

She swatted his hand away and stepped back. "Why are you
doing this?"

"If you would just let yourself be who you really are. If you'd
listen to the woman inside you—"

"Stop it! The woman inside me is the same one who's standing here trying to make you understand. I don't want to see you
again. Ever."

Todd looked amused. "Don't do this, Marta."

"I just did." She turned to go, but Todd grabbed her arm.

"Tell you what. Spend the day with me. One day. You'll see.
We're meant to be together."

"NO!" Marta realized she was yelling and lowered her voice,
but not by much. "Don't you get it? I'm not interested in you.
Stay the fuck away from me."

A gray-haired man walking his dog crossed the street from
the other side and cautiously approached her. "You okay,
ma'am? You want me to call someone?"

She shook her head, embarrassed. "I'm fine."

The man looked warily at Todd and back to Marta. "You're
sure?"

She nodded. "Thank you, but I'm fine. Really. I'm sorry

about the language."

"No need to apologize." He again looked from one to the other, then chuckled. "I understand how a lover's spat can sometimes get a bit heated."

When the man was out of earshot, Todd grinned. "See. We were having a lover's spat. Can we get to the making-up part now?"

"You really don't get it, do you?" Marta said slowly. "There is no *we*. There is no anything when it comes to you and me. I don't even *like* you. You're nobody to me."

Todd stared at her. "You can't mean that."

"I do. Stay away, you hear me? I'll get a restraining order if that's what it takes."

His eyes narrowed and grew dark. "You don't want to do this, Marta. You really don't."

Carol was wrong. Todd wasn't simply lonely. He was unbalanced.

And more than a little frightening.

CHAPTER 16

"We need to leave as soon as school gets out," Alyssa told Jamie at the end of fifth-period English.

"Okay."

"I mean really quick. My mom needs me home to babysit because she's got a hair appointment."

"You told me that this morning."

"I don't want you to forget. You tend to dilly-dally."

"I do not. And nobody says dilly-dally these days. Sometimes you're just plain weird, Alyssa."

"No weirder than you."

They bumped shoulders and in unison said, "That's why we're such good friends."

It was a silly routine they'd started months ago at a sleep-over. Jamie didn't mind it much when the two of them were alone, but here, in the middle of the school day, she could only hope no one overheard them. She wouldn't normally have played along except that Alyssa was already annoyed with her for even suggesting they cover for Harmony last weekend.

"I'll get there as fast as I can," Jamie promised. "If you need to, go ahead without me. I'll walk home."

And maybe Todd will happen to pass by again.

Not likely, but it was an enticing fantasy. And about the only good thing happening in Jamie's life these days was in her imagination.

When the final bell rang at the end of sixth period, she made a beeline for her locker and actually beat Alyssa to their usual meeting place at the flagpole.

So who was the *dilly-dallier* now? She was mentally framing some clever way to tease Alyssa when she caught sight of a familiar blue car in the oval and her heart jumped.

It couldn't be.

Lots of people drove blue Nissans. How pathetic was she, letting her fantasies run wild like that? She was glad no one could read her thoughts.

Then the driver stepped out of the car and waved at her. It actually *was* him. Jamie about wet her pants.

"You want a ride?" Todd called over the din of student chatter.

"I, uh . . . sure." Jamie's heart was pounding.

Todd had come to school to give *her* a ride? And then her heart sank. Had her parents asked him to pick her up? Probably. Her mom must have talked to Alyssa's mom and learned that Alyssa needed to get right home. Her mom was big on not inconveniencing people.

But her mom didn't like Todd. She would never ask him for a favor. And her dad couldn't possibly know about Alyssa's tight schedule.

Alyssa breezed past. "Come on, let's go."

"Uh, actually, I've got another ride."

"What?" She followed Jamie's gaze. "Who's he?"

"His name is Todd."

"You know him?"

"Of course I know him. He's a . . . a family friend." A bit of a stretch but she had a feeling Alyssa would ask too many questions otherwise.

"He doesn't look like a family friend."

"What's that supposed to mean?"

"He's cute. Cool. Not like someone our parents would hang out with."

"I didn't say they hung out."

Alyssa gave her a curious look. "Well, I've got to run. If you're sure . . ."

"Yeah, no point in your going out of your way to drop me off, especially since your mom needs you home."

"Okay. See you tomorrow." Alyssa took off toward the student parking lot.

Jamie crossed to the curb. Why couldn't she have worn something besides her baggy old jeans today?

"Thanks for the ride," she said, opening the passenger-side door. "What are you doing here, anyway?"

"I was in the neighborhood. I figured it was about the time school got out."

She settled into the front seat and set her backpack on the floor. "So you came here? Just to give me a ride home?"

Todd grinned and pulled away from the curb. "You sound surprised."

"I am."

"I can count on one hand the number of people I know in town, and you're one of them. Sometimes it's nice to see a friendly face."

Jamie laughed because she didn't know what else to do.

Todd turned on the radio. "Pick a station," he said. "Show me what kind of music you like."

Jamie punched in her favorite pop station. "There's not a lot of choice," she explained. "Reception is bad around here."

"I like this kind of music. And country. You into country?"

"Some of it," Jamie said. "But not the stuff that's off key."

"No, I don't like that kind either." Todd glanced over at her. "Do you have to get right home?"

Jamie felt short of breath. "No, not really."

"You want to get something to eat first?"

CHAPTER 17

Marta looked around the bustling restaurant, which was one of her favorites. DeeDee's Cafe wasn't fancy, but the food was good and the ambiance about as classy as it got in Sterling. The old brick building had been renovated so that the interior had an open, airy feel. The tables were a sleek design of polyurethane-coated wood and bronze, and the walls were hung with artwork by local artists. Marta was always glad for an excuse to eat here.

She raised her wine glass to Carol's and offered a toast. "Here's to one year of success."

"May there be many, many more," Carol added. "Starting with Tim Whitaker and his anonymous organization."

Marta rarely drank wine during the day, especially a workday, but she and Carol were in a celebratory mood. The stated reason for lunch was the first-year anniversary of their partnership. But Carol had learned they were among the finalists under consideration by the organization Whitaker represented, and they were both heady with thoughts about their future.

Marta had her own reasons for feeling upbeat, too. It was now almost two weeks since she'd seen or heard from Todd. What's more, she and Gordon seemed to have moved beyond the rough spot of the past few months. Even Jamie had been cheerful of late. When Marta thought about her "indiscretion" in Minneapolis, which she did less and less often, she was no longer fearful, simply grateful to put it behind her.

"I wish we knew what organization he's scouting for," Carol said. "I've tried to weasel it out of him, but he insists he's sworn to secrecy."

They had Googled Tim's name, with no useful results. "Well, we know it has to do with children's health," Marta said. "That's something we could get behind. I mean, it's not like we'd be spearheading a campaign to encourage smoking or legalize dog fighting."

"If we land this job, it could be the beginning of a whole new era for us. We're bound to net other big clients as a result."

"Let's not get ahead of ourselves," Marta cautioned. "We're more likely *not* to be chosen than chosen."

"Who *wouldn't* want us. We're the greatest."

"That we are," Marta agreed with a laugh. "We could be on the brink of something really big."

"We'll have to hire an assistant."

"Several assistants," Marta amended. "And we may need an office in New York."

"As well as Paris."

Marta nodded. "Definitely Paris. And I'll need an entirely new wardrobe."

The waitress brought their soup and sandwiches, but in Marta's mind she was already chicly dressed and dining at a café on the Champs-Élysées.

By the time Marta was back at her office desk, she remembered why she avoided drinking wine in the middle of the day. She was feeling sleepy and fuzzy-brained. There was no way she'd get anything creative done the rest of the afternoon. Instead, she decided to clean up her digital files, a boring and tedious task that was long overdue.

She deleted drafts and older versions of documents, renaming them when necessary, and moving them into the proper folders. She mentally chastised herself for letting things go so long. Cassie was not the only one who had trouble staying organized.

She was finishing up with loose ends when she came across a photo Todd had sent her from the humane society fair. He was mugging for the camera with Chester, the pooch he'd been playing with when she ran into him. She took a moment to study it and was relieved to find she experienced none of the heart-racing rush she had in the past.

Ready to hit delete, her cell phone sounded with the distinctive tone that signaled Jamie was on the line. Marta pulled her phone from her purse.

"Hi, honey. What's up?"

"Is it okay if I go home with Alyssa and stay for dinner?"

"It's a school night. What about homework?"

"I'll get it done. We've both got a history test tomorrow so we can study together."

Marta had never found studying with a friend particularly helpful, and she suspected the upcoming test would be a small part of what Jamie and Alyssa talked about. But with Jamie, it was best to pick her battles.

"If you'll really study—"

"We will."

"Okay. But you can't make a habit of this. What time shall we pick you up?"

"Alyssa will bring me home."

"That's not nec—"

"It's fine," Jamie insisted. "She doesn't mind."

"Her parents might."

"Why do you have to make such a big deal about everything?" Jamie's tone had turned petulant.

Marta relented. Maybe wine at lunch was the key to dealing

with a teenage daughter. "Be home by nine o'clock at the latest."

"Will do." There was a moment's pause. "Thanks, Mom."

Marta replayed the last two words in her mind and smiled. It wasn't often Jamie thanked her for anything.

Carol breezed over to Marta's desk with a sheaf of papers in her hand. "You have a minute? Tell me what you think about . . ." She reached Marta's desk and stopped cold. "My God."

"What's the matter?"

Carol's eyes were focused on Marta's computer screen. "Where did you get that?"

"The photo? It's from the Humane Society's Adopt-a-Friend Fair." Marta decided it best not to mention that the man in the photo was Todd.

"That's him," Carol said.

Busted. "I was just getting ready to delete it." Carol probably thought Marta was sitting there dreaming about the guy. "I'm going to wipe Todd out of my life once and for all."

"Todd?" Carol sounded confused. "That's Todd?"

Marta nodded.

"No it isn't. It's Tim Whitaker."

"Whitaker? The man representing our prospective new client?"

"Yes. That's him."

"Are you sure?"

Carol nodded. "Absolutely."

Marta felt her stomach drop. Would Todd stop at nothing?

Carol turned to her. "I hope you haven't blown this for us, Marta."

"What are you talking about?"

"Our big chance. You told him to get lost."

"Of course I did. He wouldn't leave me alone."

"But we need him. He's our connection to the big time."

Marta wanted to scream. "Don't you get it? Todd . . . Tim . . . whoever he is, he's crazy. He's not representing any big client. He's trying to get under my skin."

"You? Why assume this is about you?"

"Because it is."

"Don't you find that a wee bit egotistical?"

"Think about it. When did he contact you? It was after I met him, right?" Marta stood and started pacing around the small office. "And why us? You really think he's heard great things about the breakout work we do with local pet adoptions and school funding campaigns? This whole scheme of his, representing some mysterious but *big and influential philanthropic charity* is as phony as a goose that lays golden eggs."

Carol dropped down into the chair across from Marta's. The color had drained from her face. "No," she insisted weakly. "That can't be."

"We were delusional. How could we think we had a chance at some national account?"

"You must be mistaken." Carol sounded more wistful than hopeful.

Marta shook her head. "What do you know about this Tim Whitaker? Nothing, right?"

"He said he was being discreet, but that he represented an influential group looking for a fresh approach. They wanted to remain anonymous until they made their final selection."

"And when we Googled him? Nothing. Just like I never found anything on Todd or his wife's murder."

"That doesn't mean anything. Not everything shows up on an Internet search."

"But we never considered the possibility that he was lying. Tim and Todd, Whitaker and Wilson. It's all a game to him, even the names. How did we never make the connection?"

"I don't believe this," Carol said.

"But you believe me, don't you?"

Carol looked at her.

"Don't you?"

"I . . . It's just that . . ." She stood and marched to her own desk. "Let me see if I can get to the bottom of this."

"How?"

"I'll call him."

"He'll lie."

Carol's expression was troubled. "You want to simply give up?"

Marta was shaken. Carol didn't understand.

Todd had scored again.

CHAPTER 18

Jamie hurried through the crowded hallway, Alyssa close at her heels. As usual, the school was a frenzy of activity at the end of the day. Against the din of slammed locker doors, students darted in all directions, calling out to friends and grabbing books to stuff into their already bulging backpacks.

"I still think this is a bad idea," Alyssa said.

"No, it isn't."

"What if your mom calls?"

"She won't. I already told her I was having dinner at your house." Jamie crammed her history notes into the top of her bag. She hoped she'd have time to give them at least a quick look before tomorrow's test.

"She might call. What if there's an emergency."

"In that case, she'd call my cell."

"And you'd answer?"

"If I don't, she'll leave a message."

"Not if it's a real emergency. She'll call my house."

"Stop worrying, would you? This is a big deal for me."

Alyssa grabbed books from her own locker two down from Jamie's. "What are you guys going to do for all that time, anyway? You're not . . . you know . . . going to do something you'll regret, are you?"

"Hardly." To Jamie's disappointment, Todd hadn't even kissed her yet—despite ample opportunity. He touched her back, her arm, her leg, and while even those small gestures made Jamie weak in the knees, they were more casual than sexy.

"Well," Alyssa said, "I still think what you're doing is wrong."

"How's it wrong?"

"You're sneaking behind your parents' backs, for one thing. You could get into trouble, for another."

They started down the main stairway. "You're jealous," Jamie told her.

"I am not. Why would I want a boyfriend who was *old* anyway?"

Jamie could think of hundreds of reasons she'd choose Todd over any seventeen-year-old kid. But she was tired of defending herself to Alyssa.

"He's not *old* old," she told Alyssa. "And he's not my boy-friend."

"Oh, girl, you are so delusional." Alyssa gave her a hip bump, then took off for the student parking lot. "Be careful," she called out over her shoulder.

Jamie ducked into the restroom to comb her hair and put on a little makeup. She'd never even worn lipstick until a couple of weeks ago, but now she had a little satchel filled with lip gloss, blush, and mascara. Todd was worth the effort.

Then she headed for the spot on the west side of campus that had become their regular meeting spot. He was already there, waiting for her.

"Hey, Princess. How was your day?"

"Better now that you're here." She'd practiced that line, hoping to sound playful and flirtatious, but she wasn't so sure she'd pulled it off. "How was yours?"

Todd grinned. "Better now that you're here."

Okay, maybe she'd handled the line better than she thought. Jamie tossed her backpack into the backseat and grinned at Todd.

He'd picked her up most afternoons since that first time

almost two weeks ago. They usually stopped for a soda or something to eat, and then he'd take her home, always dropping her off a block from her house. That was her idea but Todd agreed it was probably best. No telling what her mother would do if she found out. She'd practically bitten Jamie's father's head off when he told her that Todd had invited him to a ball game.

Her father hadn't gone to the game, of course. It seemed like all her mother had to do was look at him cross-eyed and her dad folded. Jamie didn't understand why he let her boss him around like that. But then her father wasn't really much of a sports fan, so maybe he hadn't cared one way or the other. And to tell the truth, she couldn't imagine what her father would have in common with Todd.

"Did you manage to get some extra time today?" he asked softly.

Jamie nodded and let the thrill of anticipation wash over her. "My parents aren't expecting me home until nine."

Jamie worried they would run out of things to talk about. That there would be long, awkward silences and that Todd would get bored. But it didn't turn out that way at all. They started with a drive in the country, then stopped to wander around one of the small, quaint towns they discovered, chatting easily about everything from favorite foods to Hollywood celebrities.

"I want to buy you something," Todd announced as they strolled the main shopping street.

"Why?"

He laughed. "Because I like you, that's why. What would you like?"

Jamie was stymied. He asked her questions like that sometimes, out of the blue. What's your favorite color? Where are you most ticklish? It became a game with them, but this was different. "Surprise me," she said.

And he had, dragging her into a boutique and buying her an etched silver locket on a fine mesh chain.

Jamie was overwhelmed. "I can't take this."

"Why not?" He clipped it around her neck.

She could think of a thousand reasons, but with Todd grinning down at her, only inches away, and her skin tingling like crazy, all she could say was, "Thank you."

Later, back in the car, he asked, "What's the most dangerous thing you've ever done?"

Being with you. "I jumped off a roof once. On a dare."

"How high?"

"Only one floor. I guess I'm not too adventurous."

"I beg to differ. I find you quite adventurous."

"What about you? What's the most dangerous thing you've done?"

He laughed. "You don't want to know."

They ended up at a restaurant, where dinner was now winding down and Jamie's coach was about to turn back into a pumpkin.

"You have room for dessert?" Todd asked as the waiter cleared their dishes.

Jamie always had room for dessert. And she'd been thinking about the bittersweet chocolate cake she'd seen on the menu all through dinner. But she didn't want Todd to think she was a pig.

"I don't know," she said. "I'm kind of full."

"How about we split something?"

Jamie smiled. "Perfect. What do you want?"

"You choose."

She made a show of studying the menu. "They all look good." She hesitated. "Do you like chocolate cake?"

"My favorite kind."

"Okay, let's get that."

"Just what I'd have chosen myself," Todd said.

Jamie felt a warm glow inside. It was the way she felt when she answered a question correctly in class, only much better.

Todd placed the order, adding coffee for himself. Jamie would have liked milk, but opted for tea instead. Milk was for kids.

"Do you have a special boyfriend?" Todd asked when the waiter left.

The question caught Jamie by surprise. She almost choked although she had nothing in her mouth. "Not really."

"Keeping all the guys on a string, huh?"

Jamie lowered her gaze. "Hardly." She wasn't about to admit that Oliver was the only boy who even knew she was alive, and he was hardly boyfriend material.

Todd waited until she raised her eyes again, then smiled at her. "That's good. For me, I mean."

A tingle of pleasure spread across her shoulders, almost as though she'd been tickled with a feather.

Their dessert arrived, along with two forks, and they took turns digging into the thick, fudgy cake. It was delicious, even better than Jamie had imagined. It was all she could do to hold herself back and not outpace Todd, bite for bite. She tried to take small forkfuls, but noted with dismay that she seemed to always end up taking twice as much as he did.

"You know," Todd said, setting his fork down and sliding the rest of the cake toward Jamie, "boys your age have a remarkably juvenile taste in women."

"What do you mean?"

"If they didn't, they'd all be crazy for you."

Jamie blushed. "I don't think so."

"You're mature for your age, Jamie. So many high school girls are shallow and superficial. Guys, too. You're not like that. I imagine the boys at school must seem pretty silly to you

123

sometimes."

"Most of the time," Jamie shot back, although it wasn't really true. Until she'd met Todd, she wouldn't have described any of the boys at school as *silly*. Some of them were a little odd, like Oliver, but there were many who were really hot. It was just that those boys didn't look twice at girls like her.

Todd's eyes lingered on hers, and he seemed about to say something more, but instead, he checked his watch. "Time to get you home."

"I wish I didn't have to go so soon."

"Me, too." He paid the bill and readied to leave, and then, with his hand firmly on Jamie's lower back, guided her toward the door.

"Thank you for dinner," Jamie said once she was settled in the car. The imprint of Todd's hand on her back still burned warm in her mind.

"You're welcome."

Then, because her *thank you* sounded so prim, she added, "I had a great time today."

"Me, too," Todd replied. "Maybe we can do it again. If you'd like, that is."

Jamie's stomach did a joyful flip. "I would like that. Very much."

Todd didn't say anything more, but he looked pleased. In the dim glow of the passing street lights, Jamie could see his mouth curl into a satisfied smile.

She could hardly wait until the next time.

As usual, Todd parked a block from Jamie's house. They sat in the darkened car for a moment. Jamie was hoping he'd kiss her, and worried she'd mess it up by not knowing how to kiss back.

Todd looked down the street and frowned. "Shouldn't I drive you all the way home this time? It's late and it's dark. I'd hate for anything to happen to you."

"Don't worry. This is Sterling. It's safe."

"Well, okay then." He gave her a quick smile. "Sweet dreams."

Jamie reached for the car door, and then on impulse, leaved over the console and kissed him on the cheek. "Thanks again. For everything." She slid out the door without waiting for a reply.

CHAPTER 19

Dinner was over and the dishes were done. Gordon was in his study, Jamie was at Alyssa's, and Marta was feeling restless and fidgety.

Todd passing himself off as Tim Whitaker was a frightening new wrinkle. Who knew what he'd come up with next? Marta was troubled and hurt by Carol's reluctance to take her at her word. Was that Todd's intention?

Carol had been her lifeline to sanity since moving to Sterling. She was Marta's closest confidant, as well as her business partner. That Carol would doubt her cut to the quick.

She couldn't talk about it to Gordon. And Cassie—well, discussing it with Cassie would mean admitting her involvement with Todd. It would also be pointless. Her sister operated in a world where duplicity and distrust were everyday occurrences.

Finally, Marta decided to take a walk. She slipped on her jacket and scarf, told Gordon she was going for a walk, and headed out.

The night was clear and brisk, the air sweet with the scent of jasmine. She was halfway down the block when her neighbor Linda called to her.

"Can you wait a minute?" she called from her garage. "I've got a letter for you. It was delivered here by mistake. I was going to bring it by in the morning."

Delivered-by-mistake mail was an appallingly frequent event

in Sterling. "Sure. I was just out for a walk."

Linda went into the house and returned moments later. She handed Marta a square-ish envelope that appeared to be addressed by hand, although it was hard to tell in the dim light of the street lamp.

"We've been out of town," Linda said. "Came back to two weeks' worth of mail, most of it junk. I hope that's not an invitation or something time-sensitive."

"I'm sure it's nothing important," Marta said, tucking the envelope into her jacket pocket. "Anyone who needed to hear from me would have tried the phone or email. How was your trip?"

"Great. But now we have to catch up on everything that didn't get done while we were gone."

"That's always the way. I won't keep you. Thanks for the mail."

She took a familiar route around the neighborhood, staying on well-lit streets. As she turned the corner toward home, she caught sight of Jamie going into the house. Picking up her pace, she hurried home only minutes behind.

"Hi, honey," Marta said, taking off her jacket.

Jamie jumped. "What are you doing here?"

Marta laughed. "I live here."

"I mean, at the door. Where were you?"

"Out for a walk. I saw you at the door when I turned the corner."

Jamie's eyes widened. Surprise, and something else, maybe fear, crossed her face.

"At the door, not before?"

Marta nodded. "Did you and Alyssa get a lot done?"

"Yeah."

The response was so noncommittal, Marta had her doubts. "You don't make Alyssa do all the work, do you?"

Jamie edged toward the stairs. "Of course not."

"It's just that you're spending an awful lot of time with her lately."

"She's a friend, and it's more fun to study together." Jamie turned toward the stairs. "I still have stuff to do," she said, and quickly headed to her room.

When her daughter was younger, Marta had sometimes craved a quiet moment to herself. Now she felt she barely saw Jamie most days.

She popped in to see Gordon. "How's it going?"

He looked up from the computer. "Good. I'll probably work late into the night so don't bother to wait up for me."

"I may read a bit but Jamie's home so I'll lock up."

The walk had done Marta good. She got ready for bed and climbed in with her book. Then she remembered the envelope in her jacket pocket, trudged downstairs again, and retrieved it.

The envelope was thin, but stiffer than a sheet of paper. And the address was indeed handwritten.

She slipped her finger under the flap and opened the envelope, pulling out a photograph.

Of her. In Todd's Minneapolis hotel room, lying naked on a bed of rumpled sheets.

Her heart slammed against her chest. She felt dread rise up in her throat. Oh, God. Full-color proof. What other photos did he have? Would he show Gordon?

She turned the photo over. On the back he'd scrawled a message.

I'll never forget.

Marta thought she might be sick. She tore the photo into tiny pieces and flushed it down the toilet. Then she splashed water on her face and crawled back into bed.

But she couldn't read, and she didn't sleep.

CHAPTER 20

Carol punched in Tim Whitaker's number. She'd tried calling him yesterday when she was still reeling from having learned he was the man Marta knew as Todd. Now, she was glad she hadn't reached him because she'd been so angry she would have done nothing but scream.

She was still angry, but calmer. And determined to stay that way. She'd be more likely to get answers if she managed to keep her cool.

He picked up on the third ring.

"Good morning, Tim," she said brightly. "This is Carol Hogan from C&M Advantage. I have a couple of new thoughts I was hoping you'd pass on to your organization. Perhaps we could meet later today to go over them."

"Uh . . ." Tim hesitated. "Actually, getting together isn't really necessary."

Did that mean they'd landed the contract? Carol felt the tingle of excitement. "Why is that?"

He cleared this throat. "I'm afraid things aren't looking so good for you."

The tingle turned to dread. "What do you mean?"

"The board made a decision. They went with another agency."

His words echoed in her head. "But just a few days ago you said we were among the finalists."

"Things change quickly in this business."

Did they ever. Carol thought fast. "Any chance they'd be

interested in farming some of the job out to us as subs?"

"I doubt it."

That was it then. Maybe Marta had been right. "Were we ever really among the finalists?"

"Yes, of course." He sounded so sincere that for an instant Carol forgot her suspicions.

"The organization liked your plan," he added. "Liked it a lot. But you were facing tough competition. Firms with a national track record, larger staffs, that sort of thing."

"I see." It did make sense. Why would a national nonprofit choose their small agency over a larger, more experienced one? But then, why had they even been considered among the finalists? If they really had been.

"Tell me," Carol said after a moment, "did Todd Wilson have anything to do with the decision?"

Her question was met with stark silence.

"You do know Todd Wilson, don't you, Tim?" Despite her resolve to remain calm, Carol's anger bubbled to the surface. The job wasn't theirs; she didn't have to be nice to him any longer. And she wanted to know the truth.

He sighed. "I was afraid this might become an issue."

"An issue?" Carol's outrage grew, as did the volume of her voice. "An issue? Are you actually associated with a legitimate nonprofit?"

"Of course." He sounded offended.

"Then what's with the two names?"

"I prefer to keep my business and personal lives separate."

"Most people manage that without adopting different identities."

Tim laughed weakly. "Maybe I went a little overboard, but they swore me to secrecy. It was important to them that nobody would be able to trace my inquiries back to them."

"That still doesn't explain the two names. Which is it,

anyway? Tim Whitaker or Todd Wilson?"

"Listen, Carol. You're making this into something it's not."

"It's a surprising coincidence that you'd end up here in Sterling to see about hiring our firm right after you . . . after your fling with Marta."

Another beat of silence. "She told you about that?"

"Of course she did. And everything that's happened since."

He made a guttural sound, part sigh, part groan. "I had no idea she worked with you. In fact, I have my suspicions that you two set this whole thing up. Maybe I'm the one who should be ticked off."

"Set up what whole thing? You called *me*, remember?"

"I don't know what your relationship with Marta is, but you need to watch out for yourself. She's a loose cannon."

"What do you mean?"

"She told you what happened in Minneapolis?"

"Yes." Hadn't she just said that?

"But probably not the whole story."

Carol switched the receiver to her other ear. The conversation was giving her a headache. "Why don't you enlighten me," she said coolly.

"I was there on business. I'd come from a late meeting. All I wanted was to relax and have a drink before heading off to bed. Next thing I know, there's this woman—Marta—staring at me, smiling, that sort of thing. Giving me *the look*."

"Are you saying *she* picked *you* up?"

"She certainly initiated it. She claimed that being away from home was her *playtime*. Seemed like innocent enough fun to me. I won't say I didn't enjoy myself, but I thought that would be the end of it. I didn't think she'd make it into a big deal. And I certainly never expected our paths to cross professionally."

Carol couldn't remember exactly what Marta had told her,

but she was sure that Marta's version of the evening had a very different spin to it. "If what you say is true, why are you still pursuing her?"

"Is that what she's told you? That I'm pursuing her?"

"Well, that you were until recently."

"I think your friend has an overactive imagination."

"What are you implying? You did send her flowers."

"I what?" He sounded stunned.

"I saw them," Carol said. "It was right after she returned from Minneapolis."

"I never sent her any flowers."

"I saw the card, too."

"I don't know anything about flowers or a card. Maybe she sent them to herself."

Carol recalled Marta's agitation when the flowers were delivered. Besides, what would be the purpose of pretending an affair? Tim hadn't even contacted their agency at that point.

"You also tried to be all chummy with her husband," Carol pointed out.

"Oh, for God's sake. I met the guy once, then ran into him again and we had lunch. There's some law against that?"

Carol was getting nowhere. She wasn't even sure anymore what she'd been hoping for.

"You see what I mean about being a loose cannon?" Tim asked pointedly.

No, she did not see. Marta was her friend. It was true that she was sometimes . . . well, less disciplined than Carol, but certainly not depraved.

"Look, I'm sorry you lost out on this contract," Tim said. "I really am. I thought your ideas were spot on. But it wasn't my decision."

"I guess not." Assuming there'd ever been a decision to be made.

"I'll keep your name out there," he offered. "Maybe one of the other organizations I work with will be interested. But you might want to keep Marta out of it. I think I'd have trouble giving an honest recommendation if she was involved."

The guy was nuts, Carol told herself. Totally untrustworthy. Still, the conversation left her feeling unsettled. She couldn't help wondering if there might be a grain of truth to anything he'd said.

The printer had called while she was on the phone with a question about the font for the museum flyer. She returned the call and was just finishing up when Marta bounded into the office and set a homemade blueberry muffin on Carol's desk, along with a slender vase of lilac stems.

"Spring is on its way," she said. "It's in the air. I can feel it."

"We didn't get the job."

Marta hooked her jacket on the coat stand. "What job?"

"The job Whitaker was interviewing us for. What job did you think I meant?" Carol realized she sounded sharp but she couldn't help it. What if it *was* Marta's fault?

Marta leaned against the door jamb. "We didn't really expect to get it, did we? After yesterday, I mean. Tim, Todd, whoever he is—it's pretty obvious he's not legitimate."

"We don't know what he is."

Marta stepped forward. "Wait. You talked to him? What did he say?"

"For starters, his take on your . . . relationship differs from yours."

Marta scowled. "How so?"

"He claims you came onto him at the bar that night. That he's not pursuing you at all."

"That's a lie!"

"He more or less implied that you're nuts."

"That *I'm* nuts?"

"A loose cannon is the term he used."

Marta put her hands on the desk and leaned forward. "You don't believe him, do you?"

Carol rubbed her temples. "All I know is that we lost out on a big opportunity."

Marta shook her head in disbelief. "There wasn't any opportunity. There is nothing legitimate at all about him."

"I guess you're probably right."

"Probably? That's the best you can do?"

Carol felt ill. "It's just that I'd so hoped—"

"I can't believe you'd even think of believing him over me!"

"I don't necessarily believe him," Carol said. "But—"

"But what? He was messing with us, Carol. He's . . . he's unbalanced. Or at the very least, devious. He may even be evil."

Carol backed off. Marta was her friend, after all. Tim-Todd was a slimeball in addition to whatever else he was.

"Forget him," Marta said irritably. "We're good at what we do, and our clients are happy. If something big comes our way, wonderful. If not, we still run a damn good business."

"I can't forget," Carol said. "I don't like being played for a fool."

"You're being ridiculous."

Carol stood and grabbed her purse. "I need some time to think."

"About what?"

Carol ignored the question. "I've got a friend who's a P.I. Let me see what he can find out."

And maybe then she'd have a better idea if there was a side to Marta she didn't know about.

CHAPTER 21

The following week, Marta was loading the dishwasher when Gordon, humming cheerfully, came up behind her.

"Last night was fun," he said, kissing her cheek. "We should do it again soon."

Marta smiled. She wasn't sure what part of *last night* he was referring to, but she had her suspicions. They'd gone out for pizza and a movie, then topped off the night with the kind of sex they hadn't had in months. She hoped it signaled an easing of the recent tensions between them.

"Any time," she said lightly.

"I'll hold you to it."

In the thick of things, she hadn't realized how deeply the whole *incident* (as neutral a term as any she could think of) with Todd had upset her and, by extension, her relationship with Gordon.

But now, finally, Todd was gone from her life, and Marta no longer lived every moment in fear of being exposed. She'd been a nervous wreck worrying about the photo he'd sent until she realized it had been sitting in her neighbors' mailbox for a week or more before she got it. If he hadn't already followed up, maybe he never would. Each day that passed with no contact from Todd brought her greater peace of mind.

Gordon seemed happier, too. And Jamie was practically bubbly. If only Carol wasn't still agitating about Todd, or Tim, or whoever the hell he was, Marta's world would be back to normal.

She had tried to convince Carol that he wasn't worth wasting energy over. Sure, he'd raised their hopes about landing a big contract, but their business hadn't suffered any real setback. In fact, it was doing quite well. C&M Advantage might not be the big success they'd sometimes let themselves dream about, but they hadn't really imagined it would be except on rare evenings of wine-fueled fantasy.

Carol insisted it wasn't simply about disappointment or lost opportunity. They'd been manipulated and made to look like idiots. Besides, there was something very fishy about the man. While Marta agreed, she was more than willing to put the humiliation behind her. Carol was not.

She sensed that Carol was angry with her, too, but in the name of harmony had channeled her wrath toward Todd. Most of it anyway. Sadly, there was still an undercurrent of tension between them that Marta seemed unable to mend.

"I've got to run," Gordon said, setting his cup on the counter. "Have a good day."

"You too." She dumped the cold remains of Gordon's coffee into the sink and placed his cup in the dishwasher.

Jamie flew into the kitchen clutching her backpack by one strap. She poured a glass of orange juice and gulped it down.

"You really should eat," Marta noted.

"I'll grab something at school."

"That's not the same. Those energy bars are high in sugar."

"So you've told me. About a hundred times."

And Jamie continued to ignore her. Marta decided to forego another lecture. She wasn't going to ruin her daughter's recent stretch of happiness.

Jamie had even sought Marta's opinion about clothes—twice in the past week, a record-setting milestone. Saturday they'd gone to the mall to pick out a couple of new tops for spring. Marta was so pleased to be included, she'd gone overboard, agreeing to a pair of leggings, a soft drape cotton sweater, and a turquoise jersey tunic that made Jamie's eyes sparkle but cost as much as the other two purchases combined.

She'd always been thankful that Jamie wasn't one of those air-brained girls who thought about nothing but clothes and makeup. On the other hand, she was secretly pleased to see her daughter taking an interest in her appearance.

"I'll probably be a little late today," Jamie said. "Alyssa and I are going to study together after school."

"Again? You're becoming quite the student."

"Aren't you always after me to do well? Grades for college and all that."

Marta didn't think that *always* was fair. "School is important. I'm glad to see you taking it seriously."

"Sounds like you've been watching Dr. Phil or something," Jamie muttered, setting her glass on the counter. "But don't expect too much. Alyssa is the brain, not me."

Marta ignored the glass that had not made its way to the dishwasher. She was on the verge of explaining she simply wanted Jamie to do her best, then realized she'd only feed into the Dr. Phil thing.

"Speaking of Alyssa," she said instead, "maybe she could come here for a change. You've been spending a lot of time at her house lately."

"It's cool. We'll probably stay at school anyway." Jamie snagged a pen from the drawer under the phone. "I've got to go." With that, she was out the door.

Marta finished up in the kitchen, took a quick shower, and headed off to work. On her way to the office, she called Carol. "I'm going to stop for coffee. I'll pick something up for both of us unless you've already done that."

"I'll be in late today. Thanks for the offer, though."

"Are you feeling okay?" Carol sounded hollowed out. And she was never late. She ate, slept, and breathed the business.

"Mark and I got into an argument last night. I didn't get much sleep."

"What?" Carol and her husband didn't fight. They had what Carol claimed was an *ideal* marriage. Marta assumed that was because they hadn't gotten past the honeymoon stage. Nobody had an *ideal* marriage, did they?

"What happened?"

"It's complicated, and probably silly." Carol paused, then seemed to mentally change directions. "If Chuck calls about the layout for the next mailing, tell him I'm on it and he'll get a draft later this afternoon."

"Will do." She wanted to say more, but with the strain between them, she hesitated. "Take care of yourself," she added instead.

Marta would have skipped coffee herself and gone straight to the office but by then she was already parked in front of The Daily Joe.

The line was short and moved smoothly. She exchanged pleasantries with Donna, the barista, while she waited for her latte, then capped the cup and moved to leave.

"Marta," a voice called from her left. Alyssa's mother, Elaine, waved to Marta from the tiny table where she sat with a large coffee and an open book. "I haven't seen you in ages. How have you been?"

"Good," Marta said, moving closer. "How about you?"

"Can't complain. Well, I could, but I won't." She laughed. Elaine was a marriage and family therapist who readily admitted she hadn't been able to follow her own advice. She'd been divorced for ten years and had never remarried. Marta didn't know her well—their lives rarely crossed except through their daughters—but she liked her.

"You caught me enjoying an infrequent quiet moment to myself," Elaine said. "Have a seat."

"Just for a minute. I have to get to the office." Marta pulled out a chair and sat. "I hope Jamie's not been too much trouble for you."

"Trouble?"

"Well, work. She's been spending so much time at your house lately you should probably charge us rent."

Elaine looked at her blankly. "I haven't seen Jamie in weeks."

"Didn't she have dinner at your place only a few days ago?"

Elaine shook her head. "No. Like I said, not in weeks. I assumed Jamie was busy with other things."

Marta felt a soft buzzing in her head, the sort of lightheadedness she sometimes experienced when she stepped out of a dark interior into the bright midday sun. "I . . . I guess I was confused." It would be embarrassing to have Elaine know that Jamie had lied to her.

"I know the girls are going to study together after school today," Marta added. "At the library. I probably assumed they were at your house before."

Elaine looked down at her coffee and frowned. "Alyssa has a dentist appointment this afternoon."

"Oh."

"Maybe Jamie meant she'd be studying with Harmony."

"Harmony?"

Elaine looked up. "Harmony Shaw. She and Jamie have apparently become quite the friends."

"Mmmm. I wasn't aware of that." No avoiding embarrassment this time.

"Teenagers feel the need to distance themselves from their parents," Elaine reminded her kindly. "It's a normal part of growing up. I wouldn't worry about it."

"Thanks." Marta was willing to bet that Alyssa didn't lie to *her* mother.

Elaine cleared her throat. "I guess you might not know about the boyfriend, either."

Elaine's tone was gentle and nonjudgmental. Marta gave up any pretense of looking like a mother in control. "You're right, I don't. Tell me."

"I don't know more than that. I've heard Alyssa mention him in passing. In truth, I assumed that's why Jamie hadn't been around so often."

Marta smiled weakly. "I guess I should be happy for her."

Elaine nodded with a smile of her own. "Although it does bring a new set of parenting challenges, doesn't it?"

"Thanks for filling me in. The part of me that's not embarrassed is honestly grateful."

"I hope you're not angry with me. I'd want to know if the roles were reversed."

A boyfriend? Marta rolled the idea around in her head as she made her way to the car. That would explain Jamie's new interest in clothes and makeup. And her recent attachment to her cell phone. She'd started carrying it with her everywhere, even in the house. And she was constantly checking for messages.

But why hadn't she said anything? Was he one of the school's troublemakers? Someone she knew her parents would disapprove of? Is that why she'd kept quiet? Or maybe it was a crush rather than a real boyfriend. One of the popular boys Jamie could only admire from afar. An athlete, maybe. Was Jamie hanging around watching his practices, hoping he'd notice her?

Marta recalled her own teen years. She'd had her share of crushes but no actual boyfriend. And she certainly hadn't discussed any of it with her parents. Still, she wished Jamie hadn't felt the need to lie about it.

CHAPTER 22

When Mr. Vaughan finally turned his back to the class and began scratching the homework assignment on the chalkboard, Jamie slid her phone from her pocket and peeked at the screen.

Nothing.

Not a single new text or email since yesterday morning.

She looked to make sure she had cell coverage, even though she'd checked not fifteen minutes earlier.

Why was Todd ignoring her? Had he lost interest already? Had he *ever* been interested in the way she wanted?

Usually he sent her a text first thing in the morning and again at night. Nothing like the *can't stop thinking about you* kind of message she dreamed about, but if he hadn't been thinking about her, he wouldn't have sent any messages at all, right?

She had cleared the afternoon with her mom, even though she hadn't heard from him last night. He'd probably just been tied up with work or something, she decided. But she hadn't heard anything this morning, either. His silence gnawed at her. She couldn't get it out of her mind. She didn't want to appear clingy, but by the end of first period she'd worked herself into such a desperate state that she'd broken down and sent him a text—*Hey.*

As soon as she'd hit send she realized how juvenile she sounded. No wonder he wanted nothing to do with her.

But she hadn't stopped checking her phone. She made herself wait until she couldn't bear it anymore, and then checked again.

Mr. Vaughan turned back to the class just as Jamie tucked the phone under the hem of her sweater. He looked right at her and she was afraid she'd been caught, but a moment later she was saved by the bell.

"I saw you sneaking to look at your phone," Oliver said as they neared the door. He always shadowed her from math to English. "You're lucky Vaughan didn't catch you."

"I know." Being caught would have meant detention or, worse, having her phone confiscated. But she hadn't been able to stop herself.

"You've been really antsy all morning. Is something wrong?"

Jamie looked at him sharply. "What do you mean, wrong?"

"I don't know. Like maybe you're worried. Or expecting an important message from your mom or something."

Her mother? How typically Oliver. "No," she said. "I'm just bored. Hoping for anything to break the monotony."

"You could try paying attention." He grinned.

Jamie's phone pinged with an incoming text. At last! Heart pounding, Jamie grabbed her phone and eagerly checked the screen.

Alyssa.

Can I use your Spanish book, I forgot mine.

Jamie's disappointment was so sharp it stung. *Sure. I'll bring it to English.*

"Breaking news?" Oliver asked.

"Alyssa forgot her Spanish book. She wants to borrow mine."

"You're a good friend."

Jamie shrugged. Not such a good friend lately, she thought with a twinge of guilt.

"Alyssa is lucky," he said wistfully.

"How so?"

"You know, to have someone she can count on to help her out."

"Doesn't everyone?" It was just a book, after all.

"Not really." Oliver shifted his backpack to one shoulder.

"I'm your friend," Jamie said lightly. "You can borrow my book any time you want." Not that Oliver would ever forget his book.

"Thanks." He smiled but sounded sad.

Jamie knew he'd been talking about more than borrowing a book. She promised herself she'd make an effort to be nice to him. He was really a pretty decent guy.

Harmony scurried up from behind and shouldered her way between them. "Can I talk to you for a minute?" she asked Jamie, turning her back to Oliver.

"If you can make it quick. I've got to get to my locker before the next class."

"I'll walk with you."

Oliver pulled ahead and walked on alone. Jamie wanted to call after him to make up for Harmony's rudeness, but before she could figure out what to say, he was lost in the crowd.

"TJ is having sort of a party Friday night," Harmony said. "Kids who've been out of school a while. You know, older kids. Why don't you come and bring your friend?"

"Alyssa?"

She laughed pointedly. "No. Your boyfriend."

"My—"

"The Hottie."

Harmony had been dropping subtle, and sometimes not so subtle, hints ever since she'd seen Todd at school last week. Who was he? How well did Jamie know him? How did they meet?

"He's not exactly my boyfriend," Jamie said, then immediately wished she hadn't. Harmony was clearly impressed.

"I guess he's not really a boy, is he?" She laughed at her own cleverness. "Your adult male friend then."

Not a boy, but not the sort of male friend Harmony meant, either. Jamie wasn't sure what their relationship was. She knew what she wanted it to be. But Todd was, as Harmony pointed out, not a school kid. He was older. Experienced. He'd probably had dozens of girlfriends over the years. Dozens of lovers, in fact.

Jamie knew he was attracted to her. She could tell from the way he looked at her. The way he talked and listened and remembered little things she'd told him. The fact that he met her every day after school.

And the way he touched her. Not romantically, exactly, but it was like he went out of his way to find reasons to touch her. He didn't have to put his hand on her back when they crossed the street. Didn't have to brush a stray hair from her cheek or rest his arm along the seat back so that it just grazed her shoulders. He didn't have to spend time with her at all.

She thought maybe he was worried about taking advantage of her. She had tried to make him see he wouldn't be.

She wanted more. She wanted him.

"Anyway," Harmony said, "do you think you can make it?"

Jamie pulled herself from her daydream. She couldn't imagine Todd at a party of just-out-of-high-school guys. Besides, she didn't want to share him with anyone. Least of all, Harmony. "I don't know. I'll have to see."

"Try, okay?"

They reached Jamie's locker as the warning bell rang.

"Shit," Harmony said. "I wanted to dump my jacket but I'll never make it to my locker in time. Can I leave it here until lunch?"

"Sure." It was cool the way Harmony sometimes acted like they were good friends. Too bad none of the *divas* were around to notice.

Jamie slid into her desk in English as the final bell rang. She tried to catch Oliver's eye but he pretended not to see her.

Her phone pinged again, loudly enough that a few heads swiveled. But thankfully not Mr. Darby's. He was still busily filling out the attendance card.

Jamie glanced at the screen.

Todd!

Meet U after school? he asked.

Jamie couldn't wait. *Sooner?*

Not a good idea.

Plse.

Lunch?

Mr. Darby looked up. "Jamie, is your phone on?"

Jamie blushed. "Sorry, I forgot. I was just turning it off."

"Do it then."

Jamie managed one last message. *C U.* She hoped it sent before she hit the off switch.

The minute the lunch bell sounded, Jamie sent a quick text to Harmony with her locker code so she could get her jacket, then ran out of class and raced down the stairs to the parking lot. When she didn't see Todd, her heart fell. Maybe he hadn't gotten her final message. Or maybe he wasn't interested.

Then she spotted his car at the far end of the drive and raced to climb in.

He greeted her with a smile and a hug.

She leaned her head against the headrest and smiled back. "Thanks for rescuing me."

"Your day that bad?" He seemed amused.

"I couldn't wait to see you." She'd meant the comment to sound light, not desperate.

"Is something wrong?"

She shook her head. "It's just that I miss you."

A pulse fluttered in his jaw. "Ah, Jamie," he said after a moment. He touched her thigh. "Jamie," he said again. "I miss you, too."

"You do?"

He nodded.

Jamie was afraid to breathe. "You didn't text me yesterday," she said after a moment.

"I had a problem with my phone."

"Oh." Now that he was here she felt like an idiot for sounding so needy.

"Did you think I was ignoring you?"

She shook her head, but she could see Todd wasn't buying it.

He tilted her chin so that her eyes met his. "You're not someone I can forget, Jamie. Even when I try."

"Why would you try?"

He looked at her a moment, then dropped his hand from her chin and turned to start the car. "What time do you have to be back at school?"

"I don't."

Todd raised an eyebrow. "What about your afternoon classes?"

"I can skip them."

"You sure?"

"Positive."

He seemed lost in thought until he asked, "You want to take a drive?"

"Sure. Where are we going?" She didn't really care. She'd have gone to the city dump if that's where Todd wanted to go.

"There are a couple of old bridges I've wanted to capture." When Jamie looked perplexed, he added, "Photography is a hobby of mine."

"Cool. I keep thinking that's something I'll learn someday."

"Perfect. Maybe I can give you some tips."

★ ★ ★ ★ ★

It was almost dinner time when Todd dropped Jamie off at home. A block away, as usual. He got out of the car and opened the door for her.

"Are you ever going to let me drive you all the way home?" he asked.

"What does it matter?"

"You're not embarrassed to be seen with me, are you?"

"Of course not! It's just that my mother—"

"Doesn't like me." He grinned, like it didn't matter to him whether she did or not.

"She'd probably think you were too old for me," Jamie explained.

"I probably am."

"Don't say that. Ten years is nothing."

"Eleven," Todd reminded her.

"Only because you just had a birthday." Jamie wished she'd never mentioned the age thing. The afternoon had been wonderful and she didn't want to spoil the mood.

But Todd grew suddenly serious. "Come here."

He pulled her closer and kissed her. A long, slow kiss that left Jamie breathless. She'd never been kissed like that, ever.

Then he traced a thumb over her lips and kissed her forehead. "You tempt me, honey. That can be dangerous."

"Not dangerous," Jamie insisted. "Not when I want what you want."

He shook his head. "That's where eleven years starts to mean something."

"It doesn't have to."

"You don't know what you're saying, Jamie. You have no idea."

"But I do. Please don't be that way." What was he trying to

say? He couldn't be leaving her. Not now. Not after the day they'd had.

She threw her arms around him and pressed herself against him. She didn't care who was looking. "Please, Todd. I want to keep seeing you."

She felt close to tears. Todd's body was warm, soft, and solid at the same time. His strong arms encircled her as he held her close. She could feel the beat of his heart in her own chest.

"I want to keep seeing you, too, Jamie."

"You do?"

He pulled away and nodded. "Just remember, I still think it's a bad idea."

"Text me," she said as she left. "I'll show you it's not a bad idea."

Jamie felt like skipping down the street but of course she didn't. Todd was watching. She skipped in her heart, instead.

She hoped her mom wasn't home yet. But when she stepped inside, her mom was in the kitchen.

"Can I talk to you for a minute?" she called.

Uh-oh. Had the school called about her afternoon absence? Jamie didn't think they did that until things got really bad. She took a breath and braced herself. Then wiped her mouth for any traces of Todd's kiss.

Her mother was at the stove stirring spaghetti sauce. The aroma of tomato and spice permeated the room. It was a homey smell, usually welcoming. Today Jamie just wanted to get to the privacy of her room where she could relive her conversation with Todd.

And she really *didn't* want to have whatever conversation her mother was about to embark on.

"I tried calling you right when school got out," her mother said casually.

The call Jamie had ignored. She'd known from the ring tone

that it was her mother.

Todd had been posing her at the edge of an old bridge when her phone rang. "You're a good model," he'd told her moments earlier.

"All I'm doing is standing and looking where you tell me."

"Exactly. And you're lovely."

She'd lifted her chin, lowered her chin, tilted her head to the left and then to the right, all the while Todd was busily clicking away with his camera.

"I thought you wanted pictures of the bridge," she'd teased.

"The bridge will be here another day. You might not."

I'll be here any day you want.

Her mother had been the farthest thing from Jamie's mind.

"I must not have heard it," Jamie said now, still standing near the doorway. "Why were you calling?"

"To see if you needed a ride home."

"A ride?"

"You told me this morning that you and Alyssa were going to study after school. But I ran into her mother. Alyssa had a dentist appointment this afternoon."

Jamie thought fast. "Yeah, she forgot."

"So you went to the library anyway?"

Oh, God. Had her mother called the library, too?

"For a bit," Jamie said. "But since Alyssa wasn't there, we couldn't work on our project. So I went with some other kids for a soda."

Her mother brightened. "That's nice. Did one of them give you a ride home?"

Jamie nodded, afraid to say more.

"Someone I know?"

"What's the matter with you today?" Jamie asked. "You're acting crazy. I'm home by dinnertime, aren't I?"

Her mother took a moment to answer. "Alyssa's mother said

she hadn't seen you in quite a while. That you and Alyssa hadn't been spending much time together at all lately." She paused. "I was under the impression you'd been at her house a lot."

Jamie didn't say anything. She couldn't. Her mind was frozen.

"What is it you're keeping from me?" her mother asked.

Jamie thought she might cry out of sheer frustration. She'd had such a perfect afternoon, and now this? She couldn't think of a single excuse that wouldn't sound totally lame.

"Is it a boy?"

"A boy?"

"Alyssa's mother thought you might be seeing someone."

"I'm not really *seeing* anyone," Jamie protested.

"But there is a boy in the picture?"

Jamie looked down at the floor.

"I'm happy for you, honey. I wish you didn't feel you had to be so secretive about it."

"It's no big deal."

"Who is he? Anyone I know?"

Jamie latched onto the only name she could come up with. "His name is Oliver."

"Oliver Glick?" Her mother sounded pleased. "I've met his mother. Nice woman."

As if that mattered. "He's not my boyfriend or anything, though. We're just friends."

"Of course. But anytime you want to bring him by the house . . . well, he's welcome. Your dad and I promise not to hover."

"Thanks."

"We do hope to get a chance to meet him."

Jamie turned and escaped to her room, trying desperately to hold onto the warm glow of her afternoon with Todd.

CHAPTER 23

Gordon was looking out the kitchen window, thinking about his upcoming lunch with Todd, which he hadn't told Marta about, and mentally running through *The Lost Colony of Roanoke* lecture he would be giving at the graduate seminar next week. Marta was chattering in the background, making a salad before she left for an evening meeting.

This past week she'd been going on about Jamie and her new boyfriend. Jamie herself didn't talk about him much, but when she was out of earshot, Marta could barely contain herself.

Jamie seemed so happy lately, she told him. Had Gordon noticed? Did he think they ought to talk to the young man's parents? Not that there was anything to worry about—Marta knew the mother and the boy was a top student, but still, kids today were so much more open to sex than in their day.

Gordon was pleased for Jamie, who had felt more or less on the margin of things since their move to Sterling. And like Marta, he worried about the temptations that came with high school romance. But he couldn't imagine a conversation with the boy's parents would change anything. And it would certainly embarrass Jamie. Marta had finally agreed to have a cautionary talk with Jamie.

Gordon appreciated his wife's bubbly nature. It balanced his own tendency to shut down and withdraw. He was generally more than happy to let her carry the conversation while he bobbed along listening to a stream of stories and observations

151

that required only an occasional acknowledgment from him. But tonight he was finding her energy difficult to deal with.

She was on a tear about a call she'd received from the school vice-principal. It seemed that Jamie had been cutting classes and her grades were slipping.

"And," Marta added. "She had drug paraphernalia in her locker."

Gordon put his Roanoke thoughts on hold for the moment. "They must have her confused with another student."

"They know who their students are."

"But it doesn't sound like our daughter," he protested.

"No. It doesn't. That's why I'm worried."

"What does Jamie say?"

"That it was all a mix-up. And there was only one test she really messed up."

"Well, there you have it."

"I don't think it's that simple, Gordon. Jamie was . . . evasive. Like she was making up excuses on the fly." Marta ran the dishrag across the counter, brushing crumbs into her cupped palm. "I worry that the boyfriend may be at the root of this."

Gordon was confused. "I thought you were happy Jamie had a boyfriend."

"I am. But young love can be so"—Marta looked off into space—"so delicious."

"That's a problem?" Gordon had little experience with young love. He'd been too shy in high school to even talk to girls, and while he'd suffered through a few awkward dates in college, he'd never been in love until Marta came along.

"Not a problem per se," Marta said, "but we don't want Jamie to be so gaga over him she's not thinking straight."

"No, of course not. But it doesn't sound like that's what's happening. She's got a good head on her shoulders. She's not going to do something stupid."

"I don't know about that."

Gordon wasn't sure what Marta wanted from him. "Maybe she needs another dose of motherly guidance," he offered at last.

"I tried, for all the good it did. She didn't want to hear a word I had to say."

Gordon nodded sympathetically.

"She was full of excuses," Marta continued. "And then she got angry. At me. Like it was all my fault."

"Well, she *is* a teenager," he pointed out.

"What's that supposed to mean?" Marta snapped.

"Aren't teen years the rebellious years?"

"We're still her parents."

"Of course we're her parents. But Jamie's always been so responsible."

Marta turned to face him directly. "Maybe if you talked to her. Maybe she'd listen to you."

"Me?" Gordon could feel himself resisting. He loved Jamie with all his heart, and wanted more than anything to protect her. He worried about her too, just as Marta did. But he didn't know how to talk to her. Not anymore. And most definitely not about a subject as fraught with pitfalls as boys. Or drugs. "I'm sure I wouldn't have anything to add to what you've—"

"Please, Gordon. This is important."

"You had the sex talk with her, right? You've opened the door already. Isn't this just an extension of that?"

Marta glared at him.

He sighed. "All right. I'll see what I can do."

"Thanks, honey. You'll do great." She gave him a quick peck on the cheek. "I have to run or I'll miss the start of the meeting. Casserole's in the oven, salad is ready except for the dressing."

"You meeting Carol there?"

"I'm handling this evening myself. No reason we both need to attend."

The library committee was one of Marta and Carol's long-standing clients. Usually they both went to the meetings and then went out for a glass of wine afterward—as much a girl's night out as business. Given tonight's break from tradition, Gordon guessed the rift between the two women wasn't fully mended.

It had something to do with Todd, although Gordon didn't understand what the fuss was all about. So the guy used a different name professionally. It wasn't like he'd been trying to cheat them. But apparently Carol found it suspicious. She'd even hired some investigator who also sensed "something fishy," whatever that meant. Marta hadn't liked the guy from the moment Gordon had introduced them, so he couldn't understand why she and Carol weren't on the same page.

Gordon tried to stay out of it. He did find it something of a coincidence that Todd and Marta had crossed paths professionally, but life was full of coincidences. He liked Todd, and had continued to meet him for lunch now and then, even knowing Marta wouldn't approve. He didn't tell her which friends she could or couldn't see, so why should she dictate his?

After Marta left, he turned on the TV and caught the last half of the national news. He wondered if he should go up to Jamie's room and talk to her now, get it over with.

No, he decided, that would be a *talk*. Much too serious. Better to wait until dinner and then try the casual, off-hand approach. He wasn't sure what Marta thought he could do. He suspected she was overreacting anyway, but he did agree that Jamie couldn't just blow off school.

Jamie breathed a sigh of relief when she heard her mother's car pull away from the house. Even a few hours' peace was a relief.

Last week had been *Boyfriend Mania*. Her mother was full of questions—artfully disguised at first, and then more direct. What was Oliver like? Shouldn't they meet him? Did he treat her with respect? Worse were the cautionary warnings about sex, especially unprotected sex. God, it was so embarrassing. Like Jamie didn't know anything.

She'd tried explaining that she and "Oliver" were just friends, but the long afternoons she spent with Todd—which her mother assumed were spent with Oliver—led her mother to think otherwise. She'd look at Jamie with a smirky smile and say, "Of course you're friends."

Her mother could be *so* annoying sometimes.

She felt bad using Oliver the way she was, but he provided even better cover than Alyssa. She knew she should say something to him, though. Warn him in case word got back to him. She liked Oliver. Not romantically (the very thought made her gag), but he was a friend and she didn't want to embarrass him.

Boyfriend Mania had been bad enough, then this afternoon her mother had hit her with *The Call* from the school. The way she reacted you'd think Jamie had been arrested for some major felony. Cigarette papers weren't even against the law, although she was angry at Harmony for leaving them in her locker. And so what if she'd missed a few classes? Some days she wanted to spend more time with Todd.

Just thinking about him made her insides feel all tingly. She couldn't ever get enough of him. Ever since that afternoon he'd kissed her and told her how much he liked her, she'd been able to think of nothing else. Her notebooks were filled with hearts she'd drawn in pink and purple ink, with anagrams of their combined names, and with initials. JLW - Jamie Louise Wilson. And sometimes simply Mrs. Todd Wilson.

They would meet after school, or during school on the days

Jamie skipped class. Usually they went somewhere for a snack then drove around and ended up in a secluded spot, where Todd might snap some pictures, which were often of her. But mostly they talked and touched and kissed. And Jamie never could remember afterward what they'd talked about.

"Jamie," her dad called from downstairs. "Dinner's ready."

"Okay, I'll be right there."

It was just her and her dad tonight. He'd probably bring up *The Call,* but she could handle him. It wouldn't be that bad.

CHAPTER 24

Marta was at her desk later that week when Cassie phoned. She might have let the call roll over to voice mail, but she'd just finished proofing a marketing brochure and welcomed the excuse for a break.

"Hi," Cassie chirped in an unusually upbeat voice. "I'm not disturbing you, am I?"

"Not at all." Marta wondered fleetingly if Cassie's cheerful mood had anything to do with drugs. "What's up?"

"I think my life might finally be on the right track."

"That's wonderful. Is there a guy involved?" Marta had seen Cassie go down this path before.

"Well, yeah." Cassie laughed. "But it's not just that. My job is working out okay and I've been pretty regular about my AA meetings. I think I'm really going to make it this time."

"Good for you! I really hope it works out."

"That's part of why I'm calling. I know I can be a pain sometimes, and you've been really good about standing by me. I've done some stuff I'm really sorry about."

"Are you talking about alcohol?"

"Well, that, but things that involve you, too. Some sisters would have washed their hands of me."

You can't imagine how many times I've been tempted, Marta thought, knowing she never would have followed through. Cassie might be hard to take at times, but she was a little like the cute shelter pet you couldn't help wanting to rescue. And she

157

was the only family Marta had left.

"It means a lot to me," Cassie continued.

"Is this part of your twelve-step program?" The words were out of Marta's mouth before she knew it.

"Why do you have to be cynical? That's not why I'm doing this."

"I'm sorry. Really, I am. I have a way of saying the wrong thing."

"I know." Cassie laughed again. "But see, this is the new me, I'm not even angry with you."

Marta wondered again if her sister might be high. "I just want you to have a good life," she explained. "I worry about you."

"I know you do. And I know I've been a screw-up my whole life. But I've finally got my head on straight."

Marta was afraid to ask how this momentous change had come about. Afraid to jinx it by believing it might actually be true. "That's wonderful. You sound really good."

"Hey, let's celebrate. I'm going to be in Vegas in a couple of weeks. Why don't you meet me there? We'll have some girl fun."

"Las Vegas? Why?"

"Long story, but it's connected with my job."

"The plumbing supply company?"

"Yeah, more or less."

Maybe it was better not to push further. "I'd like to," Marta said, meaning it, even though she didn't much like Vegas. It had been almost a year since she and Cassie had spent time together. "Trouble is, I need to keep an eye on Jamie."

"What? Gordon is there, isn't he? Besides, she's not exactly a child anymore."

"No, not a child," Marta said pointedly. "She's a teenager, and therein lies the problem."

"Don't you think—"

"There's this boy she's involved with and she . . . well, let's just say, I don't trust her judgment anymore."

"You need to lighten up. She can't do anything worse than I did." Cassie chortled and then stopped abruptly. "I guess that's not exactly a reassuring thought, is it?"

"No, it's not." Cassie had discovered alcohol and boys early on. She'd somehow managed to avoid getting pregnant—as far as Marta knew—but she'd partied her way through her teens.

"What is she doing that's so bad?" Cassie asked. "Staying out all night and that kind of stuff?"

"No. Not yet anyway. But she's being evasive and sneaky. It's affecting her schoolwork."

"I suppose you've tried to talk some sense into her."

"She doesn't listen to me at all. Gordon had a sit-down with her a couple of days ago, but that was a waste, too. Jamie told him everything was fine and he took her at her word. He's clueless."

"What's the boy like?"

"I'm sure he's basically a good kid."

"What's that supposed to mean? How does he treat her? Is he the responsible type or not? Surely you must have some sort of impression."

"I don't know," Marta admitted reluctantly. "We haven't met him."

"Never?"

"Kids these days don't go on dates the way we did. They hang out. And text." It annoyed Marta the way Jamie had become glued to her phone. Yesterday Marta had threatened to take the phone away if Jamie couldn't leave it in her room during dinner.

"Sounds like whether you're there or in Vegas for a couple of days won't really matter. And I'd love to see you. We have so much to catch up on."

Marta wanted to go but she wouldn't enjoy herself if she was worried about Jamie. "Let me think about it, okay?"

When Marta was growing up she used to envy Cassie. Maybe not envy, exactly, because Cassie was often in trouble, and Marta knew even then that her sister's wild abandon was not something to be emulated. Still, Cassie knew how to have fun. She didn't care much what others thought of her, didn't berate herself when she screwed up, didn't worry about anything but the moment. And people liked her.

Looking back at Cassie's struggles over the years, Marta could see that her sister's life had not been charmed at all, but she did understand the lure of throwing caution to the wind. And she worried that Jamie did, too.

Carol was still hunkered down working when Marta was ready to leave for home later that afternoon. The chill between them had warmed some, which was a relief. Without Carol's confidences and contagious enthusiasm, the days felt as flat and gray as the winter sky.

Carol's back was to her but Marta could see that she was deep in thought—her head bent forward and pressed against her fingers. Marta hesitated, reluctant to disturb her. *What the hell*, she thought. Before the blowup over Todd she wouldn't have thought twice.

"I'm about ready to leave," Marta said, stepping around to the front of Carol's desk. "Anything we should go over first?"

Carol looked up. She hadn't been concentrating on work. She'd been crying.

"What's wrong?" Marta asked. Carol wasn't given to emotional swings.

"Nothing." Carol sat up straighter and forced a thin smile.

"It can't be nothing. Is it a client? Something about the business?"

"It's nothing, really. Mark and I had another fight."

"Want to talk about it?"

Carol shook her head. "It will blow over."

Carol's voice was a little too bright to sound believable but Marta didn't want to badger her. "If you're sure—"

"I am."

"Okay, I'll be going then. See you in the morning."

Carol cleared her throat. "Don't you want to know if my investigator found anything on Todd?"

Mostly Marta wanted to put all memories of the creep behind her. It pained her to think what a fool she'd been. But she also wanted to mollify Carol, who seemed unwilling to let it go.

"I assumed you'd tell me if he discovered something important." Marta paused. "Did he?"

"Not yet, but he's convinced there's something odd going on."

"I thought we already knew that." Marta's take on Todd wasn't the same as Carol's, but they did agree he was something of a con-man, even if they weren't sure what the con was. And now that she and Carol had patched their differences, she didn't want to dig further. "Is it really worth pursuing?"

"Yes," Carol said emphatically. "It is. It's not right that he get away with lying like he did."

"Okay. Tell me what your investigator found."

"Todd's cell phone is registered to someone named J.D. Conrad."

"Another alias?"

"I doubt it. Conrad is in his sixties."

"You think he stole the phone? Or maybe Conrad's identity?" Marta was trying to sort through the logistics. Surely Conrad would know if he'd lost his phone or was getting bills that weren't his.

"I don't know. But makes you wonder."

"I guess so." Curious, yes. Maybe even criminal. But Marta didn't see that it was their concern. Besides, she was more perplexed by Carol's tears than anything Todd was up to.

CHAPTER 25

Marta was setting the table for dinner when she spotted Jamie strolling down the street toward home.

"Hi, honey," she called out when Jamie came through the door. "You didn't walk all the way from school, did you?"

"I got a ride most of the way." Jamie dropped her backpack in the hallway on her way into the kitchen. "And no," she added, anticipating Marta's next question, "it's not anybody you know. Just some kids from school."

"They can't bring you all the way home?"

"It's fine, Mom. I live out of their way and I don't mind walking a few blocks." Cell phone in hand, she opened the refrigerator and grabbed a can of soda.

Her phone pinged. Jamie glanced at the screen and tapped out a response, thumbs flying at a speed that awed Marta, whose own fingers never seemed to hit the right letter.

"Was Oliver one of them?" she asked when Jamie had finished.

"Huh?"

"Was Oliver—"

Another ping, and once again Jamie focused on her phone.

Irritated, Marta asked, "How was school today?"

Jamie didn't respond.

"Can't you ignore that damned thing for a few minutes? We're having a conversation."

Jamie didn't look up from the phone. "We're not actually having a conversation."

Marta could feel her blood pressure rising. "I'm trying to have one."

"Why?" Jamie tossed her head, a habit that she'd only recently adopted. She reached for a glass, filled it with ice, and poured in the soda. "What's for dinner?"

"I made that chicken dish you like with artichoke hearts."

"Yum."

"It's just the two of us tonight. Your dad is having dinner with one of his colleagues. It's just about ready."

"Good, I'm starving." Jamie sat down at the table, tossed her head again, and guzzled down half her soda.

Fleetingly, Marta caught site of a splotchy reddish bruise on her daughter's neck. She looked closer. It had been a long time, but she recognized a love-bite when she saw one.

Flustered, she turned away. How was a mother supposed to react? She was happy Jamie had a boyfriend, but the thought of her daughter locked in the arms of a young man wasn't something she was ready to contemplate.

She put the salad on the table, dished out the chicken, then joined Jamie at the table.

"I talked to Aunt Cassie today," she said, and tried like the devil to keep her eyes from returning to the mark on Jamie's neck.

"More trouble?"

Marta shook her head. "No, it sounds like she's doing well."

"Great." Jamie picked up her fork and dug in, keeping one eye on her phone.

"Please put it away. You know the rule. No phone during dinner."

"What does it matter? It's just you and me tonight."

"I don't count?" Marta kept her tone light but the comment hurt.

Jamie rolled her eyes. "What's the big deal? It's not like we ever talk about anything interesting. You should be happy I've got friends."

"I am happy for you, but they shouldn't become your whole life."

Jamie ignored her.

"You've never been this consumed with talking to Alyssa."

"So?"

Marta wanted to handle this the right way but she didn't have the foggiest idea what that was. "I understand what it's like to be young," she said after a moment. "What it's like to have a new boyfriend. It's . . . it's magical."

Jamie looked at her like she had two heads.

"We didn't have cell phones in my day, of course, but I do remember how nothing else seemed to matter. Still, there are times—"

Ping. Jamie grabbed her phone.

"I'm talking to you, young lady!"

"Whatever."

Without thinking, Marta snatched the phone from Jamie's hand.

"Give me that!" Jamie shrieked.

"You're like an addict with this thing. Your behavior is rude. And it's unhealthy."

Jamie lunged for the phone, knocking over her glass and sending soda across the table and onto the floor. She made no effort to stem the flow or mop it up.

"You've no right," she screamed. "That's mine!"

Marta pulled back, holding the phone out of Jamie's reach. "Your father and I paid for it and we foot the monthly bill. The phone is yours only so long as *we* say so."

"So I'll get a job," Jamie cried. "I'll pay you back. Now give it to me."

"Is this how Oliver acts?"

"Who cares how Oliver acts?" Jamie was screeching, her arms flying in an attempt to retrieve her phone.

Marta had had enough. "Maybe I should call him right now, talk to him myself."

"Don't you dare!"

She felt her anger rising. She'd never seen Jamie like this. Was it Oliver's influence?

The phone pinged again, and Marta glanced at the screen. She blinked and looked again. Her heart hammered in her chest.

Not Oliver. Todd.

She scrolled down. Text after text from Todd.

Marta could barely speak. "Why is Todd sending you text messages?"

"Because he wants to." Jamie crossed her arms and glared.

Marta's head was pounding. A ferocious anger bubbled up inside her.

She scrolled through the most recent messages. There was an intimacy to the tone that sent her head spinning.

"It's Todd you've been seeing, isn't it? Not Oliver."

Jamie's smirk told her everything she needed to know.

Marta's stomach clenched with a deep, nauseous fear. This couldn't be happening. "How long has it been going on?"

"A while."

This was so wrong on so many levels, Marta didn't know where to begin. "Well, it's going to stop. Right now. You are not to see him or talk to him again. Understood?"

"I can talk to whoever I want!" Jamie tried to wrestle the phone from Marta's hand.

Marta pushed back. "No. You cannot. I forbid you to have any more contact with him. Do you understand? As of this minute, your phone stays in my control."

"You can't!" Jamie lunged for her, but Marta held her own. She stepped to the side, over the spilled soda, and held the phone tight.

"I love him," Jamie sobbed. "He loves me. What's so wrong about that?"

So much Marta didn't know where to begin. "He's too old for you, for one thing."

"He's only twenty-eight. That's not so old."

"He's much older than twenty-eight, Jamie. But even that is too old for you."

Jamie's face was red with rage. "You can't do this to me. I'm happy for the first time in . . . practically forever!"

The phone pinged again. Marta tossed it into a drawer and stood squarely in front. "He's using you, Jamie."

"He is not. You just don't want me to be happy."

As angry as she was, Marta was also heartbroken for her daughter. She wanted to wrap Jamie in her arms and protect her. "I know you can't see this now, but   "

"You can't stop me!" Jamie screamed hysterically, pounding Marta with her fists. "You can't keep me away from Todd. You may think you can, but you can't! You're nothing but a dried-up old prune."

Marta grabbed Jamie's wrists. "He's using you, Jamie. He doesn't care a wit about you."

"How can you say that?"

"Because it's true. He's using you to get at me."

Jamie stepped back. "What? Are you delusional?"

She needed to shut up. She'd already said more than she'd intended. But exasperation mixed with fear and a sense of helplessness. She had to make Jamie understand.

"It's true. I met Todd on a business trip. We went out for drinks, then dinner, and we . . . ." No way could she tell Jamie what had really happened. "We kind of flirted," Marta continued. "It was my birthday and I was feeling sorry for myself because no one remembered or cared. I just wanted to have some fun. But for some reason Todd thought it was serious. He's in Sterling because of me. To see me."

"You are such a liar."

"I'm telling you the truth, Jamie. He's angry because I rejected him, and he's using you to punish me."

"Have you lost your mind? You expect me to believe that just because you two had drinks one night—" Jamie stopped mid-sentence. Her eyes grew wide. "Oh, my God. Did you sleep with him?"

Marta felt the blood drain from her face. "No. Absolutely not."

"You're disgusting. You're beyond disgusting."

"Honey, please—"

"I hate you." Jamie ran from the room.

Marta was shaking. What a mess she'd made of everything. She'd handled it badly. Horribly. Jamie hated her. Gordon would hate her, too. She'd have to tell him now.

She sat at the table and put her head in her arms, choking back tears. What other choice had she had? She had to make Jamie see Todd for what he was. It was Marta's job to protect her daughter whatever the cost to herself.

By nine o'clock, when Gordon wasn't yet home, Marta decided to take a hot bath and then crawl into bed with a book. She'd cleaned up the kitchen, then done nothing but fret all evening, and she was worn out.

She stopped by Jamie's room and knocked on the door. She wasn't going to apologize—she had nothing to apologize for. But the rift with her daughter was tearing her apart. She wanted to try once more to explain.

When there was no response, Marta knocked again, more loudly. "Jamie, can I come in? Please. I feel terrible about the way we left things."

Silence.

Marta hesitated, then turned the door knob, half expecting it to be locked. But the door opened easily.

The room was empty and Jamie's window was wide open.

CHAPTER 26

In the darkness of night, Jamie didn't recognize Todd's car until he pulled to a stop right in front of her. She heaved a sigh of relief. He had come for her.

She had sneaked into her dad's study and used the home phone to call Todd. When she couldn't reach him, she left a message. She was afraid he wouldn't get it, more afraid he wouldn't show up. She worried her pleas and tears had frightened him away.

She'd never done anything remotely like this. She had never even called Todd, much less asked for his help. She'd never climbed out her bedroom window, either. But she'd been out of her mind, shaking and sobbing like a crazy person. Her own mother! How could she?

Jamie's whole day had been awful, but the scene with her mother was the crowning blow. She needed to get away. She needed Todd.

"Get me out of here," she said, flinging herself and her packed bag into the car.

"What's wrong?"

"Everything. Please, just go."

Todd looked wary. "Where to?"

"I don't care." Jamie leaned back, closed her eyes, and tried to quiet her tears. "Take me away."

"Away?"

"As far as possible."

"Not until you tell me what's going on." He seemed oddly uncomfortable, not tender and caring as she'd hoped. Jamie wondered if he was mad at her for disrupting his evening.

Or maybe what her mother said was true?

No. No way. Jamie could tell that Todd wanted her, not her mother.

"I climbed out my bedroom window," she told him.

"You what?"

"I'm leaving home."

"Jamie, for God's sake—"

"I'm upset."

"Yeah, I get that. But why?"

She wiped her eyes. "My mom. I hate her. I really fucking hate her."

Todd was looking at her, waiting for her to continue.

"Would you just go! I want to get away from here."

He drove to the next block, pulled to the curb, and parked. "Let's try this again. What happened?"

"My mom got hold of my phone," Jamie said. "We had a big fight, and she just grabbed it out of my hand."

"That's it?"

Wasn't that enough? "She saw your texts. She knows we've been seeing each other."

"Does she?" Todd didn't seem worried. In fact, he sounded almost amused.

"She thought I was seeing a boy at school. When she found out it was you, she got really mad."

"I bet she did."

"She says you're too old for me," Jamie added.

"I am too old for you. I've told you—"

"Don't say that." Jamie felt her throat tighten, her eyes again fill with tears. "Please, don't keep saying that."

"It's true." He fell silent, tapping the steering wheel with his fingers and staring off into space.

Jamie was sure he was going to tell her they had to stop meeting. Maybe he'd even confirm her mother's outlandish story and admit it was her mother he loved. Jamie's longing for him was so deep it hurt all the way down to her bones. She couldn't bear to lose him.

"A few years doesn't matter," Jamie insisted. "It's how we feel that's important."

A muscle in Todd's cheek twitched. He had retreated into some private place, his face unreadable. He was silent for what seemed like forever, then he leaned closer and touched her face. "If I were a better man, I'd stay away from you. But I can't. I'm falling for you. Big time."

Jamie's heart swelled. Todd didn't think she was silly or fat or childish. He liked her. He was interested in her. He was *falling for her.*

But her mother's ugly words echoed in her head. "My mom said you were just using me."

"Mothers worry a lot."

"She said she met you on a business trip," Jamie said. "That you had dinner and . . . that she slept with you." She knew this last part was true no matter how much her mother had denied it. "She says you don't care about me at all, you're just trying to punish her."

"Wow." He brushed her forehead. "No wonder you're upset."

"Is it true?" Jamie held her breath.

Todd shook his head. "No." He took a minute to look out the darkened window before turning back to her. "Not in the way she made it seem."

"What does that mean?"

"We did meet. I'd had a long, hard day. I just wanted to have a drink and relax. Your mother came on to me, all flirty and seductive. She seemed a little old for that kind of stuff but she said she wanted to celebrate. So I bought her a drink."

"And?" Jamie couldn't breathe.

"That's it."

"That's all? You didn't come to Sterling to see her?"

"Is that what she told you?" Todd laughed. "No, I came on business. I ran into your father when he was in the garage working on that car of his. I didn't even know your mom was his wife."

"She thinks you wanted to see her again."

"I don't know what kind of head trip she's laying on you, but she's full of it."

"Why would she do that?"

"I don't know. Probably because she's a desperate woman."

"Desperate?" Could that really be it?

"I'm sure she's nice enough and all, but a woman gets on in years and maybe things aren't going so well in the marriage, or maybe she just begins to feel her age. She might feel the need to convince herself she's still hot. It's sad, but I've seen it happen before."

"So you didn't sleep with her?"

"Good God, no. She's way too old for me, and she's not my type anyway. It wouldn't surprise me, though, if she's rewritten the evening in her own mind to make herself feel better. But lying to you, that's inexcusable."

"I can't believe she'd be so mean to me." Jamie was hurt and angry. But she also felt a little sorry for her mom. She'd never seen her as pathetic until now.

"She's probably jealous," Todd explained. "You're young and pretty, and you've got your whole life ahead of you. Some women can't take the competition."

"Yeah, probably." It made sense. Jamie put her hand on Todd's thigh. She was tired of talking about her mom. "I'm falling for you, too, you know."

Todd gave her a sweet, lopsided smile. "Yeah, I kind of thought so."

"So what are we going to do?"

"First thing, we need to get you home. Your parents must be worried."

Screw her parents. "I *can't* go home. Don't you understand? They'll never let me see you again."

"We'll find a way," Todd assured her.

He didn't get it. "Let's leave. Let's go away where they can't find us."

"You're a minor, Jamie."

"I'm almost eighteen."

"Not for another four months."

"Lots of kids leave home. My parents probably won't even care."

"Honey, we can't just—"

She crawled onto his lap, facing him. The steering wheel dug uncomfortably into her back. She didn't care. She kissed him on the mouth and pressed herself against him. "Please Todd, I need you so much. I want you so badly." She put her hand between his legs, and immediately felt him stir. He shuddered and his breathing grew swifter.

"Honey, don't." The words might have seemed a warning, but his tone begged her not to stop.

Jamie unbuttoned her shirt and placed his hands to her breasts. Slowly, she rocked back and forth. The movement came naturally, she couldn't imagine from where. Soon she stopped thinking and lost herself in the sensation.

Todd kissed her ear, nibbled at her neck. His breathing grew hotter and heavier. He made a half-hearted effort to push her away but she only pressed harder. Finally, he took her hand in his and rubbed it hard against the swell of his crotch.

Faster, harder until at last he whimpered. "Oh, God, Jamie.

Oh, God." He buried his head in her neck, clinging to her.

"You'll take me away?" Jamie asked in a whisper. "So we can be together?"

"Mmm."

"For sure?"

"For sure."

CHAPTER 27

Gordon wasn't much of a drinker, and his mind was still clouded by the wine he'd had with dinner when Marta greeted him at the door, visibly agitated.

"Where have you been? It's almost ten."

"I had a working dinner, remember? I told you about it." He hadn't dared admit he was meeting Todd because he knew she'd have a fit. But Todd had been interested in hearing about his conference presentation, and besides, Gordon enjoyed the guy's company.

"I've been trying to reach you," Marta howled.

He'd expected her to be asleep, or at least in bed with a book. Instead, here she was practically yelling at him before he was even inside. "I've been calling you and calling you. Why do you even have a cell phone if you're not going to answer it?"

"I turned it off during dinner. What's wrong?" Clearly something was. Marta was not usually given to hysterics.

"Jamie's gone."

"What do you mean? Gone where?"

"I don't know where, but she's gone."

Marta was obviously upset but Gordon was having trouble understanding what was wrong. "Have you tried calling her?"

"She doesn't have her phone. I do."

"Let's take this from the top." Gordon went to the sink and poured himself a glass of water, as much to give himself time to focus as to quench his thirst. "Tell me what happened."

"I went to Jamie's room to say goodnight, and she wasn't there."

"What time was this?"

"About nine. Her window was wide open and the screen was on the floor."

Maybe Gordon had drunk more than he realized. "You think she climbed out the window? Why would she do that?"

"In order to sneak out without my knowing. Or maybe she didn't go out the window, I don't know. But she's gone."

"You've checked the rest of the house?"

"Why are you asking stupid questions. Of course I've checked the rest of the house!"

Gordon sat down at the table and unlaced his shoes. He'd worn his dress shoes this morning in anticipation of the dinner, and his feet were killing him.

"I must be missing something," he said. "Why would Jamie climb out a second-floor window?"

"It's only a floor and a half where her bedroom is, and it's an easy drop to the porch overhang."

"Still . . ."

Marta laced her fingers and flexed them several times before continuing. "We had a fight at dinner and she stormed off to her room."

A fight. That made the picture a bit clearer, but still didn't explain why Jamie would sneak off late at night. It wasn't like they'd never fought before.

Marta lowered herself into the chair next to him and reached for his hand. "Gordon, I'm scared. I'm angry but I'm also really, really scared."

"She's probably at a friend's house." It wouldn't be the first time she headed there after a fight with her mother.

Marta shook her head. "I called."

"You can't have called everyone she knows."

"It doesn't matter. I'm sure she's with Todd Wilson."

"Todd?" Gordon looked at her in surprise. Had Marta lost her mind?

"I'm not making this up." She withdrew her hands and folded them in her lap. "That's what our fight was about. Jamie's been seeing him."

"Seeing Todd?"

"The 'boy' she's been spending time with? It's not Oliver Glick. It's Todd."

Gordon shook his head in disbelief. "You must be mistaken." He'd just spent the evening with the guy. Jamie's name hadn't come up. Besides, it made no sense.

"No mistake. I saw the texts." Marta got up, opened a kitchen drawer, and handed him Jamie's cell phone. "Here, look for yourself."

Gordon hesitated. No father wanted to imagine his daughter romantically involved with a guy, no matter who it was. But the notion that she was seeing Todd was outrageous. He reached for the phone and scanned the most recent exchanges.

He was stunned. It was true—Jamie and Todd, texting. Frequently. How did they even know each other? As far as Gordon was aware, they'd only met one time, the same night Gordon met Todd.

He scrolled down. The messages weren't overtly sexy, but there was an implied intimacy that turned his stomach.

"They could just be friends," he offered lamely.

"They're more than that. Jamie confirmed it."

"Confirmed what?"

"She claims she loves him."

Love? Jamie wasn't old enough to be in love.

"I told her it had to stop," Marta added. "That we wouldn't allow it. That's when she stomped off to her room. And that's why she snuck out."

Gordon tried to envision Jamie with Todd. She'd always been so cautious, so obedient, and honest to a fault. She wasn't a risk taker, and sadly not much of a dreamer, either. She took after him in that way. He couldn't imagine her sneaking off in the middle of the night to be with a man twice her age.

And he couldn't imagine Todd being interested in Jamie. "What makes you think she's with Todd now?"

"Since I had her cell, she used the land line to call him. I checked outgoing numbers. The last one called was his. At a little before eight."

Gordon recalled the call Todd had received over dessert. They'd met for an early dinner because Todd had to be someplace later that evening, but the call had seemed to catch him by surprise. He hadn't taken it, but he'd listened to the message. Could it really have been Jamie? The timing worked. But why hadn't Todd said something to him right then?

"We need to contact the police," Marta said.

"The police?"

"She's run away."

"Or maybe just slipped out to see her"—Gordon choked—"him."

"Todd's an adult. We have to put a stop to this."

"Absolutely. But there's not much we can do until she comes home." And then he was going to ground his daughter and have a serious, in-your-face talk with Todd. Jamie might have a foolish schoolgirl crush on the man, but Todd was old enough to know you didn't encourage that sort of thing. Decent men did not prey on young girls.

"She's not going to come home," Marta insisted. "She packed clothes and other stuff."

"Do we really want to involve the cops so soon?" Jamie would be furious.

Marta stomped to the phone. "I don't see that we have a choice."

The reality had been slow to sink in, but now hit Gordon with the force of a cannon. His baby girl had run away. She was gone.

"You're right," he admitted. "I'll get on the extension." Jamie might have run to Todd, but he clearly hadn't brought her straight back home. That was worrisome.

Marta made the call and explained what had happened. The police dispatcher was kind but not overly concerned. It wasn't yet midnight, he pointed out. It wasn't uncommon for teenagers to occasionally ignore parental rules. That Todd was older than Jamie caused the dispatcher to mutter disapproval but did not spur him to action.

At some level, Gordon felt vindicated. Marta was overreacting. On the other hand, her agitation was contagious. The call calmed neither of them.

"Let's step back for a moment," Gordon said when they were off the phone. "Maybe Jamie does have a crush on Todd. But why would a good-looking guy in his thirties be interested in our daughter?"

Marta shot him a pointed look. "You know why."

"Todd's not like that."

"How the hell would you know?"

Guilt punched him in the gut. He'd continued to stay in touch with Todd when she'd specifically asked him not to. This was the moment to come clean, but he couldn't bring himself to do it. Especially not now. Hell, he'd been sitting right there when Todd had taken his daughter's call. He felt dirty, as if he was somehow complicit in her running away.

"Anyway, it's more complicated than that." Marta started to say something more, then stopped. She paced the length of the kitchen, then back again. Looking nervous and uncomfortable, she gripped the back of the chair. "I need to tell you something, Gordon. I want you to promise not to be angry."

He waited while she took a couple of deep breaths.

"What I mean is, I know you'll be angry, but please don't shut me out. I couldn't bear that. Not right now."

"Why would I be angry?" Then, in a flash, Gordon had an inkling of what she might say. He hoped to God he was wrong, but feared he wasn't.

Gordon knew he would never sleep so he didn't even try. Marta had offered him the bedroom but he insisted on taking the couch in the den. Now he lay awake, alone, staring at the ceiling and running the tape of his wife's confession over in his mind.

She'd met Todd on her trip to Minneapolis. She had gone for a birthday drink and allowed Todd to join her. Somehow things had gotten out of hand.

"I promise it was just that one time," she said, pleading for him to believe her. "I'm so sorry. I didn't mean for it to happen, and I've felt awful about it ever since."

Gordon didn't see how something like that could *just happen*. People made decisions. Acted on those decisions. They might regret them later—or they might not. But at the time, they chose freely.

And he didn't see why Todd would be here in Sterling if there hadn't been more to the night than Marta laid out. "Why would Todd follow you here if you didn't do anything to encourage him?" he'd asked.

"I don't know. I think he might be a little nuts."

Gordon wasn't buying it. Or maybe he was just hurt by his wife's betrayal. It stung so much he had trouble breathing. His own duplicity in continuing to get together with Todd paled by comparison.

But he also felt like a real chump. He'd considered Todd a friend, and the guy had been screwing his wife. *And* in all likelihood, his daughter.

He turned to his side and looked at the clock. Three a.m. and Jamie still wasn't home.

Was she actually with Todd? What if she wasn't? That possibility frightened Gordon even more. Anything could happen to a girl wandering the streets alone at night.

Finally, he gave up the tossing and turning and stood by the window, hoping to see Jamie stealing home through the shadows.

The street remained empty, the night quiet except for a lone train whistle far off in the distance. Quietly, he climbed the stairs to Jamie's room and opened the door. *Please let her have come home without my hearing. Please let her be here.*

When he first saw the lumpy form on Jamie's bed his heart soared. But stepping closer, he realized it was Marta, not their daughter.

"This way I'll know if she comes home," Marta said flatly. "I couldn't sleep anyway."

"Me either."

She rolled to face him. "I'm sorry, Gordon. So, so sorry."

"Sorry doesn't change what happened."

"No, it doesn't."

"It doesn't excuse it either."

"I know that." She sat up, pulling the covers to her chin. "I can't undo what I did. If I could, I would. You believe me, don't you?"

"That's not really the point, is it?"

"What do you mean?"

He turned toward the door. "Forget it. I'm not up to talking about this right now."

"Please don't hate me, Gordon. I need you. Especially now."
He left the room without looking back.

Marta couldn't remember when she'd ever felt more afraid.

Or more alone.

She wondered again if she'd done the right thing in telling Gordon the truth. She'd intended to hold back. To tell him just enough so he'd understand Todd was unbalanced. That what was happening wasn't about Jamie at all. But the words rushed from her mouth in an unbidden wave of anguish.

She'd only made things worse.

CHAPTER 28

They waited until eight the next morning, then called the police again. It was a different dispatcher this time—a woman—but she offered the same reassurances before taking their information and advising them that runaways weren't a priority, particularly those who were approaching their eighteenth birthday.

"Two and a half million kids," she told them. "That's how many runaways there are each year. If we chased after them all, we'd never have time to go after the bad guys."

The number was staggering but Marta refused to believe that Jamie was one of them. "What about an Amber alert? Aren't they used for missing kids?"

"For abducted kids. And not even all of those. I suggest you check with her friends to see what they know. And call the runaway hotline." She gave them the number. "Parents can sometimes do more to find a missing teen than the cops."

"But—"

"She's not armed, is she?" the dispatcher asked.

"No."

"Or in danger?"

"Of course she's in danger," Marta said angrily. "She's a seventeen-year-old with a man in his thirties."

"But she went with him willingly?"

Marta reluctantly conceded that was the case. "Are you saying there's nothing you can do?"

"We'll add her to the list of missing kids and spread the word to neighboring jurisdictions. You'll need to come to the station and file a report. Bring a recent photo and any contact information you have for her friends."

When the call ended, Marta looked bleakly at Gordon. "What are we going to do?"

She'd assumed that reporting Jamie missing would be a first step, a big step, in finding her and bringing her home. She'd thought the police would mobilize their resources and mount an all-out effort. She realized now how naive she'd been.

"We're going to begin by filing a police report," Gordon said. He appeared hollow-eyed and pasty, and had yet to meet her gaze directly.

She was sure Gordon hadn't slept any better than she had. He was dealing with the double blow of a missing daughter and an unfaithful wife. Marta supposed that the torment of her regret and guilt didn't hold a candle to that.

"I'd better call Carol to tell her I won't be in today. And I'll ask her for the name on Todd's cell account."

Gordon turned. "What do you mean?"

In her worry about Jamie, Marta had forgotten to tell him that Todd's phone was registered to a sixty-four-year-old man by a different name. "Carol's P.I. traced Todd's cell account," she explained. "It's registered under a different name but I can't remember what it is."

Picking up her phone, she noticed she had unread texts. She hadn't even checked since leaving work yesterday. What if Jamie had been trying to reach her?

Quickly, Marta scanned the list. No Jamie, but there was a message from Carol.

Very interesting discovery about our friend! Call me if you get a chance, otherwise I'll explain in the morning. I may know more by then, anyway.

"Carol left a message," she told Gordon. "She discovered something interesting about Todd. Maybe it will help us locate him."

She punched in the number. When Carol didn't answer she left a short message. "Hi, it's me. I'll try you on the office phone."

Before she could end the call, Carol's husband, Mark, picked up. "Marta, is that you?"

Okay, so maybe Carol wasn't yet at work. Or maybe she'd left her cell phone at home by mistake. "It's me, I'm trying to reach Carol."

There was a moment's silence. "I have terrible news." His voice was raspy. "Carol's dead."

"What?" Marta must have misunderstood.

"Dead. She's dead." He choked back what sounded like sob. "I'm sorry, I'm having trouble getting my head around this."

How could Carol be dead? "What happened?"

"A hit-and-run. It happened last evening, probably on her way home from work."

"Were there any witnesses?"

"No one who has come forward. She was apparently getting out of her car in the parking lot at the mall. One of the grocery employees found her body when he left work about eleven."

Marta's chest felt tight. "I don't know what to say. I'm numb."

"I can't believe it, either. I keep hoping I'll wake up and discover it was all a bad dream."

"How did you find out?"

"I called the cops, actually. I didn't get home until almost eleven myself. When she wasn't here, I got worried. And she didn't answer her phone. I kept telling myself I was getting worked up about nothing—I've done that before. But this time I was wrong."

"I'm so sorry, Mark." Marta searched her mind for something

more to say, but there was nothing. Her own shock and sadness made it hard to think.

Mark asked if Carol usually shopped at that particular mall.

"I've never heard her mention it." The area was a dated, lower-end strip mall that appealed largely to the agricultural workers who lived east of town. Marta couldn't imagine Carol, who favored designer clothing and gourmet specialty foods, shopping there. "Maybe she had car trouble or something and needed a convenient place to pull over."

"It's not convenient, though," he pointed out. "Not if she was on her way home. And she never called to say her car had broken down. I was hoping you'd know if her being there had anything to do with a project at work."

"Nothing I can think of off the top of my head, but I'll check her notes." Marta paused, feeling torn. "I don't think I'll be able to do it right away, though. We have our own crisis here. Jamie has run away."

"That's tough. No telling what kids will do." Mark sounded like a man in shock.

"The reason I called . . ." Marta knew she was going to sound insensitive, but it couldn't be helped. "Carol contacted a private investigator in order to get background on a potential client. Would you know how to get in touch with him? I think he might have information that would help us find Jamie." It made no sense, but hopefully Mark was too distracted to notice.

"I remember her saying something about it, but if she ever told me the guy's name, I don't remember it."

"When you get a chance, could you take a look? Maybe Carol wrote him a check or made note of his name. I wouldn't ask if it wasn't important."

"Yeah, sure. When I can."

"And let me know about . . . about plans for Carol's service. I don't know what you're thinking, but if I can help at all . . ."

"I haven't gotten that far yet," Mark said. "I'm still . . . reeling."

"If there's anything I can do for you, please let me know."

Marta said goodbye and clicked off, then instinctively turned to Gordon and burst into tears. "Carol's dead. She was hit by a car on her way home from work last night."

When he hesitated for a moment before putting his arms around her, she remembered he was barely speaking to her. She was grateful he hadn't turned away.

"How terrible," he said when she'd relayed what little she knew.

Marta nodded and blew her nose. "I can't believe it. She was at her desk yesterday afternoon and now she's dead. It's just so random. So unexpected."

"It really is." Gordon hesitated and looked at his watch. "I don't mean to be insensitive, but we need to get to the police station. I can go alone if you're not up to it."

"Of course I'm coming!" Carol was a friend, but Jamie was her daughter, for God's sake. How could Gordon think she wouldn't put Jamie first?

Possibly because this whole mess was her fault.

The officer who took their report was a middle-aged man by the name of Phillips. He had a full, fleshy face and smelled of cigarettes. He sat at a desk littered with stacks of manila folders, and appeared mildly bored as he covered the same ground the dispatcher had.

"We gave all that information to the woman when we called," Gordon explained.

Phillips nodded. "I've got her report right here."

"Then why are you asking?" Marta felt the urge to yell at him but she kept her voice even. She wanted the police to be on their side, after all.

Phillips didn't seem offended. "Sometimes new details emerge. You'll remember something you forgot earlier, or you'll lay it out differently. It all helps."

In that case, wouldn't it be best to go through the exercise over and over, like a *Groundhog Day* nightmare? But Marta wasn't about to challenge him.

She handed him a photo of Jamie. She and Gordon had debated between her recent school picture and a candid taken over Christmas. They'd finally decided on the school photo because it made Jamie appear younger.

"Has your daughter done this before?"

"Done what?"

"Run away."

Jamie hadn't simply *run away*. Why couldn't the police get that through their heads? "No, she hasn't," Marta said.

"How about other trouble? Problems with drugs, acting out, that sort of thing."

"No, Jamie's not like that." Marta hesitated, then added. "She's cut a few classes recently, but that's all."

Phillips scratched his cheek. "Any problems at home?"

Marta hesitated and glanced at Gordon. "Nothing out of the usual, but Jamie and I did have a heated disagreement last night."

His ears perked up. "What about?"

"A man she's been seeing behind our backs."

"We think that's who she's with," Gordon said. "He's much older than she is—in his thirties."

"He goes by the name of Todd Wilson," Marta added, "but that might not be his real name. Here's his cell number." She handed Phillips the number. "We've tried calling but he doesn't answer. You can track him using cell towers, can't you?"

"With a court order. Assuming he's naive enough to use his phone."

Gordon looked puzzled. "How about the FBI?"

Phillips rolled his pen between his palms and took a moment before answering. "A seventeen-year-old who leaves home isn't the same as an abduction. I'm sorry. I know that's not what you want to hear, but this sort of thing happens more often than you'd believe. It's not something the FBI generally gets involved with."

His words echoed those of the dispatcher, and they weren't encouraging. Marta felt a grip of panic at the thought that they might never see Jamie again.

Chapter 29

The days that followed were a blur of fear and confusion, each more agonizing than the one before. Marta felt trapped in a nightmare that wouldn't end.

They were almost certain that Jamie was with Todd, nonetheless, they couldn't rule out other possibilities. Maybe she'd simply run off because she was angry and hurt. Or maybe she'd intended to go to Todd and something terrible had happened in the interim. And even if she *was* with him . . . well, those possibilities were frightening in their own right. Marta couldn't get the stories she'd heard about sex slaves and forced prostitution out of her mind.

As the police suggested, she and Gordon contacted the runaway hotline immediately. The staffers were supportive and offered helpful tips, but none of their suggestions guaranteed Jamie's return. Gordon took on the task of combing through Jamie's computer and cell phone records while Marta focused on contacting her friends. She began with Alyssa, calling as soon as they'd returned from the police station Saturday morning.

"You still haven't heard from her?" Alyssa asked.

"No. We're fairly sure she's with an older man she's been seeing behind our backs." Marta paused pointedly. "I take it you know about that?"

Alyssa groaned. "I told her it wasn't a good idea."

"What do you know about him? Do you have any idea where

they might be?"

"No idea. Jamie didn't say much, but I could tell she was ape-shit over the guy. Sorry for the language."

"That's okay. All I care about is information."

"I wish I could tell you more, but she kept pretty quiet about him. I know he picked her up most days after school, but I don't know where they went. Jamie told me they mostly just drove around."

Not likely, Marta thought. "Did she ever say anything about running away with him?"

"Not a word. I thought she was smarter than that. I mean, I knew she shouldn't be seeing him, but I didn't want to rat out my best friend. If I'd known she was going to . . ." Alyssa's voice faded into a quivery whimper. "I'm really sorry. I should have said something."

Marta didn't have time for hand-holding. Besides, her own behavior fairly reeked with *should haves*. "Can you give me the names of other friends I might not know about?"

"Sure."

Marta took down names as Alyssa dictated. Most were familiar to her, a few were not, but those, Alyssa explained, were more school acquaintances than real friends.

"Promise you'll call me the instant you hear from her?" Marta asked. "It's really important."

"I doubt she'll contact me."

"Why's that?" At one time Jamie and Alyssa had been practically inseparable.

"He's all she thinks about." Alyssa sounded sad. "We hardly talk anymore outside of school."

Marta called the list of her daughter's friends, none of whom had heard from her, or had any idea where she might have gone. Most didn't even know she was seeing anyone.

The exception was Harmony Shaw, who'd known Jamie was

seeing an older guy, but hadn't seen anything wrong with it.

"He picked her up practically every day after school," she said with something approaching envy. "Really cute guy. She seemed to like him a lot."

"Did she ever talk about going away with him?"

"Not specifically."

"But she hinted at it?"

Harmony laughed, a smirky sort of humorless guffaw. "Doesn't every girl when she's got a hot boyfriend?"

This was the reason Marta hadn't wanted Jamie hanging out with Harmony. The girl was incorrigible. In fact, she seemed impressed by Jamie's boldness.

Marta saved Oliver Glick for last.

"You think she ran away?" he asked, dumbfounded. "Why?"

"She's been seeing an older man, and we told her it had to stop."

"Oh." Oliver sounded both aghast and hurt. "He's like, her boyfriend?"

"I'm afraid that's how Jamie sees it."

"You think that's who she's with?"

"It seems that way."

Oliver took a moment to digest what he'd learned. "Is she . . . in trouble? I mean, is this guy bad news?"

"She went with him willingly, so we're hoping she'll be okay. But we have to find her."

"Of course. Gosh, I can't believe it. Jamie, of all people. She's like one of the few sensible girls."

"You're friends with her, right?"

"I don't know if she'd say that, but yeah, we talked at school and stuff. She was nice to me. I think of her as a friend." He sounded wistful and a little sad.

Marta recalled how thrilled she'd been when she thought Jamie was seeing Oliver. How she wished she'd been right.

"You'll let me know right away if you hear from her?"

"For sure. But I'm pretty sure I'm the last person she'd contact."

Gordon turned up nothing useful from Jamie's electronics. Yes, she'd been seeing Todd, but nothing about plans to go away or hints about where they might be. The police continued to offer verbal support, but little more. Following the initial, limited burst of news coverage, the media went on to other stories. The all-out effort to find Jamie that Marta had hoped for never materialized.

As long as she and Gordon focused on Jamie, they managed to get along. Otherwise, he avoided her. He wasn't outwardly angry or accusatory. Marta would have preferred that. At least then the issue of her infidelity would be out in the open. Instead, it lurked like the proverbial elephant in the room. They stepped around it but never acknowledged it.

Wednesday morning, Marta got up early to make waffles and fresh-squeezed orange juice for breakfast. She set the table with a small vase of violas she picked from the garden. She hoped she could woo Gordon into at least acknowledging her presence.

"I'm not hungry," he said, walking past the table to pour himself a cup of coffee.

"You usually enjoy breakfast."

"These aren't usual times."

"No, they aren't. But you're making them worse."

He turned to glare at her. "Me? Whose fault is it that Todd Wilson came into our lives?"

"I made a horrible mistake, I admit it. And I'm so sorry. I've told you that over and over. I've begged for forgiveness. I don't know what else I can do."

"Maybe there's nothing you *can* do."

He might as well have slapped her. "Please, Gordon, don't

say that. I need you, now more than ever."

"You didn't need me when you were in Minnesota."

Would he ever forgive her? "Haven't you ever done something you regret? You've never made a mistake?"

Gordon straightened and his face flushed. He seemed on the verge of answering, then thought better of it. He sipped his coffee and avoided looking at her.

"I told you Todd was trouble," Marta reminded him. "That day he showed up pretending to look at the house down the street, remember? I told you, and you wouldn't listen. You kept saying what a nice guy he was."

"I didn't have your *intimate* knowledge of his true nature." Gordon set his cup on the counter. "Besides, it was your argument with Jamie that caused her to run away."

"What was I supposed to do? Tell her she had our blessings to keep seeing him?" Marta was suddenly through begging. "Maybe if you'd been home instead of out schmoozing with friends from work—"

"I've had enough! I'm going to the campus." He grabbed his keys and left.

Marta dumped the breakfast in the trash. She fought back tears but didn't know if they were tears of sadness or anger. Maybe both.

Her entire world had fallen apart. Her daughter had disappeared with an unscrupulous and dangerous man. Her marriage was on the verge of collapse. Her only friend had been killed, leaving Marta with both the grief of losing her and little hope for continuing the business. Worse, with the exception of Carol's death, it was all her fault.

A staggering sadness swelled from deep inside and threatened to consume her. She needed to get out of the house. Leaving the dishes unwashed and the kitchen a mess, she grabbed a sweater and her purse.

Already, people she knew in town had begun to pull away. To her face, they were sympathetic, but she knew that behind her back they whispered disapproval. She was the woman whose daughter had run off with an older man. She was the clueless mom who hadn't suspected a thing. She and Gordon were the sort of parents responsible people scorned.

Without any specific plan, she started the car and drove east, past the high school and a collection of fast-food places, past the used-car lots and auto-repair shops, to the mall near the edge of town. She didn't know exactly where Carol had been hit, but she pulled into one of the outer parking spots and turned off the engine.

What might Carol have been doing here? Mark was right that this mall wasn't on her way home from the office, so it had to have been an intended destination. But Marta couldn't imagine what interest Carol would have in any of the businesses in this small, rundown mall. It housed a discount grocery store, an odd-lot dollar store, a nail salon, and a cleaners, as well as several vacant storefronts. None of them places Carol would have patronized, much less gone out of her way to do so.

Despite the constant agony over Jamie, Marta had found time to look through Carol's client contacts and files. She found nothing that might explain what Carol had been doing at the mall. And nothing she saw now jarred a memory.

She sat there a few more minutes watching the customers come and go, and then drove off. Everything had turned sour in such a short period of time. Overnight, really. She thought back to Friday evening. Just Jamie and herself for dinner. She'd been looking forward to spending time with her daughter, and irritated that Jamie hadn't felt the same way. But the real shockers were learning that Jamie was seeing Todd, and then finding her daughter gone.

Carol had been killed that same night.

Marta knew the saying "When it rains, it pours." But still, what were the odds of so much bad news coming all at once?

Mark called that afternoon with the name and number of the man Carol had hired to investigate Todd. His name was Larry Gray and he lived in Boston.

"Thank you," Marta said. "I know you have a lot on your mind."

"Hope it helps."

"I take it there are still no witnesses?" When she'd last talked to Mark a couple of days ago, the police had come up with nothing.

"Nope. It happened at the back of the parking lot, in an area the security camera doesn't cover."

"I drove out there earlier today," Marta told him. "I was hoping I might remember something that would help explain why Carol was there. It didn't work."

"We'll probably never know."

"How are you doing?"

"Not great. But I went back to work. It actually helps."

"You'll let me know if I can do anything for you?"

"Sure."

"And thanks for Gray's name and contact info. I really appreciate it."

The minute Marta was off the phone, she called Larry Gray. She was pleasantly surprised when he picked up.

"Gosh, I'm sorry about Carol," he said when she'd explained the reason for her call. "How terrible. I'm afraid I can't help you, though."

"Why not?"

"Client confidentiality issues."

"But she's dead."

"Still, it's information Carol asked for. For all I know it could implicate you in some way. Maybe the two of you are at odds."

"That's silly. We were business partners and friends." Marta had an idea. "What if her husband gives you permission?"

"It still wouldn't be right."

Marta felt her cheeks grow hot. Frustration. "I can find someone else to get the information for me," she said. "But in the interest of time, it would be better if you could help me out. Please, I'll pay you. Pretend I'm hiring you right now."

Gray hesitated, then sighed. "Never mind paying me. Carol's retainer more than covers it. Just give me a minute." Over the phone Marta heard footsteps and then the shuffle of papers. "Here it is," Gray said. "The cell number she gave me belongs to someone named Conrad. J.D. Conrad. Sixty-four years old."

"She told me that much. What else?"

"He's a senior partner at Morgan, Thomas and Webb in New York. As far as I can tell he specializes in business and finance."

"Any relation to Todd Wilson or Tim Whitaker?"

"Not that I was able to find. I'll give you the same advice I gave Carol. Forget it. It's probably a stolen phone or a hacked account. Digging further along those lines is liable to be like stirring up a hornet's nest."

If that's what it took to find Jamie, Marta would do it. "What about the names Todd Wilson and Tim Whitaker? What did you find on them?"

"Absolutely nothing. Neither is an unusual name. I searched a lot of databases, but nothing seemed to match what Carol had given me."

"That's it?"

"Afraid so."

That didn't make sense. "But she left me a message right before she was killed. She said she'd learned something 'very interesting' about him. Those were her words."

"It wasn't from me."

How else could she have learned it? "Can you keep looking?" Marta asked.

"Without something more to go on, it would be a waste of time. I'm sorry. I wish I could have come up with more."

Marta was sorry, too. But at least she had Conrad's name and number. It was a starting point.

CHAPTER 30

Marta's hand was shaking as she punched in Conrad's number at the law firm. Did he know Todd? Would he know how to find him?

She expected a layer of secretaries, and worried she might not be able to talk her way through, but after asking the receptionist for J.D. Conrad, her call went straight to the attorney himself.

"Conrad, here," he said, picking up on the second ring.

She introduced herself, then launched into the reason for her call. "You might find this question odd, but it's important. I'm calling to ask about a cell phone listed in your name." She read off the number. "Is it yours?"

"What I find odd," Conrad said after a moment, "is that you are the second person in the past week to contact me about this."

"Was the other person Carol Hogan?"

"The name rings a bell." His voice was low and gravelly and not particularly warm.

"I'm sorry to bother you again, but she—"

"I take it you are acquainted with her, so you must know I can't help you."

"Carol was killed a few days ago," Marta explained. "We didn't have a chance to talk about your conversation before she died." Marta paused, waiting for Conrad to jump in. When he didn't, she added. "So I don't know what you told her."

"I told her that the name on the wireless account is mine, but it's not a phone I use personally."

"I see." Although she wasn't sure she really did. "Can you tell me who does use it?"

"I'm not at liberty to say."

Marta hadn't anticipated this. "He uses the name Todd Wilson," she said. "It's probably an alias. He sometimes goes by Tim Whitaker. I need to reach him. Please, it's important."

"Your friend mentioned something about a potential client and some irregularities. As I explained to her, I'm unable to help."

"But you must know who uses that phone," Marta insisted.

"My answer stands. Now if you'll—"

"Wait. Please hear me out. My daughter was abducted by this man."

Conrad was silent a moment. "Abducted?"

"Right." As good as abducted, Marta told herself. She was more than willing to bend the truth if that would help find Jamie.

"Recently?"

"Five days ago. We've contacted the police, of course." She hoped the threat of police involvement might make him more inclined to help.

Conrad sighed heavily. "I'm truly sorry," he said, and hung up.

When Gordon returned home, Marta filled him in on her conversation with Conrad. She'd been pacing circles for the past hour, waiting for him. "Why would the account be in his name if it's not his phone?"

"Could be for a son," Gordon offered, "or a friend without a credit history of his own. Or maybe it's a number associated with the law firm. That would explain why he's so secretive about it."

"Whatever the reason, you'd think he'd be nervous about covering for criminal activity."

Gordon frowned. "Maybe he knows nothing criminal happened."

"But Jamie—"

"Wasn't actually abducted. Remember? She ran off on her own."

Left unsaid was the accusation Marta knew was never far from Gordon's mind: *Ran off with a man you brought into our lives.*

"But if he—"

"We don't even know for certain she's with him," Gordon reminded her. He folded his arms and glared. "We don't know what's happened to her."

"But she called him."

"After an argument with you."

"Gordon, please. I feel guilty enough without your rubbing my face in it all the time."

"All the guilt in the world won't bring Jamie home."

He grabbed an apple and went upstairs, coming down again shortly after. Without a word, he marched out to the garage to work on his Mustang.

Marta bit back tears. She understood that he'd needed to go into work this morning. She even accepted that he might want to tinker in the garage. But she'd never felt so alone.

She clung blindly to the hope that he'd eventually forgive her, because she couldn't bear the thought it might not be true.

When the doorbell rang, she jumped to answer it. A uniformed police officer stood on the porch. He wasn't anyone she recognized, and he'd come alone. Did that mean good news or bad?

Her heart was in her throat as she opened the door.

"Sorry to bother you," he said.

"No problem. Finding Jamie is all I care about." She was surprised how calm she sounded because she didn't feel calm. Opening the door wider, she invited him in. "Shall I get my husband? He's in the garage."

"Actually, I'm here about the death of your business partner, Carol Hogan."

"Carol? Not Jamie?" Marta felt weak with relief, but also oddly disappointed.

"I'm sorry, I wish I had news about your daughter."

Thank God he was aware that Jamie was missing.

Handing her his card, the officer introduced himself as Officer Beck. He followed her to the living room where he sat stiffly on the edge of the couch. He was tall and thin and relatively young. He cleared his throat before speaking.

"Are you aware of anyone who had a grievance against Ms. Hogan?"

"A grievance? We do public relations, mostly for nonprofits and small businesses. If a client isn't happy with our work, we revise it until they are. It's really a cooperative effort."

"What about her personal life?"

Marta shook her head. "People liked her."

"How about family?"

"She had a brother she didn't see very often. Her parents live in Florida. She didn't talk a lot about them but I think they got along." Marta could only imagine what they must be going through right now.

Officer Beck cleared his throat again. "And at home? How was her marriage?"

"Good. She and Mark had only been married a couple of years. A second marriage for Mark, a first for her."

"No hint of infidelity?"

Marta shook her head, trying to ignore the irony of asking *her* about infidelity. "They were like newlyweds really. Except . . ." She hesitated. "I don't think it's anything important, but Carol was upset the other day. Said she and Mark had a fight. I was surprised because I didn't think they ever fought."

Beck seemed to ponder that. "Did she say what it was about?"

"Something to do with his long hours, I think. Why all the questions? Her death was an accident, wasn't it?"

"That's what we're trying to determine."

"She was hit by a car," Marta reminded him.

"Not just hit; more like run over."

"You think it might have been deliberate?"

"That's a possibility."

"My God." Marta sat back in her chair. Who would want to hurt Carol? It wasn't uncommon for the police to suspect a spouse in the case of a suspicious death, often with good reason, but Mark? "You really think someone might have done it on purpose?"

Beck was already on his feet. "Be sure to give me a call if you think of anything."

"Of course." As she walked him to the door, she remembered Carol's message the night she was killed.

"It may be nothing," Marta said, "but there was one person Carol had a disagreement with. A potential client." A stretch of the truth, but a convenient one. "He's the man we think my daughter might have run off with."

She explained as best she could, leaving herself out of it.

"Ms. Hogan was having him investigated for using an alias?" Beck looked perplexed.

"We need to know who we're dealing with."

The answer seemed to satisfy him. "Did he threaten her at all?"

"Not that I know of. But she sent me a text the evening she

died. She said she'd discovered something 'interesting' about him."

Beck scratched his chin. "You're not by any chance telling me this so that we'll double down on our effort to find this man, are you?"

"No, it's true. I'm not sure it means anything, but it might."

"We'll keep that in mind." He trotted down the steps to his car.

Carol's death intentional? Marta shuddered. Who would do such a thing? Mark? She couldn't imagine it, even with the recent fights. But then again, the marriage might have been rockier than Carol let on. Todd? Possibly, although it seemed a stretch. But if he had . . . might he hurt Jamie, too?

Another thought hit her. Had Jamie been there when it happened? It was, after all, the night she'd run away with him.

No. Jamie couldn't have been involved in Carol's death. Please, not that.

Marta and Gordon had already torn Jamie's room apart. They'd searched her computer, her emails, her Facebook page, the messages on her phone, and turned up nothing that would help them find her. But Marta wanted to look through the messages again in light of what she'd learned about Carol's death.

She took Jamie's phone into the den. There were two new texts. One was from Harmony, who was "testing" to see if Jamie would respond. The second was like a hammer to Marta's chest.

A message from Todd.

She clicked on it.

Hey, Marta. Miss me yet? Don't say I didn't warn you.

CHAPTER 31

The house was quiet when Gordon came in from the garage to wash up. There was no sound of activity in the kitchen despite the fact that it was dinner time. No radio or television playing in the background. No response when he called Marta's name.

Was she hurt? Mad that he wasn't more forgiving? He felt guilty about meeting Todd behind her back, but she'd been unfaithful. On the scale of wrongs, she won hands down.

He wasn't ready to forgive Marta yet, but he didn't want to lose her. She and Jamie were the best thing that had ever happened to him, and bottom line was, he still loved her.

What if she'd left him? Or been attacked? They didn't really know where Todd was or what he was up to. What if he'd abducted Marta, too? Mother and daughter.

Gordon called out again, louder, and again there was no answer.

Alarmed, he made a sweep of the rooms. No sign of her, but nothing was disturbed. Finally, he noticed the back door was ajar. He stepped outside, half expecting to find her beaten or dead.

Instead, she was sitting on the deck steps, arms wrapped around her knees, staring into the yard.

"Marta?"

She turned with a blank expression. "I didn't hear you come in."

"You had me worried. I couldn't find you anywhere."

"I came out to get some air." Her voice was as flat as her expression. Gordon wondered if she'd downed a handful of sleeping pills.

"Have you been out here long?"

"I don't know. What time is it?"

"Almost seven." He sat on the steps next to her. The setting sun was below the horizon and the air had turned chilly. "Has something happened?"

"We got a text. Or rather, I did."

"From Jamie?" His pulse quickened.

She shook her head. "From Todd. He sent it to Jamie's phone."

"You mean she's not with him?"

"She's with him." Marta handed him Jamie's cell phone. "See for yourself."

Hi Marta. Miss me yet? Don't say I didn't warn you.

"Are you sure this is from Todd? It's not his cell number."

"Of course it's from Todd. It's probably a disposable phone."

Gordon read the short message again with rolling waves of understanding. Instinctively, his gut knotted at the intimation of Marta's affair, brief though it might have been. He wasn't proud of the fact that he thought of himself before his daughter.

"He doesn't say Jamie's with him."

"He doesn't have to say it."

"We should call the police."

"I did. They didn't seem much interested."

Given the obscure nature of the message, Gordon could understand why. "Maybe we should try texting him back."

"And say what?"

"How about, 'Let us talk to Jamie.' "

"He's not going to let us talk to her. This is a game to him. Why give him the satisfaction of playing along?"

"We need to do something," he pointed out.

She stood and brushed the dirt from the seat of her jeans. "Let's go inside. There's more news, and I could use a drink."

"News about Jamie?"

"About Todd. Sort of." She moved into the kitchen.

"A cop came by when you were in the garage. He's looking into Carol's death. He asked if I could think of anyone who might be angry with her. He even asked about Mark. They think her death might not have been an accident."

"They think she was murdered?"

"They're not sure." Marta went to the fridge and pulled out an open bottle of Pinot Grigio.

"Is that a good idea?" Gordon hadn't ruled out the possibility of sleeping pills. Her lifelessness scared him.

She turned to glare at him. "Are you my keeper?"

"I'm worried about you."

"Oh, that's rich. Why would you worry about me when you can't stand me?"

"I don't want to fight, Marta."

"Fine, we won't fight." She poured herself a glass. "You want one?"

He started to say no, then changed his mind. "Yes, please."

"At first I couldn't think of anyone who'd want to hurt Carol," Marta continued. She poured a second glass and handed it him. "Then I thought of Todd."

Gordon looked at her, puzzled.

"Carol hired that investigator to dig up information on Todd. And we know that she talked to the attorney, J.D. Conrad, the man listed on Todd's cell account."

"Are you suggesting the attorney had her killed?"

"Not the attorney," Marta said. "Todd."

"Why would he kill Carol?"

"I don't know, but she was trying to dig up information about him. Maybe she found something. She left me a message implying that she had."

"That's quite a leap." But not out of the realm of possibility. Gordon was beginning to realize he hadn't known Todd at all.

"What if he's ruthless as well as crazy? If he killed Carol . . ." Marta looked at him with an expression that sent a chill down his spine.

"We have to find Jamie," he said.

CHAPTER 32

"You want anything to eat?" Todd asked when they pulled up to the gas pump.

Jamie shook her head. They'd been driving all day, and mostly she was tired. The only radio stations they could pick up were either religious, which neither of them wanted to listen to, or country, which Todd liked but Jamie hated. She decided their taste in music was very different. He'd never even heard of Daft Punk, Robin Thicke, or Kelly Clarkson.

"You might want to pee," he said with a nod toward the station. "With a full tank of gas we ought to be able to make it the rest of the way without stopping." He got out of the car and began to pump the gas.

She did need to pee, although she didn't relish the idea of using the restroom here. The station was in the middle of nowhere and looked like it had been around since cars were first invented. But she followed the sign that pointed her around the side of the stained stucco building. At least she hadn't had to ask the attendant for a key.

Todd wanted to keep a low profile. That's why they were sticking to back roads and winding through out-of-the-way places. They figured her parents, and maybe the police, would be trying to find her. She wished she could let her mom and dad know she was okay. More than okay, really. Even though the past few days hadn't exactly lived up to her fantasies, she was happier than she'd ever been. Being with Todd was all that mattered.

She took care of business and got back to the car just as Todd headed for the restroom himself.

The motels they'd stayed in were a lot like this gas station—old and tacky. They were clean enough, but not all that comfortable or inviting. It hadn't mattered to Jamie, but Todd felt bad.

"You deserve to be pampered," he'd tell her every night when they stopped. "I want to treat you like the princess you are. But for now, these places are safer."

"We're together," she always said. "There's nothing else I want."

Except, she'd add silently, *for you to love me as much as I love you.*

In bed, she could tell that he was crazy about her. His hands and mouth were everywhere. He couldn't get enough of her. One night the bed squeaked like crazy. An older couple in the room next to theirs had pounded on the wall and told them to keep it down. Jamie was embarrassed but Todd had laughed.

"They're envious," he'd told her.

But when they weren't in bed, he sometimes seemed almost bored. She worried she was disappointing him somehow. He'd go for hours without speaking unless she asked him a direct question, and on a couple of occasions he'd disappeared without telling her where he was going. The first time was on the night she'd left home. He had deposited her in a motel and then taken off. She'd been afraid he might not come back. He'd been in a big hurry, explaining that he had a lot on his mind and needed to come up with a plan. Jamie hadn't seen why they couldn't work one out together.

"All set?" he asked now, climbing back into the car.

She smiled. "All set."

"That's my girl." He patted her on the knee.

★ ★ ★ ★ ★

Several hours later they pulled up to a multistory condominium complex not far from the freeway. There were office buildings on one side and a Denny's restaurant on the other.

"This isn't San Francisco," Jamie noted, trying to keep the disappointment from her voice.

When Todd had asked her where she wanted to go, Jamie said the first thing that came to mind. She knew San Francisco from iconic photographs and movies, but she'd never been there. She'd been excited when Todd agreed. But a few minutes ago, she'd seen a sign announcing they were in someplace called Emeryville.

"San Francisco is close," Todd said. "Just across the bay." He pointed to the horizon where Jamie could make out the lights of a bridge and a city beyond.

"Come on, let's go up," he said. "I'll come back for our stuff later."

They took a glass-walled elevator to the tenth floor. Jamie held her breath in awe at the vast array of sparkling lights below them. The city looked like a magical kingdom in the distance. She thrilled at the thought of how exciting it must be to live there.

The inside of the condo was impressive, too. All sleek and modern, with a wide expanse of windows and an even more breathtaking view.

"Wow," Jamie gushed. "Look at all the lights."

Todd hugged her. "I thought you'd like it."

"You're sure your friend won't mind?"

"He's out of the country for a few weeks so it works out perfectly."

When Todd went down to move the car and get their bags, Jamie walked through the apartment. She ran her hands over the dark green granite counter in the kitchen and admired the gleaming stainless steel appliances and built-in espresso machine. It looked like something you'd see in *Architectural Digest,* a magazine she knew about because Alyssa's mother subscribed. From the kitchen, she moved onto the master bedroom with its large bed and mirrored closet doors. The bedspread was red satin—like something out of a romantic movie.

The master bath was almost as large as the bedroom and was tiled in what looked like marble. There was a double Jacuzzi tub as well as a glassed-in multi-spray shower. The towels were red, plush, and monogrammed. Jamie had never seen a bathroom like it.

Back in the bedroom, she noticed a phone on the bedside table. She touched it longingly, wishing she could call her parents. Alyssa, too. She wanted to share her excitement. But Todd had been emphatic. No calls, no contact. Not for a while anyway. Calls could be traced, he warned her. They'd both be in big trouble if the authorities caught up with them.

She wandered back into the kitchen. Todd was taking a long time. She opened the fridge and found an old chunk of cheese. She cut away the crusty outside and took a bite. Then she went into the bathroom again, filled the tub with water and turned on the jets. When she was younger her parents had taken her to Disney World. They'd stayed in a motel with a Jacuzzi but they hadn't let her use it. Now she was grown up and could make her own decisions. She undressed and climbed in.

The warm water bubbled around her. She leaned back, feeling like a celebrity. When she heard Todd return, she called to him. "I'm in the tub. It's wonderful."

A few minutes later, he showed up carrying two glasses of champagne. He handed her one. "Good riddance to cheap motels," he said. "This is the life you deserve."

"They weren't so bad."

"Not good, either." He looked at her and smiled. "You're gorgeous, you know that?"

Jamie felt herself blush. "I am not."

"Yes, you are." He pulled out his phone and snapped a photo. "A moment to be remembered." Then he set his glass down, undressed, and got into the tub with her.

Jamie had tasted beer before but never champagne. It was wonderful, sweet and sparkly in a way that beer wasn't. The warm water, Todd's hands on her body, the bubbles floating through her system—she'd never felt so good.

Todd helped her from the tub and dried her off. Jamie realized she'd drunk a lot and was having trouble standing on her own. She must have made it to the bed somehow because she woke once in the middle of the night to find Todd's body pressed against hers. She smiled and drifted back to sleep.

When she woke again, it was morning. Light filtered through the window shades and she was alone.

CHAPTER 33

Day six and still no news of Jamie. The waiting and worrying were unbearable, especially with Carol's death now considered suspicious. Marta was a nervous wreck, unable to sleep or sit or eat. She knew Gordon felt the same.

What little news coverage there had been had died off after the first few days, and the police had no leads. They had tried repeatedly to reach J.D. Conrad, the attorney, but he never returned the calls. No luck reaching Todd, either. His phone rang and rang, not even rolling into voice mail. Texts disappeared into the black hole of cyberspace.

Marta called Alyssa again, and Harmony. Neither had heard a word from Jamie.

Where was she? Was she with Todd? Was she okay?

Would they ever know?

Gordon taught his classes, but all work on his paper was suspended. He couldn't concentrate, he said. Couldn't focus on anything but Jamie. And, Marta added silently, the bitter resentment he felt toward her.

She tried to keep up with pressing deadlines at work, which were thankfully few. She, too, could think of nothing but Jamie and the state of her marriage. She tried to console herself by clinging to the hope that Jamie was happy, still bewitched by Todd and visions of love. That nothing bad had happened—yet. But it was hard to hold onto such fragile optimism. More often, her mind raced with dark thoughts. Jamie held prisoner, locked in some dark, dank space with barely room to stand. Jamie tortured. Jamie dead.

All to punish Marta.

The phone rang while she was in the kitchen, going through the motions of fixing what passed these days for dinner. It was their second night in a row of frozen pizza.

Her heart leapt, as always, at the sound. *Please let it be Jamie.*

"Just checking with you about Las Vegas," Cassie said. "Do you think you'll be able to get away? It would really be fun."

With all that had happened, the trip had skipped Marta's mind. "I'm afraid not," she said.

"Oh phooey. Because of Jamie? Are you really worried Gordon won't keep an eye on her?"

"It's worse than that." Marta had mixed feelings about sharing her troubles with Cassie, who had problems enough of her own. But she could hardly keep Jamie's disappearance from her own sister.

"Jamie's gone," Marta said. "She ran away."

"Ran away? Where'd she go?"

"We don't know."

"When?"

"Last Friday."

"And you didn't call me right away? What kind of sister are you?"

Under other circumstances, Marta might have asked Cassie the same thing. But she should have called. She realized that now, although it hadn't even crossed her mind earlier.

"Sorry. I've been kind of overwhelmed here."

"You never think about me, do you?"

"This isn't about you, Cassie."

There was a burst of static. "So what happened? Why did she leave?"

"We're pretty sure she's with the guy she's been seeing,"

Marta explained. "Turns out he's not the boy I was telling you about. He's someone older."

"No wonder she was being secretive. Do you know much about him?"

"We know he's up to no good," Marta hedged. "He has no business being involved with a naive seventeen-year-old."

"That's for damn sure. It's downright—" Cassie stopped short. "Wait a minute, how old is he?"

"Mid-thirties. Maybe a bit older."

"How did she meet him?"

Marta was too embarrassed to admit the truth. "He's someone Gordon met in the neighborhood."

"Oh." Cassie sounded relieved. "A neighbor."

"No, he was interested in buying a house that's for sale down the street." Marta recognized that she was spinning a web of untruths, but she wanted to keep the focus on Jamie, not the sordid details of how Todd came into their lives.

"You've contacted the police?"

"Of course. For all the good it's done. They don't seem to think a runaway seventeen-year-old is a priority."

"Is there any way I can help? Do you want me to come there?"

"Thanks, but there's not really anything for you to do." Marta had worries enough without adding Cassie to the mix. "How about you? Is the job still going well?"

"So far. That's how I'm going to be in Vegas. There's a convention or something. I'm sorry you can't come."

"And the AA meetings?" Marta asked.

"They're dumb."

"Does that mean you've stopped going?"

"I'm not a drunk or a druggie, okay? I've messed up a few times but that's only human."

Marta sighed. "It's your life."

"Yes. It is."

Marta's phone chirped, indicating a new text message. "I gotta go," she said, happy to bring the conversation to a close.

"Let me know if you need me," Cassie said.

The text was from an unfamiliar number.

Hey, guys. Having a great time.

Love, Jamie

There was a photo attached. Marta eagerly tapped the screen to bring it up. Her breath caught.

It was a picture of Jamie—without a stitch on. She appeared to be soaking in a whirlpool bath. She was grinning and did, indeed, seem to be having a good time.

CHAPTER 34

Todd was gone again, and Jamie was going stir-crazy.

They'd finally made it across the bay to San Francisco a couple of days ago, and she'd had a wonderful time. They rode the cable car, ate crab cocktail on Fisherman's Wharf, laughed at the harbor seals, and took a boat to Alcatraz.

Todd insisted on buying her an ice cream cone, telling her, "I've always wanted to buy a girl an ice cream cone."

"I can't be the first girl for that."

He'd laughed. "But you are. You're like no one else, Jamie."

He had been playful and sweet, and when Jamie told him it was one of the best days in her life, he'd teased her about leading a boring life.

But Jamie had been pretty much alone since. Todd would leave early in the morning, sometimes when she was still asleep, not returning until late afternoon. And he never wanted to go out again in the evening. He said they'd taken a risk being seen together, and now they needed to keep a low profile for a bit.

Fine for him to say, but Jamie was tired of being cooped up in the apartment with nothing to do but watch TV or prowl around the rooms, snooping into the private life of their host. She missed her friends and her parents. She wanted to call them but Todd said it was still too soon.

She'd tried their host's computer, thinking the Internet might help her pass the time, as well as giving her a way to communicate with her friends. But it was locked with a password she hadn't been able to figure out.

Next to her, the apartment phone rang, as it did several times a day. She knew the answering machine message by heart. *Hi, this is Charley Brooks. Sorry I'm not available. Leave a message if you want and I'll get back to you when I can.*

Few callers did, and most of those were recorded telemarketing solicitations. There had only been a couple of personal calls, but that was enough for Jamie to make a game of piecing together a picture of Charley Brooks. He was a serious guy, probably around forty. From the clothes in his closet, she decided he was a businessman with a fondness for dark gray.

Jamie heard a door shut in the outside hallway. She went to the peephole and peered out. It was the girl, a bit older than Jamie, who lived two doors down. Jamie had seen her coming home a couple of times. Now, she set her bag of laundry on the floor and used both hands to lock her apartment door, then grabbed the laundry and started toward the elevator.

Jamie couldn't stand the isolation a minute longer. She stepped into the hallway and said, "Hi."

The girl was focused on her cell phone screen, but she looked up when she heard Jamie. "Are you moving in?" the girl asked.

"Just visiting."

"I thought Mr. Brooks was out of town."

"He is. But he's letting my boyfriend and me stay here for a bit."

"That's nice." The girl gave Jamie a fake smile, turned her attention back to her phone, and continued on to the elevator.

Well that went well, Jamie thought. Kids here were as unfriendly as the ones at home. She'd been hoping they'd be different.

The apartment phone was ringing once again when Jamie stepped back inside. On a whim, she answered. She could take a message as easily as the machine, and she was starved for conversation.

"Brooks household," Jamie announced.

A moment's silence followed by, "Who the hell are you?"

"My name is Jamie. Mr. Brooks is out of town and I'm house-sitting for him."

"The hell you are! That's my house and I've never heard of you."

She quickly explained. "I'm a friend of Todd's. He's out at the moment."

"Todd?"

"Wilson. Your friend." Jamie was beginning to get an uneasy feeling about this. Maybe it was the word *housesitting* that had thrown things off. "You told him he could use your place while you were away."

"I don't know any Todd Wilson, and I never told anyone they could use my place." His voice was growing loud and sharp. "How did you get in anyway?"

"Todd has a key."

"What the fuck! I call to pick up my messages and some stranger answers my phone. I don't know what kind of scam you're pulling, lady. I'm calling the cops," he said and hung up.

Jamie had a sick feeling in her stomach. She didn't understand what was going on—probably some simple misunderstanding—but she knew she was in no position to sort it out.

If only she had Todd's new cell number. A disposable phone was safer for right now, he said. So she was stuck here alone and she had no way to get in touch with him.

Should she hide? Run? At least come up with a good explanation to offer the police?

Before she could come up with a plan, she heard the chime of the elevator in the hallway.

Were the police here already? She glanced at the balcony and thought fleetingly about climbing out on the ledge that ran around the side of the building.

Before she could move, the door opened and Todd stepped through.

"Thank God you're home." She threw her arms around his neck.

Todd pushed her away. "What's wrong?"

"The man who lives here . . . Charley Brooks . . . he called."

"What do you mean, he called? You didn't answer the phone, did you?"

"I was going to take a message. But he got mad and said he was calling the cops. He didn't know about any housesitting arrangement."

"Why the fuck did you answer the phone?" Todd grabbed her arm roughly, glowering at her.

"Because I'm bored. We never go anywhere, and you won't let me go out on my own. I haven't talked to anyone but you for days."

"Damn it, Jamie. Do you ever use your brain?"

"I'm sorry." She tried to pull her arm free but he gripped it tighter. "Let go, Todd. You're hurting me."

"Whine, whine." But he let her go.

She'd expected he might be unhappy about what had happened, but she hadn't imagined he'd be so angry. Stung, she said, "What's going on? Why didn't he know you were here?"

Todd ran his hands through his hair and cursed under his breath. "It's his wife who's a friend of mine. I made the arrangements with her. She must not have told him."

"But you said Charley was your friend." And it was the first she'd heard of any wife.

Todd was moving around the apartment, gathering his things. "I thought you might be jealous if I gave you a woman's name."

"Is she an ex-girlfriend of yours?" Jamie didn't see why she'd be jealous. The woman was married to Charley now. "Maybe you should call her and sort it out. You know, in case the cops show up."

"Nah, I don't want to cause trouble for them. Let's pack up and leave."

"Leave?"

"We don't have time for this, Jamie. Go on, pack our stuff. And make it quick." He shoved her toward the bedroom. "Get moving. Don't make more trouble than you already have."

Jamie didn't understand what was going on but she didn't have time to think about it. She found it odd, though, that there was nothing in the apartment to indicate a woman lived there.

CHAPTER 35

Marta's stomach soured as she watched Detective Phillips examine the photo of Jamie, stark naked, in the bathtub. The pose was tame by contemporary standards, but this was her daughter Phillips was staring at, not some unknown girl on the Internet. She had to remind herself that the photo was evidence and Phillips was a cop. He wasn't leering. At least, she hoped not.

Next to her, Gordon looked uncomfortable, too. "You can track the location where it was sent from, can't you?" he asked.

After a sleepless night, they'd headed to the station first thing that morning.

"The FBI might be able to," Phillips said.

"So have them do it." Gordon was practically breathing fire.

Phillips responded with something between a cough and a laugh. "It doesn't work that way." He leaned over his desk to hit the intercom. "Let me run this by our tech guy and our legal people. The phone companies won't even speak to us without a court order."

He was going through the motions, Marta gave him credit for that, but the bottom line was, the text probably convinced him that Jamie was in no danger. He might even believe she was safer and happier now than she had been living at home. Marta had learned a lot in the past week about the abuse and neglect that often drove kids to leave home.

A few seconds later, the door opened and a younger officer

joined them. Phillips introduced him as the technical specialist, Jack Pickering. He, too, examined Jamie's photo while Phillips filled him in on the background and Marta continued to squirm.

"This isn't from a number you recognize?" Pickering asked.

"Definitely not," Gordon said. "We're guessing it's from a disposable phone."

"Looks like your daughter is going out of her way to keep you from locating her."

Marta crossed her arms. "That message is not from Jamie. I already explained that to Detective Phillips."

Gordon glanced her way but kept silent. He wasn't so sure that Jamie hadn't sent it. But whether the message was from Jamie or not, he agreed they needed to find her.

"Give me a few minutes," Pickering said. He took Marta's phone and left the room.

"As we've told you," Marta explained to Phillips, "we think Jamie is with a man we know as Todd Wilson. We believe he took that picture and sent the message, pretending to be Jamie."

"What about the photo itself? It doesn't look to me like your daughter is miserable or frightened."

Gordon exploded. "She's seventeen years old, for God's sake. Whether she's happy or not isn't the issue."

"I'm just trying to get the lay of the land," Phillips said. He looked down at the file on his desk. "This Wilson is the same man you claim killed your friend Carol Hogan?"

"I didn't claim anything," Marta replied, smarting at the detective's tone. "All I said was that he possibly had a motive."

"But you did volunteer his name, didn't you?"

"It was your guy, Officer Beck, who asked if I knew of anyone with reason to harm her."

"Besides," Gordon added, "the issue is Jamie. We need to find her and bring her home."

Phillips frowned and leaned back in his chair. "Tell me again how this man Wilson came into your lives."

Marta felt her face flush. She hoped Phillips didn't notice. "I met him at a conference."

"And then I met him by chance when he was in the neighborhood," Gordon added. "We believe now that he was stalking Marta, but I didn't know that at the time."

"And you don't know anything more about him?" Phillips sounded skeptical.

"If we did, you can be sure we would tell you. He's lied to us from the beginning." Marta glanced at the door, eager for the tech specialist to return with answers. Then she turned back to Phillips. "What have you learned? Do you have any leads about where Jamie might be?"

"No responses to our 'be on the lookout for' dispatches, but that's not surprising if she's left the local area."

"You only sent them out locally?" Gordon made no effort to disguise his outrage.

"If every runaway teenager warranted a national alert, people would stop paying attention to any of them. Besides, there isn't really a system for national alerts of this sort."

Marta put a hand on Gordon's arm since he looked ready to argue. "How about the attorney, J.D. Conrad?" she asked Phillips. "What did he tell you?"

"I spoke to him myself. He wasn't any more forthcoming than he was with you. I'm afraid it's not illegal to let someone else use your phone."

"But why wouldn't he *want* to help?"

Phillips shrugged. "That I can't answer."

"So you've made no progress at all?" Gordon shook his head in disbelief.

Phillips pressed his fingers together and stared at them a moment. "As I told you initially," he said, "there's not a whole lot

226

we can do about a runaway teen. Especially one who's almost eighteen."

"She's still seventeen," Gordon reminded him.

Thankfully, the tech specialist returned. "You can have your phone back," he said, handing it to Marta. "I've downloaded what I need. I'm not sure what I'll come up with, though."

She imagined Jamie's nude photo was among the files downloaded.

Phillips rose from his seat, signaling the end of the interview. "I'll be in touch if we learn anything." He walked them to the door. "And just so you know, Todd Wilson *is* on our radar. We're not letting him off the hook."

"Great," Gordon said hotly. "Meanwhile, our daughter is still missing."

As they left the station, Gordon muttered, "That was useful."

Marta nodded. "It's like they don't care."

"They don't. To them, Jamie's just some boy-crazy teenager who can't stand her parents." He stopped to face her with a level stare. "And maybe that's not far from the truth."

"What? You know that's not the case."

"Do we?" he said bitterly. "Perhaps she's more like her mother than we imagined." Gordon looked at her pointedly, then turned. "I've got to get to class."

"That's not fair, Gordon. Please don't be like that." But he was already heading to his car.

Marta blinked back tears. Gordon refused to talk about what had happened between her and Todd, but he didn't shy away from rubbing her nose in it. She had it coming, but it hurt all the same.

There was no solace to be found. Her daughter was missing and her husband hated her. All because she'd made a foolish, impetuous mistake. And now it looked like her best friend's death might be her fault, too.

The chaos she'd caused, the boundless pain—Marta felt physically ill. She clung to the hope that Jamie was still alive.

As Gordon headed across campus to his office, he spotted one of his students. The young man waved and Gordon waved back, then picked up his pace, hoping to avoid becoming embroiled in conversation. He had too much on his mind for idle chitchat.

Try as he might, he couldn't get the photo of Jamie out of his mind. His little girl, stark naked, grinning like some wannabe starlet while the creepy guy behind the camera gawked at her. It made his blood boil.

Worse, the creep was Todd Wilson. Someone Gordon had considered a friend.

He had seemed like such a nice guy. Gordon wondered now how long Todd had been coming on to Jamie. He'd probably been laughing at Gordon the entire time. *Hey dude, I'm doing your daughter and you don't even have a clue.*

Of course he'd also been doing Gordon's wife. Probably laughing even harder.

Gordon kicked a loose stone on the path, sending it onto the grass. He was so angry at Marta he found it difficult to be civil. Angry, and of course, hurt. Devastated, in fact. He'd never, in all the time they'd been together, had any reason to doubt her. Marta was grounded, loyal, kind. She wasn't flighty, or even flirtatious. Her behavior with Todd was totally out of character.

Or maybe he didn't know his wife as well as he thought.

CHAPTER 36

Between Jamie's running away and Carole's death, not to mention the trauma of her failing marriage, Marta had let work slide. She wasn't taking on new projects, even for existing clients, but she couldn't in good conscience abandon work already contracted for. Reluctantly, she headed into the office.

The room was stuffy and stale when she entered, and it felt horribly empty. Carol's outspokenness might have grated at times, but she was an easy partner and a good friend. Her death was a profound loss.

On top of so many other losses.

And if Todd was responsible . . . Marta's throat tightened. It all came back to her and her fatal misstep.

As she gathered the mail and checked phone messages, she wondered if she'd be able to keep the business going. Or if she even wanted to.

Now was not the time to think about that.

She decided to start with Carol's files since it was a task that needed to be done and didn't require creativity or serious concentration. Gordon's barbed comment as they left the police station that morning still stung. He'd made her sound like a brainless floozy, and she wasn't.

Okay, maybe the brainless part fit. She had committed adultery with a man she'd met only hours earlier. That was the sort of airhead thing Cassie did, not Marta. Again, the weight of her guilt settled over Marta like a dense, dank fog. Her world was collapsing around her.

She took a moment to catch her breath and focus, then settled at Carol's desk. Three of her projects were active and Marta was familiar with all of them. She opened the first file and began to bring herself up to speed.

She'd just begun a letter laying out her thoughts about how to proceed when Alyssa's mother, Elaine, called. They'd talked only once since Jamie's disappearance, and for a brief moment, Marta harbored a flicker of hope that Alyssa had heard from her.

"How are you holding up?" Elaine asked. "Have you heard anything?"

"Nothing. I was hoping you were calling with news."

"I wish I was. I know you must be going through hell right now."

Hell might have been preferable. Marta was on the verge of telling Elaine about the recent text and bathtub photo when she thought better of it. "It hasn't been easy," she replied instead.

"I imagine not." Elaine hesitated. "I want you to know . . . I had no idea Jamie was seeing an older man. I thought it was a boy at school. I don't want you to think I was concealing anything. I would have told you if I'd had any inkling that wasn't the case."

"Of course." Marta didn't know Elaine well enough to have an opinion one way or another, but it was clear that Elaine needed to set the matter straight.

"It's been weighing on me. I mean, someone quite a bit older really puts a different spin on it."

It did, but there was more wrong with Todd than his age. "Tell me," Marta said. "In your work as a therapist, have you ever had a client who was a stalker? Or maybe a client who was being stalked?"

"Not in terms of a criminal investigation, but unwanted or

obsessive attention can play a part in many therapeutic cases. Why?"

Having opened the door to the subject, Marta decided to go for broke. "The man Jamie is with initially developed a thing for me. When I made it clear I wasn't interested, he went after Jamie as a way of punishing me."

A moment's silence. "You think that's what's behind this?"

"Obviously. What else?"

Elaine cleared her throat. "Men do sometimes fall for young girls. And vice versa."

Marta wondered if she'd already said too much, but she couldn't let Elaine's comment stand. "That's not what's going on here. I met the man on a business trip. He began sending me messages, flowers, photos, and then he unexpectedly showed up here in town, hoping to convince me we were meant for each other."

"Well, that does fit the pattern. It's not unusual for a stalker to feel entitled to an intimate relationship with someone who has caught his interest. But substituting Jamie for you is a bit of a twist. It borders on sociopathic."

"What does that mean?"

"Sociopaths are manipulative and controlling. They're incapable of normal emotional attachments. What's important to them is winning. And they win by diminishing the lives of others."

"Like being a bully?" Marta asked.

"I suppose they are bullies on some level. But they are usually also quite charming, and often fancy themselves irresistible. The controlling behavior emerges in subtle ways at first. That's how women, and it's usually women but not always, get trapped in relationships with these individuals. A sociopath can sweep a woman off her feet. She's so enamored she doesn't recognize the abusive behavior, or she makes excuses for it."

"Or maybe," Marta noted, "there are enough trade-offs, she's willing to overlook it." She knew women who were happily married to men she found impossibly manipulative.

"Right. Relationships are never simple. I know that as well as anyone." Elaine laughed. "Some of these men are simply narcissists, but others can be dangerous, especially because they tend to feel invincible."

"Dangerous?" Marta's heart skipped a beat.

"I had a client, a young woman who broke off her engagement at the last minute when she learned her fiancé had been married twice before. Both former wives died under suspicious circumstances."

Marta gasped. "He killed them?"

"Possibly. Probably, in fact. And my client might have been next. The man had wooed her with attention and flattery, convincing her they were destined to be together. He claimed he'd been terribly hurt in past relationships. Said his experiences had turned him off to love, but that she made him feel worthwhile again. When she called off the marriage, he spread horrible, untrue rumors about her and married her best friend less than a year later. He's now in prison for that wife's murder."

Marta shuddered. The description sounded a lot like Todd. "How does a person deal with someone like that?"

"By staying as far away as possible."

"It's a little late for that," Marta pointed out.

"I'm sorry, I didn't mean to worry you. It's just that you asked and I guess when it comes to psychology, I sometimes get carried away. Jamie's probably not in any physical danger. The man I was describing was an extreme case."

Marta wasn't so sure. Todd was unpredictable. Who knew what he was capable of?

She thanked Elaine for calling, so few people had, but she couldn't get off the phone fast enough. She tried to get back to work, but Elaine's words echoed in her head, making it impossible to concentrate. She boxed up the loose papers from Carol's desk to go through at home and left the office.

CHAPTER 37

"How much farther?" Jamie asked.

"We're almost there." Todd sounded annoyed, as though she'd been bugging him all day like an antsy five-year-old, which she hadn't been. She'd barely said anything the entire trip. He must have realized how he came across, because he added, "I know this has been a difficult day for you."

Not so much difficult as confusing. She didn't really mind their hurried departure from the condo or the long drive that followed, but it bothered her that Todd seemed angry, like she'd done something terrible and he blamed her for it.

"I don't see why you couldn't have called the guy back and explained that you arranged the stay through his wife," Jamie had said when he'd hurried her out the door of the condo.

"Drop it, Jamie. I don't want to hear another word out of you." And then he'd barely spoken to her for the next five hours.

She remained quiet, curled up tight inside her skin, wishing she could make herself invisible. Why was he so upset with her?

They were headed for a fishing cabin that had been in Todd's family for years. Jamie had no idea where they were at this point since she'd fallen asleep along the way, but they'd left the main highway and were winding up into the mountains.

"Smell that mountain air," Todd said. Now that they were getting closer, his mood seemed to have improved.

Jamie relaxed a little. "Do you spend a lot of time at the cabin?" she asked, eager to make conversation.

"I used to. Haven't been there in years, though. There's a stream not far from the back porch and at night the sky is something to behold."

Jamie would have preferred to stay in the city, but she'd gradually warmed to the idea of a remote, romantic getaway. "Sounds pretty."

"It is. Also, very secluded and private."

"A family compound." Jamie knew the term but she wasn't quite sure what it meant. Rich families had them, and important politicians.

"Not quite." Todd looked amused. "Not like the Kennedy compound, that's for damn sure."

"A stream sounds nice."

"I used to catch frogs in that stream," he said. "Lots and lots of frogs."

"What did you do with them?"

He shrugged. "They were frogs. Not much you can do with them but catch them. My grandfather used to take me squirrel hunting, too."

"You killed squirrels?" Jamie was appalled. Squirrels were cute.

"Yep."

"What for?"

"Fun mostly. Sometimes my grandfather made squirrel stew."

"Yuck."

He laughed. "I promise, no squirrel stew."

It was the first time he'd laughed since they'd left the condo and it made her feel better. Maybe he didn't hate her after all.

"The cabin's up there, just around the bend." He pointed ahead through the trees, which looked like all the other trees they'd seen.

They'd left the paved road several miles back and were now bouncing long a rutted dirt lane. Jamie continued to peer into the distance where Todd had pointed. Finally, a small log cabin came into view.

"It's a bit rustic," Todd said. "But that's its charm."

Rustic, yes. Charm, maybe. Jamie was withholding judgment. On closer inspection it looked more like a shack than a cabin. And definitely not a compound.

Todd parked in a small clearing near the side of the house. Jamie eased her stiff legs from the car while Todd retrieved the key from its hiding place under the porch.

"Still here," he said with obvious relief. "I had visions of having to break in."

Remembering the fiasco at the condo, she looked at him in alarm. "You didn't check with whoever owns it?"

"I own at least part of it. I don't think anyone has been here in a while, though."

The door stuck a bit and Todd had to push it open with his shoulder. He stepped inside and Jamie followed.

The interior was dark, and her eyes took a few minutes to adjust. The cabin consisted of a single room with a kitchen area at one end and a wood-burning fireplace at the other. The furnishings were sparse and the windows bare. A ladder led to what Jamie assumed was a loft. The place looked cold, dark, and dusty.

"Let's open up before we bring our stuff in," Todd said. "I'll turn on the propane and fill the water tank."

"Water tank?"

"It's either that or pump the stuff from the well." He looked around and grinned. "Once we get the place cleaned up, it will be great."

This was the cheerful Todd she knew and loved. Maybe he was embarrassed about messing up the arrangements for the condo, which he'd intended as a treat for her. He'd wanted to please her and it hadn't worked out. She was touched knowing he cared so much.

She turned and gave him a kiss. "It's awesome," she said.

Three hours later, as she stood at the stove stirring the pan of canned chicken soup they'd found in the cupboard, she could think of many words more fitting than "awesome."

They'd swept, wiped, and scrubbed, plowing through layers of grime that stubbornly resisted the hardest scouring. She'd dealt with plenty of spiders and mouse droppings, too. With some effort (and swearing) Todd had managed to coax the gas refrigerator and lights to work. He'd found supposedly clean sheets and sent Jamie up the ladder to make the bed. She was almost glad the light was poor in the loft because she didn't really want to get a good look at the mattress.

When the soup was hot, she poured it into mismatched bowls. Todd had the fire lit in the fireplace, although the flames were thin and the fire smoky. He brushed his hands on his pants.

"Good thing dinner's ready," he said. "I'm starved."

Jamie set the bowls on the small, rickety table. "Not too starved, I hope. It's not much of a dinner."

"I thought there was more stuff here, okay?" His tone verged on angry again.

"I wasn't complaining."

"Could have fooled me."

She bit her lip.

He sighed. "I'm sorry, Jamie. I wanted this to be fun."

"It will be," she said with faked enthusiasm.

He poured bourbon from a dusty bottle into two chipped glasses and handed her one. "Anyway, we've got booze. Super-aged in fact. This stuff must have been here for years."

He lifted his glass in a toast and Jamie did the same. "To us," he said.

She took a small sip. The liquor was bitter and burned her throat.

"I know we didn't exactly plan on this trip to the cabin, but I'm glad it happened. The place has special meaning for me. It's nice I can share it with *someone* who's special to me." He touched her chin. "You're a wonderful and amazing girl, Jamie. I don't know how I got so lucky."

She was the one who was lucky. A sexy guy like Todd, and he'd chosen her. She still couldn't believe it. She just wished she knew what he expected of her. She took a second small sip of whiskey. It didn't burn as much as before. In fact, it emboldened her. "You must have known lots of wonderful girls," she teased.

"Not so many as you might think."

"But there had to have been one or two special ones, no?"

Todd set his glass on the rickety table and lowered his gaze. "There was someone I thought was special. But turned out she was just using me. I was heartbroken. It put me off all women." He looked up and smiled. "Until you came along."

Jamie melted inside. If only they were someplace nicer than this creepy, buggy cabin, she'd be the happiest girl on earth.

The next morning Todd was out of bed and dressed before Jamie even woke up. When she opened her eyes, he was standing over the bed and pulling on a jacket.

"Where are you going?" she asked.

"To town for supplies."

She must have slept longer than she thought. There was so little light in the cabin it was hard to tell what time it was. "It'll only take me a minute to get ready."

"No need for you to come."

"But I want to." She had assumed they'd go together. It was part of the adventure.

"Better that you stay here. Someone might see you in town."

"So?"

"Jamie, we're hiding out. Remember?"

"No one in town is going to recognize me, or even care."

"We can't take that chance. You're not coming."

Jamie sat up, gripped in fear. What if he left and never came back? There was nothing around but wild animals and wilderness. She'd die of fright if not starvation.

"Please? I'll wear a hat or something."

"Jesus, Jamie. Get a grip. I won't be gone long. Maybe you can clean the place up a bit more while I'm in town." With that he headed downstairs and out the door.

Jamie didn't get out of bed, even when she heard the car pull away. She was too miserable to move. How could Todd be so sweet one minute and so . . . so mean the next?

She didn't want to be alone in the stupid cabin. She didn't really want to be here at all. Through the haze of last night's whiskey and the crackle of a fire, the cabin had seemed adventurous and oddly romantic. But the reality was that the toilet was filthy, the water ran at a trickle, and the whole cabin smelled. During the night she'd heard howling in the woods, and when she'd woken Todd, he'd turned his back to her. "It's just coyotes," he'd said. "They won't hurt you."

And then this morning he'd left with barely a word. Even if he didn't want her to go to town with him, why did he have to act like he was mad at her again?

Afraid to think how Todd would react if he came home and found her still lying there, she got up.

He wanted her to clean some more, so she would. Maybe then he'd be nice to her again. She washed the dinner dishes in the rust-stained sink, dried them, and put them away. She swept the floor and restacked the logs by the fireplace. There was nothing else for her to do. The cabin was beyond cleaning. It needed a bulldozer.

When she heard Todd's car rumbling down the road, she ran

outside to greet him, relieved beyond reason.

"You're back!"

"Shit hole of a store." He pulled a couple of grocery bags from the car. "They've got nothing there."

"Maybe there's a better store farther on." She reached to help him carry a bag and he practically threw it at her.

"Yeah, if we want to drive for an hour." He slammed the car door shut.

Jamie followed him into the cabin and began silently putting the groceries away. Mostly cans: canned beans, canned stew, canned pasta, more soup. He had bought eggs, instant coffee, bread, and more whiskey. No meat and not a single fresh fruit or vegetable.

"Next time we'll go together and make an outing of it," she suggested. "An hour's not so far and we can explore along the way. I'll wear some sort of disguise if it will make you feel better."

He ran a hand across the shelf where the whiskey bottle was stored. Jamie could see the dust fly up in the air. "What the hell did you do all morning?" He grabbed her by the arm. "I thought I told you to clean up."

"I did."

"Not so as you'd notice."

Jamie felt the prick of tears. "Why are you being so mean?"

"Why are you being so difficult?"

"Difficult? What am I doing wrong?"

"How about you just stop whining and do what I tell you."

Hadn't she just cleaned up? And she wasn't whining. In fact, she'd made an effort to sound upbeat about his whole stupid plan. "Maybe I should go home," she said angrily.

"It's not that simple."

"What do you mean?"

"I went out on a limb for you. Don't you forget it."

"I haven't. But I don't see why—"

"You are *not* going to hang me out to dry. Is that understood?" He headed for the door. "I'm going to split some wood. See if you can do something about the dust."

Jamie had dusted yesterday, but the whiskey shelf was too high for her to reach easily, and there had been plenty of other places that screamed for her attention. Besides, what did it matter if the shelf was dusty? It wasn't like they were putting dishes or fresh food there.

Her great adventure didn't seem so great anymore. She missed Alyssa. She missed her family. She missed the sweet Todd she'd known back home. Nothing was turning out the way she thought it would.

Still, she'd better dust the stupid shelf. She grabbed a chair to stand on. Then she noticed Todd's jacket on the table where he'd tossed it in anger when he came home from the store.

Going to the window, she glanced outside. He was at the woodpile, ax in hand.

Jamie lifted his jacket as silently as she could. She reached into the pocket for his phone and turned it on, praying for reception.

Her prayers were answered with two bars. Good enough. She called home.

CHAPTER 38

The phone was ringing when Marta opened the door. Balancing the box of Carol's papers in her arms, she hurried to answer it. She only made it to the hallway when the answering machine picked up.

"Mom? Are you there?" Jamie's voice was tentative and pleading. "Mom, pick up. Please."

Marta dropped the box where she stood, sending papers and folders flying onto the floor in a heap, and raced to the phone.

"Jamie? Thank God. Honey, are you ok? Where are you?"

"I'm fine. It's just . . . Mom, I think I made a mistake."

Marta was frantic. She wanted to reach through the phone, hold Jamie tight, and never let her go. "Are you with Todd?"

Jamie made a sound that Marta took to mean yes.

"You're sure you're okay?"

"I'm not hurt." Her voice broke. "I want to come home."

"Of course. Tell me where you are. We'll come get you right away."

"I don't know where I am. The woods somewhere. About five or six hours from San Francisco, but I don't think we took a very direct route so it might be closer."

"Okay." Marta's mind raced. "Do you know which direction you headed?"

"No. But we're sort of in the mountains. There are trees. Pines and some other stuff. And there's supposed to be a stream nearby."

That didn't narrow it down much. "What about landmarks along the way?"

"We went through a bunch of little towns." Jamie's voice was soft, almost a whisper. "I slept for a lot of it. But there was an old-fashioned gas station in one of the towns. And a mobile home park called Royal Gardens or something like that."

Royal Gardens. Marta wrote down the name. "What about other houses?"

"There's nothing around. I think . . ."

Jamie grew suddenly silent. Marta heard the squeak of a door in the background and the sound of footsteps approaching. Jamie whimpered, then a male voice said, "What the fuck?"

There was a scuffling noise and the phone clanged to the floor.

"Jamie?" Marta's voice rose. "Talk to me, Jamie."

Nothing.

Then Jamie cried out in pain.

"Jamie!" Marta screamed into the phone.

Finally, she heard breathing on the other end of the line. Her heart raced.

"Jamie?"

"You had your chance, Marta."

She recognized Todd's voice instantly. "Please, don't do this, Todd. Let me speak to my daughter."

But she was talking to dead air.

Hoping to keep the line open, she didn't end the call until the damned recording told her to hang up and try again. She punched *69, hoping the call-back function would connect her again. She got another recording.

She called 911. "What's your emergency?" the dispatcher asked.

"I need to talk to Detective Phillips. Right away."

"This is the emergency number, ma'am. You need to call the

main number."

"Please, this is urgent. Can't you transfer me?"

"I can give you his number, if you'd like."

Marta knew she should have called Phillips directly, but she hadn't wanted to waste time looking up the number. Now she'd squandered even more precious minutes.

Thank God, he picked up when she called. Marta told him about Jamie's aborted phone call.

"Did you get the number?" he asked.

"It came through as 'Name not found.' Can't you pinpoint the locale?"

"Not after the fact. Even during the call, we'd need a longer connection time than you had. But we should put a tap on your phone in case she calls again."

"Okay." Although Marta felt certain Jamie wouldn't get the chance to call again. Todd would watch her like a hawk. God only knew what he would do about this call.

"I'll set things up on this end," Phillips said. "Someone should contact you shortly."

"But what do we do now? We have to find her. All she was able to tell me was that she was in the mountains with trees. That covers a lot of territory."

"Six hours from San Francisco, right?"

"Approximately. Jamie wasn't sure of the timing. She slept for some of the drive."

"We'll start by alerting the authorities in the San Francisco area."

Where Jamie no longer was. The elation Marta had felt initially at hearing her daughter's voice gave way to a heavy heart. Jamie might as well be in the middle of the ocean.

"She wants to come home," Marta reminded him. "Todd Wilson is holding her prisoner. He physically attacked her. I'm worried about her safety."

"I understand. Without more to go on, however, our options are limited."

Gordon was in class right then, which meant his phone was probably turned off. Marta called and left a message. Then, ignoring the mess of papers in the hallway where she'd dropped the box, she sat down at her desk and got to work. She couldn't simply wait, worry, and hope for the best.

She started by Googling Royal Gardens Mobile Home Park. She found listings for Florida, Louisiana, and southern California, nowhere near mountains or trees. She tried mobile home parks in northern California, but nothing for Royal Gardens showed up.

For the next several hours, Marta faxed and phoned every newspaper, television, and radio station she was able to find in the San Francisco area. She sent them a press release she'd written herself, a photo of Jamie, and pledged to be available for an in-person interview should they decide to do one. She attached a flyer and asked them to make it available to the public.

Then she got out a map, drew concentric circles around San Francisco, and was in the process of repeating the fax and phone outreach to smaller towns in rural areas when Cassie called.

"I can't talk right now," Marta told her. "I'm in the middle of sending a press release to every town in California."

"Wow, a big new client?"

"No. Jamie called."

"What? That's great news. So she's okay?"

"Not really."

"What's that mean? Where is she?"

"She doesn't know. Probably somewhere in California, but maybe Oregon. Or Nevada. She wants to come home." Marta told her about the phone call.

"This man is holding her captive? Like a prisoner?"

"That's what it sounded like. The police are taking it more

seriously than before, but there's still not a lot they can do. That's why I'm contacting media outlets myself. Our only hope of finding her is to get the word out and pray someone recognizes her."

"My God, how awful."

"She sounded so scared, Cassie. I have to help her."

"What can I do?"

"Nothing. I need to go to California and make a stink. Rattle the airwaves until she's found."

"I'll come with you," Cassie said.

"What about your job?" Marta wasn't sure she wanted to deal with the chaos of her sister.

"Screw my job."

"Cassie, you can't—"

"I can and I am. Jamie is my niece. Besides, two of us can do twice as much as one."

It was a decent point. "If you're sure—"

"I am. The job is no great shakes anyway."

Another time, Marta would have called her sister out for walking away from a job, but she didn't have time for Cassie's problems. "Okay. Thanks."

"Only thing is, I'm a little short on cash right now. Can you lend me the money for a ticket?"

At least one thing in Marta's world hadn't changed.

CHAPTER 39

Gordon concluded his lecture and dismissed class ten minutes before the end of the hour. He was surprised he'd managed to stay focused as long as he had. His mind was a million different places, and none of them had anything to do with American history.

His behavior toward Marta this morning had bordered on cruel. He'd known it at the time and that hadn't stopped him. But now, he regretted it. Why hadn't he kept quiet? As angry as he was, he had trouble imagining his life without Marta.

He didn't *want* to imagine his life without her. Which was why what had happened with Todd was so hard to take.

And on top of that, his daughter had run off—with Todd.

There he was again, full circle. Todd. And it was Marta who'd set the whole thing in motion.

His mind tumbled from one thought to another, from one fear to a worse fear. His chest was so tight he felt he might explode.

As he left the classroom, he ran into the department chairman, Alan Warner. Gordon cringed, caught in the act of cutting out early. But Warner didn't seem to notice.

"Any news on your daughter?" Warner asked.

"Nothing new." Gordon wasn't about to mention the photo of Jamie naked in the bathtub.

"Sorry to hear that. She's what, fifteen or sixteen?"

"Seventeen."

"It must be tough being a parent these days. I look at some of our students here on campus and thank my lucky stars my own kids are grown and settled."

"It's not easy," Gordon acknowledged. *Tough being a husband, too,* he added silently. *Tough trying to be a family.*

"I hope you get good news soon."

"Thanks." Gordon stopped at the vending machine and bought a bag of peanuts so he wouldn't have to walk the rest of the way with Warner. He had nothing against the chairman, but he didn't want to discuss Jamie, his daughter, his baby girl—how the hell had this happened?

When Jamie was young, he'd happily answered the never-ending stream of questions she threw his way. Questions about stars and bugs and the endless wonder that was a child's universe. He taught her to ride a bike and encouraged her fledgling attempts at gymnastics. He attended father-daughter cookouts with her Girl Scout troop, helped her with math homework, and together they'd painted her bedroom the bright yellow she had chosen in defiance of Marta's preference for a softer color.

He knew she wasn't a child anymore, but she was still his baby girl, his Jamie. Or she had been until Todd showed up.

The daughter he knew wouldn't have lied. She wouldn't have run away from home. She wouldn't have chosen Todd over her parents.

But that's what she'd done.

With a heavy heart, Gordon braced himself for office hours. He set his briefcase on his desk and powered up his cell phone.

A message from Marta greeted him.

Gordon arrived home to find his wife at the computer, fingers flying across the keyboard. Her hair was disheveled and her brow furrowed in concentration.

"I'm home," he said from the doorway.

She looked up, startled. "I didn't hear you come in."

"I tried calling when I got your message, but I couldn't get through."

"I've been on the phone all afternoon."

Gordon cleared a stack of papers from the extra office chair and sat down. "You really talked to Jamie?" Marta nodded.

"Is she okay?"

"I couldn't tell. We hardly talked. Todd yanked the phone from her hand in the middle of our conversation." Marta's words caught in her throat. "I got the feeling she had to sneak the call in behind his back."

"How did she sound?"

"Scared. She wants to come home."

"Thank God."

"Todd won't let her. He wouldn't even let her talk to me." Marta's voice trembled. "He hit her."

Gordon flinched as though he'd been punched himself. "Where are they?"

"They were in the San Francisco area, now they're in a cabin somewhere, five or six hours' drive from the city. In the woods. That's about all she could tell me."

"So we don't know how to find her?"

"No. What if he's keeping her locked up or something?"

His daughter held prisoner by a crazy man. Gordon could barely contain himself. "What did the police say? You called them, right?"

"Of course I called them. Phillips said they'd 'alert the authorities,' which is cop-speak for going through the motions. They don't give a rat's ass about a runaway seventeen-year-old."

"But she *wants* to come home," Gordon protested. "She's being held prisoner."

"We can't leave this to the police. We have to find her ourselves."

"We don't have the foggiest idea where she is!"

"We'll have to blanket northern California news outlets with pleas for information." Marta's eyes narrowed as they did whenever she was on a mission. "I'm trying to get her picture in every newspaper, on every television station, in every coffee shop possible. Someone has to have seen her. That's why I've been on the phone all afternoon."

Gordon was familiar with his wife's determination. When she set her mind to something, she gave it her all. But connecting with someone who knew where to find Jamie was worse than a long shot. It would be close to impossible.

"Five or six hours from San Francisco covers a lot of territory," he pointed out. He'd spent a summer there when he was in college. Three hours east took you from the ocean to the sierra. Going north, practically to the Oregon border.

"I know it's a big area, but that's all we have to go on."

He reached for a copy of the press release Marta had prepared. Seeing Jamie's picture on a "missing" poster sucked the air from his lungs.

Marta stood and began shuffling papers on her desk. "I'm going out to San Francisco to spread the word in person."

Gordon stood also. "I'll see if I can get someone to cover my classes tomorrow."

"You're planning to come?"

"You were planning on going alone?" he said, stung.

"My sister is meeting me there."

"Cassie? You're kidding. She'll be useless."

"You never give her the benefit of the doubt, do you?"

"How many times do you need to get burned?"

"She wants to help," Marta said.

"So do I!" He couldn't believe his wife would choose her

neurotic sister over him. She was a disaster waiting to happen.

"What about your classes?"

"I'll figure out something." Covering for one day would be doable. Longer than that, more difficult. Gordon had missed half his classes already this past week. But surely people would understand that his daughter took precedence.

"You're sure you should do that?" Marta asked, raising an eyebrow.

"I know that area and you've never even been there."

"You think I'm not capable of handling this myself?"

"That's not what I meant. But I do know my way around—"

"You spent *one summer* there years ago. I don't see what 'knowing the area' has to do with it, anyway."

"Don't be dense. Besides, a father's presence makes an impact in the media."

"And a mother's doesn't?"

"That's not what I said."

"Someone should stay here in case there's a break locally."

Gordon's resentment flared. "Jamie's not here. She's in California. Besides, if anyone stays here, it should be you. You're the one who caused all this with your reprehensible behavior in Minneapolis."

Marta's face closed up tight, as though she'd been slapped. A deep flush spread across her cheeks. "Low blow, Gordon."

"It's the truth." Marta could apologize until she was blue in the face but it didn't change what she'd done. Or what had happened because of it.

She crossed her arms. "What's going to happen to us if you get fired again?"

"I didn't get fired from Tufts," Gordon shot back. "My contract wasn't renewed."

"Because you were accused of sexual harassment!"

"It was a trumped-up charge, as you well know."

251

"Call it what you want. We ended up having to move to a hick town in the middle of nowhere. I had a good life there, a successful career, and Jamie had a group of friends she was comfortable with. We lost all of that because of you."

"So this is about me now? You're saying this is *my* fault?"

She glared at him. "You're the one who started with the blame game."

"I was merely pointing out a fact."

Marta took a stack of papers from the printer and set them next to the computer. "It doesn't make sense for you to go to San Francisco. At this stage, I'm just pounding the pavement. If I learn anything useful, then you can think about coming out."

Gordon gave up. He took a breath and leaned away. "When are you leaving?"

"Tomorrow. I'll send you an email with my travel information."

"Fine. Have a good trip." He turned on his heel and left the room.

CHAPTER 40

As her plane sped down the runway for takeoff, Marta couldn't help remembering the last time she'd flown—leaving Minneapolis following her precipitous and foolish tryst with Todd Wilson. She was ashamed to remember what she'd been feeling that day. Along with the guilt, she'd savored the thrill of being considered desirable. It had been a long time since she'd felt that way.

She hadn't expected to hear from him again. Hadn't wanted to. But she'd basked in the memory of a night that was as exciting as it was regrettable.

Now, that same memory made her ill. Her reckless behavior had shattered her world. She'd caused pain to those she cared about most and had put Jamie in jeopardy. God willing, her daughter would be safe. She wasn't so sure about her marriage.

Rather than brooding over what she couldn't control, Marta tried to focus on Jamie. Only one Bay Area television station had expressed interest in an interview, but she wasn't giving up on the others. She intended to make contact again, once she was there. Along with contacting radio stations and newspapers. And she wanted to visit with the local police. Detective Phillips was supposedly coordinating efforts with the SFPD, but Marta wasn't counting on his having made a forceful case for finding Jamie.

When the plane leveled off, Marta pulled out her laptop and got to work. Finding her daughter was the most important media campaign of her life.

As soon as they landed, Marta checked her phone for messages. Nothing. She felt a stab of disappointment. She'd been hoping for more responses to her inquiries from yesterday. Instead, it was looking as though the media wasn't interested.

She'd just have to persuade them.

On the way to baggage claim, she picked up a copy of the *San Francisco Chronicle,* thinking maybe the paper had run at least a short blurb based on the press release she'd sent out. She scanned the entire paper while she was waiting for her suitcase to come through, and was once again disappointed. Not a single mention of Jamie.

She took a shuttle to the hotel, silently cursing the heavy traffic that clogged the roads. She was eager to get to work.

She had booked a room through the HotDeals website because the regular price of a centrally located hotel was well beyond her budget. With the Web discount she didn't get lots of choices, but she got a decent price. The trip was still going to max out her credit card, but at least she and Cassie weren't staying in a flea-bitten motel, multiple bus rides away from the places she needed to be. The Emperor Inn on Turk was old but recently renovated. Marta was crossing her fingers that it was also clean and safe.

Cassie had arrived first, and Marta found her in the small lobby, talking to an attractive, middle-aged man in a dark suit. As usual, Cassie looked gorgeous. Her honey-blond hair was pinned loosely with a clip at the nape of her neck and her creamy skin was practically glowing. She wore dark leggings and a low-cut, turquoise top that accentuated the blue of her eyes as well as her slender figure. Looking at her, you'd think she was a Hollywood celebrity, not a hapless alcoholic who burned through dead-end jobs as fast as she did deadbeat men.

When she spotted Marta, Cassie rushed to greet her with a hug. "Oh my gosh, it's good to see you. How was your flight?"

"Boring," Marta said, feeling inexplicably annoyed. "How long have you been here?"

"Not long."

"Who was that you were talking to?"

"Just some guy I met while waiting. He's a financial analyst, whatever that is. He's got a ski house in Aspen."

"How did that happen to come up?"

"You know, we were just talking about stuff."

No, Marta didn't know. When she talked to strangers, which wasn't often, they never got past the nice-day stage. With Cassie, things were different, and had been as long as Marta could remember. As teens, whenever she and Cassie were together—at the movies, or the park, or simply walking through the mall—boys would flock around Cassie while ignoring Marta as though she were invisible.

"I hope you haven't made plans to see him while you're here," Marta said.

"Why would I do that? I'm here to help you." Cassie glanced back at the man, who was busily typing a message into his cell phone. "Besides, he's married."

"That hasn't stopped you before."

Cassie rolled her eyes and blew out a long slow breath. "Do you have to pick on me all the time?"

"I wasn't and I don't." Marta already had mixed feelings about having her sister along, but she also recognized her own hypocrisy. Being married hadn't stopped *her*.

She glanced at the reception desk. "Are we checked in yet?"

"I was waiting for you." Cassie brushed a strand of hair from her face. "You made the reservation, remember?"

A subtle reminder that Marta was footing the bill. "Why don't you watch our bags while I get the room?"

Marta handed her credit card to the receptionist, filled out the paperwork, and got their keys. "Fifth floor," she said, rejoining her sister.

Cassie wrinkled her nose. "I hope they have an elevator."

"It's around the corner."

"So what do we do first?" Cassie asked on the way up to their room.

"I've got an interview with a television news team scheduled for later today. A local affiliate of one of the major networks. I just need to call to confirm."

"That's wonderful."

"But it's the only sure thing." And even it might go nowhere. With television news, nothing was guaranteed. "I want to follow up with the places I contacted yesterday. Maybe once they know I'm in town, they'll be more willing to run a story."

Marta opened the drapes while Cassie checked out the bathroom, mini-bar, and television, then plopped into the sole armchair. "Which bed do you want?"

"The one by the window," Marta said. She'd already set her purse and carry-on there. "Let's unpack later. Why don't you begin contacting the television and radio stations I haven't heard back from." Marta handed her the list she'd compiled yesterday. "Agency and phone numbers are listed here. Contact name also, if I got one."

Cassie gave the paper a cursory glance. "What should I say?"

"Whatever it takes to get them to run something about Jamie. A missing kid always gets people's interest."

"Innocent teen led astray by smooth-talking pervert?"

"Now held against her will," Marta added.

"Got it."

While Marta called to confirm her afternoon interview, she

heard Cassie in the background pitching the story. She was surprisingly articulate and made a persuasive case. Marta felt marginally better about leaving her sister to make calls while she met the news crew.

The reporter was a young woman with short dark hair and a cheery, upbeat attitude that seemed inappropriate given the substance of the story. She talked to Marta for a few minutes while the cameraman set up.

She had suggested they conduct the interview on the waterfront by the Ferry Building, a busy area on the edge of the financial district, near the news station. Normally, she explained, the reporting team would come to her home because the personal setting made the story more compelling. But Marta wasn't at home and a hotel did not have the same impact.

Marta had readily agreed but now she worried that the waterfront might be inappropriate, too. This wasn't a tourism story. Wouldn't the clear sky and throngs of pedestrians undercut the seriousness of her plea?

"Is your husband coming?" the reporter asked.

Marta shook her head. "We decided it was better to divvy up our efforts to find Jamie. He stayed in Sterling."

"I suppose that makes sense," the young woman replied in a tone that suggested it made no sense at all.

Marta was overcome with a sudden case of the jitters. It was her fault Jamie had met Todd. If she messed up now and didn't come across as desperate enough, would she doom Jamie's chances of being found?

Once the cameraman gave the signal and the interview began, Marta grew calmer. She stayed focused on her message—finding Jamie.

"My seventeen-year-old daughter has been missing for over a week. She managed to call us two days ago and wants to come home, but she's being held captive by a man we thought was a family friend. He is in his late thirties or early forties and sometimes goes by the names Todd Wilson and Tim Whitaker. My daughter indicated she was being held in a wooded area of northern California but had previously been in the San Francisco Bay Area. She's five foot five with brown shoulder-length hair."

Marta spoke with emotion and pleaded for Jamie's safe return, urging anyone with information to call the hotline number.

It was a short interview, and would probably be shorter still when it ran on the evening news, but even a little publicity was better than none. And the reporter had promised Jamie's photo would appear on screen at the end of the interview.

Feeling newly energized, Marta walked the bustling streets back to the hotel to check in with Cassie. She found her sister lounging on the bed with a can of Coke.

"How'd it go?" Cassie asked.

"Okay. Whether it will have any effect is another story. We'll watch tonight and you can tell me what you think. How are you making out with the calls?"

"I've finished with the list you gave me. Nobody committed to an interview but a couple of the stations said they'd try to run something." She sat up. "What next?"

"I'm meeting with a detective at the missing persons bureau."

"Want me to come?"

"Let's not double up. Why don't you see about getting the 'Missing Teen' flyer posted around town."

"Where?"

"Try coffee shops, small businesses, that sort of thing. Bus stops and BART stations, too." Marta pulled a stack of flyers from her briefcase. "I had these printed up before I left home, but we can get more made here if we need them."

Cassie leapt to her feet. "Finally, a chance to see the city."

CHAPTER 41

Marta's visit with the missing persons detective went nowhere. After cooling her heels for half an hour in a sterile waiting area, she was granted a brief interview with a spiritless officer who assured her that Jamie's name and photo were in the system, and that there had been no reported sightings. He then referred her to the California Missing Children's Clearing House, reminded her that San Francisco was a mecca for runaway teens, and showed her to the door.

So much for personal contact, Marta thought angrily as she pushed through the heavy door and onto the busy street. It might carry weight in some place like Sterling, but apparently not in a big city like San Francisco.

Cassie called as Marta was trying to hail a cab back to the hotel. "I'm out of flyers," she announced. "You want me to make more?"

"All fifty of them? Wow. There was a lot of interest, then?" Maybe they didn't need the cops in order to get the word out.

Cassie sighed. "I wouldn't really call it interest. More like, 'You can leave it if you'd like.' A lot of merchants said they had a policy against posting handbills, though."

"But this is for a missing child!" Marta's frustration had about reached a breaking point.

"Don't yell at me. I'm just passing along what people said. Besides, it's taken me all this time to cover a handful of blocks. No way we can blanket the entire city. And we don't know that

Jamie was actually in the city proper, do we?"

"Not in San Francisco, per se. But she was in the area." Marta's earlier optimism had pretty much evaporated. Obviously, this trip wasn't going to accomplish what she'd hoped it would. She'd flown all the way out here, at no small expense, for one short interview and maybe a couple of mentions in the press—a drop in the bucket.

"I'm heading back to the hotel," she said. "Why don't you meet me there?"

Marta dumped her purse on the bed, kicked off her shoes, and flipped on the TV. The station she'd done the interview with ran an early evening newscast, another an hour later, and yet another at eleven o'clock. The reporter hadn't been able to tell her when the interview would run, so she settled in for a long night of local news.

Cassie arrived fifteen minutes into the first of the shows. "Did I miss it?" she asked.

"Not yet."

She got another Coke from the minibar and flopped down on her bed. "San Francisco is a cool city. We should take some time to see it while we're here."

Marta bristled. "We're not here to play tourist."

"It's just that if none of the media outlets are interested—"

"Then we keep looking until we find some that are."

"You don't have to bite my head off."

"And watch it with the Cokes. They're probably five dollars each." And would wind up on Marta's credit card.

"Geesh. Chill out a little."

And then, without any lead-in, the reporter who'd interviewed Marta appeared on the screen. "This afternoon I talked to the mother of seventeen-year-old Jamie Crawford, who is a runaway with possible ties to the Bay Area."

The camera zeroed in on Marta, and the interview was on. At the conclusion, Jamie's photo appeared on the screen for maybe seven seconds, along with a contact phone number. Then it was over, almost as soon as it had begun.

Marta was left feeling disheartened and oddly empty. Her daughter needed help, and Marta was doing little more than spinning her wheels.

"You did good," Cassie said with excitement. "You looked good, too."

How she looked hadn't been Marta's concern. "It was such a short segment. How many people do you think even saw it?"

"All it takes is one person who recognizes her."

"And then what? We still won't know where she is." The futility of her efforts was suddenly clear as day. What had she thought she would accomplish? This whole crusade to rescue her daughter was nothing but a big joke. Jamie was being held captive by a madman somewhere in the western U.S. How would they ever find her?

"It's a first step," Cassie said.

Marta fought back tears. "It won't do any good."

Cassie put an arm around her. "Don't get discouraged. You never know when a break will come. And it will, I'm sure of it."

"You can't be sure," Marta snapped. "Besides, you didn't hear how frightened Jamie sounded over the phone. You don't know this crazy person she's with."

"So you want to give up, is that it?" Cassie sat back and folded her arms. "You want to pull up stakes and go back home? What's that going to accomplish?"

"What I'm doing here is pointless."

"You're not a quitter, Marta. You can't give up."

"I'm not delusional, either." Marta found it ironic that Cassie, who habitually took the easy way out, was lecturing her about not giving up.

"Think about Jamie. You haven't even given it one full day!"

On one level, Cassie was right. But Marta was right, too. The odds were overwhelming. She was suddenly exhausted. "Come on, let's grab a bite to eat. I know it's early, but we've had a long day."

Cassie jumped up. "San Francisco is supposed to have lots of really good restaurants. We could eat out by the water or just wander around a bit until we find something we like."

Her sister seemed determined to make a vacation out of their trip but Marta wasn't in the mood. "I was thinking we'd eat in the hotel."

Cassie's disappointment was evident, but she shrugged. "Sure, whatever you want."

Marta almost changed her mind when she discovered that the hotel restaurant was an extension of the bar. The set-up reminded her uncomfortably of the night she'd met Todd.

They slid into a booth and Cassie ordered a vodka martini.

"I thought you were clean and sober."

"One drink isn't going to hurt me. It's been a hard day and I've earned it."

Marta wasn't up to lecturing, and besides, she could use a drink herself. She ordered a glass of Zinfandel.

"And bring an order of fried onion rings," Cassie told their server. She pushed the hair from her face and surveyed the room. "Take a look at the guy to your left. Blue shirt. Cute, don't you think?"

"Do you ever *not* think about men?"

"What fun would that be? Besides, I'm single. I'm allowed to look." She laughed, then added, "And more."

Marta squirmed uncomfortably, once again remembering the night she'd met Todd. "Do you ever think about finding Mr. Right and settling down?"

"Sure, but it's not like I can just make that happen."

The server brought their drinks and took their orders. Burgers for both of them.

"Not *make* it happen," Marta said when he'd gone, "but how you conduct yourself and how you lead your life plays a big part in who you meet." A major part in Cassie's case.

"Do I detect criticism?"

"It's just an observation." Marta sipped her wine and felt herself relax. "In truth, there are times I wish I was more like you."

"Hah, that's a good one."

"I'm serious."

"You're nuts. You've got it all. A career. A good husband. Granted Gordon's not my type, but he's a decent man. And you've got a great daughter who's going to be back home any day now."

Marta fingered her glass. "If only I could believe that."

"About the good life or about Jamie?"

"Both, but mostly Jamie. I'd trade everything I have for her safe return."

"She's a smart girl," Cassie said after a moment's reflection. "She wouldn't run off with someone she didn't trust."

"She's seventeen years old. No one is smart at seventeen."

"You were."

Marta looked at her sister. Cassie was serious.

"Mom always talked about you like you were perfect. Hard-working, thoughtful, responsible, an impossible act to follow."

"I'm a long way from perfect, as you well know." This was an old lament and always sounded vaguely accusatory, as though there were something wrong with being conscientious.

Their burgers arrived and Cassie ordered another martini. Marta raised her eyebrows.

"I'm a long way from perfect, too," Cassie said, and made it sound as if that was also Marta's fault.

"Besides," she said after awhile, "perfect or not, you have a pretty sweet life. Or did until this thing with Jamie. Nothing ever seems to work out right for me."

"If it makes you feel any better, my *sweet life* has turned horribly sour."

"I meant aside from Jamie. I know you're worried. I am too."

"It's not just that." Marta paused for another sip of wine. "You remember Carol, my business partner?"

"Sure."

"She was killed last week."

Cassie sat up straighter. "How awful. What happened?"

"Hit and run. The police think it might have been intentional."

"Whoa! Like someone wanted her dead?"

Marta nodded. "It's really upset me, but with everything else I haven't really had time to deal with it."

"That's understandable."

"She was my best friend. My only friend really. I miss her so much."

"Of course you do."

"My marriage isn't so good right now, either." Marta was surprised to feel herself choking up. Her whole life was a mess.

"What's wrong?" Cassie leaned forward. "You don't have to tell me if you don't want to. I know you weren't happy about moving to Georgia but you've been there awhile now, and I thought—"

"It's my fault." Marta looked down at her hands. "It's my fault that Jamie is missing, too."

"How so?"

"Remember the business trip I took to Minneapolis?"

"Right. It was your birthday. Carol got sick and you had to go alone."

"Everything went wrong on that trip. My presentation fell

flat. Gordon and I had a fight right before I left. It was over something stupid, but it put me in a pissy mood, and then Jamie was sassy when I called to check in. You and Carol were the only ones who even remembered it was my birthday."

"Gordon forgot?"

"Forgot, or maybe he didn't care. It all came together and I was feeling really bummed." Marta paused. She hadn't intended to go down this road but now that she had, she found she wanted to show Cassie just how far from perfect she actually was.

"I did something really stupid," she said after a moment. "I went to the hotel bar to have a drink, a sort of personal birthday celebration. A man came over and asked if he could join me."

Cassie's eyes opened wide. "Go on."

"He was attractive and acted like he was interested in me." That part of the evening remained clear in Marta's mind. Bold and bright, like a scene in a movie. What came after was less so. "I ended up sleeping with him," she said in a rush of emotion.

"Wow. Miss Goody-Two-Shoes is human after all." Cassie didn't seem particularly shocked.

"It was just that one time, but I should never have done it."

Cassie shrugged. "Probably not, but you were turning forty. Don't you think you deserved to have a little fun?"

"Not that kind of fun."

"So you made a mistake. Stop beating yourself up over it. Some of us make mistakes on a regular basis."

"You don't understand. That's what has caused all the trouble. When I told Gordon—"

"You what? Why in God's name did you tell him?"

"I had to." Marta swallowed hard. "The man I met in Minneapolis is the man Jamie ran off with."

Cassie looked stunned. "What?"

"The guy I slept with got it into his head that we were meant for each other. He said he was in love with me. He showed up in Sterling and kept trying to convince me to continue seeing him. He even befriended Gordon and Carol as a way to get to me. When I told him to get lost, he got angry, and to punish me, he turned his seductive powers on Jamie."

"My God." Cassie's face was white as a sheet.

"This guy is a lot older than Jamie, in his mid to late thirties. And he's unbalanced, maybe genuinely nuts. He doesn't come off that way at first, but it's obvious to me now. He may even have been involved in Carol's death."

"Holy shit." Cassie pushed her half-eaten burger to the side. She looked ill.

"You finished?"

"I guess I'm not as hungry as I thought I was."

Marta signaled for the check. "You can see why I'm so worried. It's not like she just ran off with a boyfriend, although that would be bad enough."

"You're sure that's who Jamie is with?"

"She told me as much. And I heard his voice when she called."

"Jesus. You've told the police about him?"

"Not the details of how I met him, but yeah. The problem is we don't know anything about him, even his real name. He told me it was Todd Wilson, but he met Carol pretending to be a potential client and gave her a different name."

"I heard you say his name in the interview but I never thought . . . My God, the man you met on your trip."

"You can't imagine how guilty I feel."

"I think I can." Cassie's face was drawn tight. She stared blankly at the far wall. "Holy shit," she said again.

"Holy shit is right." Marta signed the bill, charging the meal to their room. "Ready to go on up?"

"Why don't you go on. I think I'll take a short walk and see the city."

"You'll be careful?"

"Yeah. I won't go far."

"Okay. I'll see you later."

Two hours later when Cassie hadn't returned, Marta began to worry. She called her sister's cell. "Just checking to make sure you're okay."

"Yeah, everything's fine." Cassie's voice was faint over the din of laughter and the clink of glasses in the background.

"I take it you're not still walking."

She laughed. "No. It's too cold for a walk. But I'll be back soon."

Marta hung up without saying goodbye. She was furious with her sister. Furious with herself for trusting her. Cassie hadn't come to support Marta, or to help Jamie. She'd come for a free trip to San Francisco and a chance to party.

CHAPTER 42

Gordon moved restlessly from room to room, unable to settle. Marta had left for the airport early that morning, and the house felt eerily quiet. He found himself listening for familiar sounds that never materialized. Even his haven in the garage seemed foreign to him.

He'd taught his morning class, then gone to see Detective Phillips. As Marta had predicted, Phillips did nothing more than repeat what he'd told her over the phone yesterday. It wasn't that he was without sympathy, he told Gordon, but northern California wasn't his jurisdiction. He'd contacted the proper authorities there, and beyond that his hands were tied. Gordon supposed all that might be true, but he couldn't shake the sense that an almost eighteen-year-old who'd left home voluntarily didn't concern him.

From the station, Gordon had headed home rather than return to campus. He'd intended to work on his paper, but now that he was here, he found he was unable to think about anything but his missing daughter, his angry wife, and his own inability to make things right. It was easy to blame everything on Marta, as he'd been doing, but surprisingly, that didn't make him feel any better. It hadn't accomplished much, either. He felt alone and sad.

He settled in at his desk but found his mind spinning with images of Jamie locked up in some dark place, desperately hoping to be rescued. Surely there was something he could be doing. After an hour of staring at the computer screen and drumming his fingers on his knee, he gave up on the idea of working.

He had gathered up the papers Marta had dropped yesterday so he wouldn't trip every time he walked down the hall, but he'd simply dumped them into the file box. Now he decided to take a stab at sorting them and trying to restore some sense of order. If he couldn't find his daughter, he could at least help his wife.

He took the box into the kitchen and set it on the table. Then he took out all the papers and began going through them one by one, placing them in piles according to project. Luckily, Carol had been diligent about labeling and dating documents, so the task was less taxing than he expected.

He hadn't known Carol well. She was Marta's friend and business partner, and the couples didn't socialize. Gordon hadn't exchanged more than pleasantries with her on the few occasions they'd met. He was saddened by her death, but not troubled by it the way Marta was. To the extent Gordon felt any real sense of loss, it was the way Carol's death affected his wife. Still, it felt odd to be reading through her files, knowing she was dead, possibly murdered. And while it seemed far-fetched that Todd might have killed her, the thought was rarely far from Gordon's mind. It made finding Jamie all the more urgent.

Toward the bottom of the pile, Gordon came across what looked like a computer printout of a news story, something to do with the potential sale of a community bank in Texas. There was no indication which project or client it pertained to, unusual given Carol's attention to order. He scanned the article to see if the subject matter would shed any light on the issue, and when it didn't, he set the story aside. Maybe it would ring a bell with Marta.

When he'd done as much as he could, he turned on the evening news but found he cared about none of it. People were dying in far-off countries and in cities closer to home. Politicians in Washington were arguing about the number of angels who could fit on the head of a pin, or something equally inane. A warehouse burned, a private plane landed safely despite mechanical issues, an outbreak of *E. coli* sparked a recall of salad greens. None of it permeated the veil of emptiness and worry that was his own life. He tried watching a detective show, had a beer, gazed aimlessly out the window to the street. Finally, he made himself a salami sandwich and ate it standing over the sink.

Marta called as he was cleaning up. Simply seeing her name on the caller ID brightened his mood, which surprised him because he often considered calls, even those from his wife, an annoyance. Still, he was irked that she'd more or less shut him out of the trip to San Francisco. And angry that he'd allowed it to happen.

"How's it going?" he asked.

"The interview this afternoon with the TV station went okay, but in general, the response from the media hasn't been what I'd hoped. I guess the story doesn't have enough of a local angle to have legs here. Or maybe it's not heart-wrenching enough to appeal to a jaded public."

"A missing kid doesn't cut it?"

"Only if Jamie was seven instead of seventeen. Or had been snatched from the street by a stranger at knifepoint."

"You made it clear that Jamie is being held captive?"

"Of course I did." Marta sounded discouraged. "My meeting with the local cops was a disappointment, too. Jamie's name and photo are in the system. That's all they can offer."

Gordon wasn't surprised, but he was discouraged all the same. "Maybe she'll call again and we'll get a better idea where she is or how to reach her."

"That may be our only hope."

"How's it working out with Cassie?"

"About the way you predicted."

"Sorry to hear that." He felt bad for Marta, but he also took some small satisfaction in being proved right.

"She was really helpful this afternoon," Marta said after a moment. "She made calls while I did the interview and talked to the cops. And she distributed flyers to local businesses. But after dinner she went out, supposedly for a walk. When I called her a bit ago, it was clear she was in some bar. She had a couple of drinks with dinner, too. I don't think she's reformed as much as she makes out."

No surprise there. Cassie had the history of a yo-yo.

Gordon didn't want the conversation to end but he could think of nothing more to say. He longed to simply talk, as they had in the early days of their marriage. Rarely about anything of significance, but he'd found the easy companionship rewarding in ways he'd never imagined. His current neediness surprised him. He hadn't felt that yearning to connect in a long time.

Silence stretched between them. Then he remembered the papers from Carol's desk. "By the way, do you and Carol have a client involved in a Texas bank merger?"

"No. Why?"

Gordon explained his attempt to make order out of chaos.

"I'll take a look at it when I get back."

Another beat of silence. "Well," Gordon announced finally, "I should let you go."

"I'll give you a call tomorrow," Marta said. "Sooner, if I learn anything."

When they clicked off, Gordon felt more disheartened than ever.

Determined to make himself useful, he returned to the folders spread across the kitchen table. He read through the files in detail but not one referenced a bank. Or Texas, for that matter.

He picked up the news story and read it again. Citizen's Choice Bank was in talks with AG National about a possible buyout. Near the bottom of the page, an accompanying photo showed two men and a woman. The caption identified them as Frederick Winslow, Travis Winslow, and Stephanie Winslow. A checkmark was penciled in lightly at the margin. Carol's marking? It almost had to be.

The photo had not printed well. It was dark and fuzzy. But Carol must have marked it for a reason. Gordon found the original news article online and clicked on the photo.

His mouth went dry. Travis Winslow bore a striking resemblance to the man he knew as Todd Wilson.

CHAPTER 43

When Marta's phone rang at 5:30 the next morning, she was awake in an instant. She checked the caller ID—not a number she recognized.

She grabbed the phone and answered breathlessly with a pounding heart. "Jamie?"

There was no response, only soft breathing.

"Jamie, are you there?" Marta asked.

"It's me," Cassie said, after a moment.

Marta's galloping heart skidded to a stop. Her anger with her sister was now compounded by her disappointment. She almost threw the phone down in disgust.

"Sorry to wake you," Cassie said.

"Think nothing of it." Marta laid on the sarcasm. "I hope you had a delightful evening."

Cassie didn't answer immediately. "I need you to come get me," she said, finally.

"You've got to be kidding? You stay out all night partying, then wake me at some ungodly hour to come get you? What in the hell is wrong with you?"

"I messed up."

"Damn right you did. Take a cab."

"I really need your help." She sounded hollowed out, verging on desperate.

"Well, I really needed *your* help." Marta got out of bed and began pacing around the hotel room. "Which you supposedly came here to offer."

"Please." Cassie's voice trembled. "I do want to help. But right now, I need you to bail me out."

"Bail you out of what? Your bar tab?"

A moment's pause. "Out of jail."

Marta sank back down onto the edge of the bed. "How in the hell did you wind up in jail?"

"I got a little drunk, okay?"

"A *little* drunk?"

"And I sort of got into an argument with a cop."

"Good God, Cassie. You never learn, do you?"

"I had a reason," Cassie said defensively. "A good reason."

"There is no good reason to get arrested for being drunk and disorderly. You're on your own."

"Please, Marta. I have something important to tell you."

"I bet you do." Some sob story that was supposed to make Marta feel sorry for her. *Poor put-upon Cassie.*

"It's about Jamie."

"So tell me."

"Not like this. I have to tell you in person."

Marta went to the window and looked out. The stars had vanished and the sky was beginning to lighten. "I'm not falling for that load of crap. I know you, remember? I know how you operate."

"It's not crap." Cassie took a long breath. "I think I know where Jamie is."

Marta took her time showering and getting dressed, and then called for a cab. She toyed with the idea of letting Cassie stew for awhile. She hated being played for a fool, but she couldn't walk away from the possibility that Cassie might have information about Jamie, as unlikely as that was. She promised herself, however, that this was the end. From here on out her sister could sink or swim on her own.

It was after seven by the time Marta arrived at the county jail, an imposing building on a noisy and dirty street in a part of town Marta imagined few tourists ever visited. Inside, her footsteps were among the many that echoed in the cavernous stone lobby, even at this early hour.

She gave the deputy at the intake window Cassie's name. In return, he handed her a clipboard of forms that needed to be filled out, then explained her options for payment. Marta elected to write a check, mostly because she didn't want to spend hours dealing with a bondsman or waiting around for a hearing.

Eventually, a burly black cop escorted Cassie into the small room where Marta was waiting.

"You do this often?" he asked Marta.

"Isn't once bad enough?"

"She needs help," he said.

"No kidding."

"She lucked out. Detention only this time. No arrest. She shouldn't count on that luck holding in the future."

They were barely out the door when Cassie said, "He talked about me like I wasn't even there. Like I was a kid or something."

Marta continued on without saying a word. She was still fuming, but seeing Cassie's disheveled hair, rumpled clothing, and bloodshot eyes softened the ire a bit.

Cassie slumped against the wall of the elevator. "Thank you for coming," she said softly.

"You should be grateful I agreed to save your sorry ass. But this is the last time. I mean it. I'm done."

Cassie looked down. "I understand."

Marta hailed a cab and they rode to the hotel in silence. Once they were inside their room, she turned on Cassie. "What got into you? What were you thinking?"

"I was trying *not* to think."

"Congratulations. I'm sure you succeeded." Marta tossed her jacket onto the bed. "You said you know where Jamie is?"

"I might." Cassie looked at her trembling hands. "I have something to tell you first."

Some weasel tale that would have nothing to do with Jamie. Marta was already kicking herself for falling for her sister's tricks.

"You may never speak to me again," Cassie continued, "so let me say right now that I never wanted to hurt you."

"How big of you."

"I mean it, Marta." Her eyes teared up and her bottom lip quivered. "I know we have our differences, but I've never, ever felt anything but love for you."

Marta was ready to dismiss the tears, but the raw sincerity in her sister's tone caught her by surprise. "What is it you wanted to tell me?"

"The man Jamie is with . . . he's the guy you met in Minneapolis, right?"

Marta nodded.

Cassie pulled her phone from her purse, brought up a photo, and handed the phone to Marta. "Is this him?"

Marta glanced at the screen and felt her scalp tighten. She was looking at a candid shot of Todd. "Where did you get this?"

"I took it."

"When?"

"A year or so ago."

"You know him?" Marta felt totally blindsided. "How? Who is he?"

"We met in a recovery group. We were like the only two sane people there so we sort of hung out together."

Were she not trying desperately to remain focused on Jamie,

Marta would have laughed at the absurdity of Cassie and Todd as sane.

"You dated him?" Marta asked.

"Not exactly."

"What's that mean?"

She hesitated. "We hung out."

"Hung out or hooked up?"

"We might have done it one time. I honestly can't remember. I was pretty wasted that night. But mostly, we just hung. I didn't even see him all that often. He travels a lot."

The questions came fast and furious in Marta's head. She focused on the most important one. "What do you know about him?"

"His name is Ted. At least that's how I know him. People don't always use their real names in those recovery groups. I never could figure out exactly what he does, but he never seemed to be hurting for money."

Marta's mind felt scrambled. Every time she tried to make sense of what her sister was telling her, she got lost. "How weird," she said finally, "that the man I met is someone you know." And then something struck her. "How did you make the connection?"

"This is the really hard part." Cassie licked her lips, looked down at her feet. "I knew you'd met him, but I didn't know until last night that Jamie ran off with him."

"You knew I'd met him?"

"I told him where you'd be."

Marta sat down hard on the edge of her bed. "Why?"

"He was going to be there on business."

"But why mention me at all?"

Cassie pressed her fingertips together, steeple style. "We used to talk about how impossible family could be and stuff like that.

He heard me sound off about my paragon-of-perfection sister a
lot."

"Where do you get such nonsense?"

"Where do I get it?" She lifted her chin. "I've had to live with
it my whole life. Everything I did, Mom would point out how
stupid it was, and how dear, precious Marta would never make
the same mistake. 'Why can't you be more like your sister?'
she'd say, over and over. I can't tell you how sick I was of hearing those words. It wasn't easy, you know."

"So you've reminded me many times. You suffered and it's all
my fault. I still don't understand why you told him I was in
Minneapolis."

Cassie took a breath. "He bet me he could bring you down a
peg or two."

"My God! You set me up?" Marta's stomach felt sour.

"I told you you'd hate me."

"After all I've done for you! All the times I've helped you
out."

"I didn't think he'd follow you home. Like I said, I didn't
mean to cause trouble. Please, Marta. You've got to believe me."

"But you knew he was going to come on to me? And you
agreed to it?"

"I never thought you'd give him the time of day." Cassie
clasped and unclasped her hands. "I'm sorry, Marta. I'm really,
really sorry. It was supposed to be a joke."

"A joke?"

"As much on him as on you. Ted thinks he's irresistible.
Women fall for him and then he dumps them. He gets off on it.
I was sure you'd blow him off right away. I didn't expect him to
stalk you. And I certainly never expected him to go after Jamie."

Marta felt as though the wind had been knocked out of her.
"Tell me what you know about him."

"Not a lot. Like I said, we just kind of hung out."

"In Dallas?"

Cassie nodded. "I'm not sure if he actually lived there, though. He was gone a lot."

"Go on. What's he like?"

"He's a smooth talker, but I guess you know that. Fun to be around. But . . ."

"But what?"

"There's something weird about him . . . He makes stuff up. Kind of like a compulsive liar, I guess, only I think he just enjoys playing games."

Marta felt a new prick of anxiety. "Is he dangerous?" The more she learned, the more worried she was becoming.

"I don't know. I thought he was a regular guy. Maybe a little peculiar at times, but who isn't?" Cassie started pacing around the room, arms akimbo as though she was weighing her thoughts with her hands. "Ted can be unpredictable and something of a hothead. And he's got an ego bigger than the sun. But I never thought of him as dangerous. On the other hand, I never thought he'd stalk you or run off with Jamie."

"You said you might know where Jamie is."

"Ted used to talk about a family cabin. It's up north, somewhere near Shasta. Jamie told you she was in a cabin in the woods, right? That could be the place."

"Somewhere near Shasta, that's all you know?"

"I might recognize a name if I looked at a map," Cassie suggested.

"Or he could have been lying about the cabin along with everything else."

"I suppose so."

But what if he hadn't been? Marta felt the first glimmers of hope.

Hang on, Jamie. I'm going to find you.

CHAPTER 44

Jamie hummed quietly under her breath as she followed Todd along the narrow, uneven path. She had no interest in fishing but she was happy to be outside and to feel the warmth of the sun on her skin. She was happy, too, that Todd was being so sweet and attentive, trying hard to make up for his angry explosion the other day. Trying hard to show her how much he cared.

When he'd slapped her and wrenched the phone away, he was as irate as anyone she'd ever seen. Like a bull with fire in its eyes and steam rushing from its nostrils. The sting of his slap brought instant tears to her eyes, but the pain of the subsequent punches almost blinded her. At first, she'd been too stunned to do anything but cower and run her tongue around her mouth feeling for loose teeth.

When he'd told her to take off all her clothes, she'd complied without a word, shaking so badly she'd been afraid she'd never be able to get them off.

"Don't you ever cross me again, understand?"

Jamie nodded.

"Get down. On all fours like the bitch you are."

"Please, Todd," Jamie gulped between tears. "I'm sorry. I didn't mean to make you mad."

"Down. Right now."

Shivering, Jamie had lowered herself to the cold, filthy floor. Her head was pounding, whether from the force of Todd's fist or fear of what was coming next, she couldn't say.

Todd took off his leather belt and snapped it in the air over Jamie's head.

She flinched.

"You disappoint me, Jamie. Going behind my back like that. I trusted you."

She dared to look up, pleading for mercy with her eyes. "I just wanted to talk to my mom."

The belt came down with a sharp snap across her backside. Jamie cried out in pain.

"You need to be punished for what you did." Todd's voice no longer resonated with anger, but with an iciness that frightened Jamie even more. He raised the belt and whipped her again, and then again, until Jamie's back burned with an all-consuming fire and her insides turned to jelly.

And then abruptly he stopped and dropped to his knees. "Oh, my God, Jamie, I'm sorry. I'm so sorry. I didn't mean to hurt you. Jamie, honey." He began crying. "I love you, honey. I love you so much. I can't bear the thought of losing you."

Todd helped her to her feet and gathered her in his arms, gingerly so as not to hurt her further. He kissed the raw skin on her back and begged for forgiveness. "Come on, let me get a towel and I'll clean you up."

He led her to the kitchen area, gently blotted away the blood, and spread some kind of salve on it. He wrapped her in a clean towel and helped her back into her pants. Then he poured her a glass of whiskey.

"Here, drink this. It will help dull the pain."

Still stunned, she took the glass with a shaking hand and drank, trading the fire on her back for the fire in her gut. She wasn't able to form a single independent thought. Like a well-trained dog, she followed Todd's lead.

He'd stroked her check, kissed her softly. "I don't know what came over me, but I'll make it up to you, honey. I promise. I want you so much, Jamie. I can't lose you."

It still frightened her to think about what had happened, but Todd was making a real effort to show her how sorry he was. He'd been waiting on her hand and foot, as if she were royalty or something. He even called her his precious princess. At first, she'd resisted his kindness—he'd hit her after all—but now, with that awful afternoon fading into the past, Jamie found herself increasingly willing to forgive him. No one had ever cared about her like Todd did.

This afternoon's outing was a further offering from Todd, even if it did include fishing. As they approached the steep bank of the stream, he slowed and took Jamie's hand. "Careful," he said. "Watch for tree roots."

Jamie stepped carefully, steadying herself with Todd's support. He continued to hold her hand even when the terrain leveled out again. When they came to a wide, level spot under a canopy of trees, Todd stopped and slipped off the pack he carried. "How's this look for our picnic?"

"It's good. How's the fishing here?"

"We'll find out." He grinned. "Not that I really care. I just want to be with you." He spread the blanket and helped her settle in a comfortable spot. "You hungry yet?"

"Let's wait a bit. It's really lovely here. So peaceful."

"I'm glad you like it." He settled in next to her and draped an arm across her shoulders. "How's your back?"

"Better."

She'd been afraid to look in the mirror, afraid she'd see deep cuts and raw flesh. She'd been mildly disappointed to find only thin, red welts, and now even the welts were gone. All that remained was a reddish cross-hatching like she'd been scratching hard at her skin.

"I've been trying to figure out why I lost it like that," Todd said, nuzzling her neck. "I went crazy at the thought you were selling me out."

"I wasn't selling you out," Jamie protested. She'd tried explaining this before, but it wasn't easy because in some ways she *was*. She did love Todd, but at the same time she missed her family. She didn't understand why she had to make a choice.

"You were the one who came to me, don't forget. You begged for my help."

"I haven't forgotten." She had trouble remembering now why she'd been so eager to get away from her parents. It was all mixed up in her mind. Her mother reading her phone texts, making up stories about Todd, trying to turn Jamie against him. And then flat-out forbidding her from seeing him. Jamie had acted impulsively, she saw that now. But at the time, she hadn't seen any other choice.

"I went out of my way for you, Jamie. I'm not complaining. I'd do anything for you because I love you. I thought you loved me, too." Todd's voice grew husky. "It really hurt to discover you going behind my back. To think you wanted to leave me."

Jamie rested her head on Todd's shoulder and traced a finger across his palm. "I don't want to hurt you." And she didn't want to leave him. But she didn't want to leave her family, either.

"I can't help how I feel," he said.

"Neither can I. I miss my parents, but that doesn't mean I don't care about you."

He stared into space before continuing. "I've been badly burned before, so maybe I overreacted. It's been a long time since I've trusted a woman. I thought you were different."

"I'm sorry," Jamie said again. She seemed to be doing a lot of apologizing lately. Her mother was right. She needed to do a better job of thinking before she acted.

Todd kissed the top of her head. "You still love me?"

"I do."

"Good. That's all I care about."

What about what *she* cared about? Jamie kept quiet. She'd already said enough. She didn't want to set him off again.

Todd had bought a bottle of pre-mixed mimosas when he went into town and now he poured some into plastic glasses for each of them. The liquid was still icy cold and the perfect mix of sweet and bubbly. Jamie finished her glass before Todd's was a third gone.

"More?" he asked.

"Please."

After lunch Jamie dozed while Todd fished. Then she rolled onto her back, listening to the birds and watching puffy white clouds drift across the blue sky. Eventually Todd joined her on the blanket.

"Did you catch anything?" Jamie asked.

"Just a couple of little ones. I tossed them back. Let them live a bit longer."

"You're a softy at heart," she teased, and then snuggled against him while he stroked her hair.

"And you're my little princess." He kissed her chin, her eyes, then pulled her down onto the blanket.

By the time they returned to the cabin, the sun was already low in the sky.

"Did you have fun this afternoon?" he asked as he unloaded the backpack on the kitchen table.

Jamie nodded dreamily. Despite her nap, or maybe because of it, she was still feeling groggy.

"There's a little bit of mimosa left in the bottle. It won't keep. You want it?"

"I'll split it with you."

"I'd rather you have it."

Todd handed her a glass, led her to the couch, and sat beside her.

The liquid was warm now and tasted sweeter than it had that afternoon. Jamie didn't really want it, but she didn't want to hurt Todd's feelings. There wasn't much left so she drank it quickly, the way she might some unpleasant medicine. She would get up in a few minutes and brush her teeth to clear the taste.

Todd picked up her hand and drew imaginary hearts on her palm with his fingers. "You're my girl, Jamie. You're my special girl."

She smiled and tried to think how to respond. But she was suddenly too tired to care.

The next thing she knew, Todd was gone and the cabin was enveloped in darkness. Not pitch black the way it was at night, but dark enough that she realized she'd slept quite a while. She stood unsteadily and called for Todd.

There was no answer.

She went to the bottom of the narrow stairs and called again. And again, nothing.

Then she saw the note on the table.

Hey, sleepyhead. I've gone into town. Back soon. XOX, Todd

CHAPTER 45

"It was something woodsy," Cassie said, peering over Marta's shoulder at the digital map on the laptop screen.

"Something woodsy?"

"Yeah, the name of the place had a river in it. Or view. Or maybe some kind of animal."

"That doesn't narrow it down much."

"I know. I wish I could remember but I can't."

Marta moved the mouse to the north, zoomed in again, and began reeling off the town names, hoping Cassie recognized one of them.

"How about Gazelle?" Marta asked.

"Gazelle doesn't sound woodsy. Don't they live in Africa?"

Instead of answering, Marta sighed and moved the mouse to another part of the map. "What about Rio Vista? That's got both river and view in the name."

"In Spanish," Cassie snorted.

Marta silently counted to three. "How near Shasta is the cabin?"

"How should I know? I just remember that he said it was up near Shasta."

Which could mean just about anywhere in the northern third of the state. Marta moved the mouse again.

Cassie leaned forward, eyeing the screen more closely. "Wait," she said, "there. Trout Creek."

"That's where the cabin is?"

"Not right in town, but around there, I think. The name sounds familiar, anyway."

Marta zoomed in as far as the map allowed, and then switched to satellite view. The town of Trout Creek appeared to consist of a single named road and a web of winding crossroads identified only by numbers. The surrounding terrain looked mountainous and heavily forested. She switched to Zillow, thinking she might find information on specific lots and houses, but the area was too sparsely populated for that sort of detail. A cabin might not have shown up in any case, depending how remote and how rustic it was. For all she knew, the structure might not even be legal.

She switched back to Google maps, zoomed out, and calculated the distance from San Francisco. Just under five hours.

"Pack up," she told Cassie. "We're driving north."

"Can I shower first? The jail was filthy."

"Fine. But make it quick."

She sent Gordon an email, thinking that would be easier and quicker than the long, convoluted explanation that would come with a phone call. She'd call him once she knew more.

By late afternoon she and Cassie were nearing Trout Creek. The road was a two-lane ribbon winding through heavily forested mountains. They'd passed through a number of small towns on the way, many nothing more than a gas station and a bar.

"There are a lot of places to hide up here," Marta noted glumly.

"Yeah." Cassie, who'd been uncharacteristically subdued on the long drive, appeared equally dispirited. "I hope I haven't taken us on a wild goose chase."

"Me too."

"I might have been wrong about the cabin being near Trout Creek."

"But the name rang a bell with you, right?"

"I guess."

"You guess?" Marta couldn't entirely discount the possibility that Cassie was making things up as they went along.

"It does sound familiar, but I can't be sure it's the right town."

"Well, we're almost there. It's a little late for second-guessing."

"I want so bad for us to find Jamie. I never imagined Ted doing anything like this."

"So you've said."

As they approached the town proper, she could see a handful of houses built along the hillside, and a mileage sign directing them off the state road to Trout Creek in two miles.

"Wow," Cassie said. "Population one-seventy-nine."

Marta pulled up in front of a general store couched between a diner and a gas station. She turned off the engine. "We're here," she announced.

"Now what?"

Good question. "Let's go talk to people, see if we can find out anything about nearby cabins."

They started with the general store since they were parked right in front. The clerk at the register was young, probably not more than eighteen. He looked up when Marta approached.

"We're trying to find some people who have a cabin around here," she told him. "A man in his thirties and a teenage girl. Have you seen them?"

"I dunno. Sounds like a lot of folks. What's their name?"

Marta pulled out the photo of Jamie. "This is the girl."

"Nope, never seen her."

Cassie brought out her phone and pulled up the photo of

Todd. "How about him?"

"Nope."

"Are there many cabins around here?"

The kid guffawed. "You're joking, right? This is big fishing and hunting country. We get lots of folks who just want to get away from it all, too. So yeah, I'd say there's lots of 'em."

"The one we're looking for is pretty old," Cassie said. "Goes back a couple of generations or so."

"Most of 'em do. The newer places are mostly closer to town. You know, with utilities and stuff."

"Utilities?"

"Yeah, water, electricity, that sort of thing."

"The older places don't have that?"

"Nope. Most of 'em are too far away."

Jamie might be only ten or twenty miles from where they were standing, but Marta couldn't see how she'd ever find her. A backwoods cabin off the grid would be like finding a needle in a haystack.

She thanked the young clerk and moved on to the Whitefish Café next door. It was in an older brick building that looked as if it might have dated back to the town's founding. Inside, the walls were hung with photos of grinning fishermen and hunters showing off their catch. A large deer head hung over the bar area. But the room was surprisingly roomy and comfortable. And not surprisingly, largely empty at four in the afternoon. At one table, a grizzled man was bent over a large plate of eggs and sausage. At another, a couple sipped coffee while their two young kids dove into big pieces of pie.

The waitress was a middle-aged woman with thin, penciled-in eyebrows and bright red lipstick. Her name tag read "Dolores" and she greeted them with a warm smile. "Table or booth?"

Marta hadn't planned on eating but Cassie spoke up before

she could explain. "Booth, please. One by the window would be nice."

Marta shot her a look.

"We have to eat," Cassie said. "And I'm hungry."

Marta ordered iced tea and an egg salad sandwich. Cassie, a Coke and a cheeseburger. When the waitress returned with their food, Marta showed her Jamie's photo and asked if she recognized the girl. Cassie did the same with Todd.

The waitress shook her head. "Can't say that I've seen them."

"How long have you lived here?" Marta asked.

The woman laughed. "Believe it or not, I grew up around here. Moved away for a while, but ended up married to a guy who thinks this place is paradise. We've been here for twenty-five years now."

"You must know the area fairly well then."

"I like to think I do. My husband knows the back country better than me, but when it comes to people and what's going on, I leave him in the dust."

"Maybe you can help us. We're looking for my daughter. She's being held at a cabin this man's family has owned for several generations."

"Held?"

Marta nodded and launched into an abbreviated explanation, concluding with, "She made a mistake. But now she wants to come home and he won't let her."

"Goodness. Are the police involved?"

Marta hesitated. "In theory."

"I hear you." She rolled her eyes. "Our local sheriff's office is in Yreka. There's a lot of territory between here and there. He gets spread kind of thin."

Marta didn't bother to explain that she hadn't even contacted the local authorities yet. If what Dolores said was true, it might not do much good anyway.

"We think she's at a fishing cabin somewhere around here. One that isn't used much." Marta didn't know that last statement was fact, but she thought it likely based on what Cassie had said.

Dolores's face scrunched in thought. "Wish I could help. But there's a lot of old cabins stuck back up in the hills."

"What about someone in real estate?" Cassie asked. "Someone who might know the properties."

"There isn't anyone local. Besides, if the place hasn't changed hands recently, I doubt you'd learn anything from a real estate agent."

The family signaled for their bill and Dolores turned to go. "Tell you what," she said. "If you can get me prints of those photos, I'll ask around. Maybe I can even post something in the window."

"That would be wonderful." Marta resisted the urge to hug the woman. Finally, someone who was willing to make an effort to help. She wrote down her cell number and home contact information for Dolores. "Where can we get prints made around here?"

"You can't. Not officially anyway. Where are you staying?"

"Not sure."

"Closest place is the Ponderosa Pines motel. It isn't much, but it's clean and Harry's a good guy. He might be willing to help you out. All you really need is a computer and printer. I'd offer mine but it's on the fritz."

"Now, aren't you glad we decided to eat?" Cassie asked when Dolores had gone.

"Time will tell." The trouble with looking for a needle in a haystack, beyond the obvious, was that you had to be looking in the right haystack to begin with.

CHAPTER 46

Jamie was scared. Not just worried and slightly pissed the way she had been a while ago when she'd woken up and found Todd gone, but really, really scared. Evening twilight had deepened to a shadowy indigo. The cabin was dark and cold, and she was all alone.

She was afraid to tackle the gas lanterns herself. What if she did it wrong and the cabin blew up? Or she died of asphyxiation? She knew stuff like that could happen. Being in the dark was better than being dead.

She was freezing, too. The sun had warmed the afternoon air but once it set, the temperature had dropped quickly. She thought about starting a fire, but the stack of wood was outside, and not only was she afraid to go out, she couldn't find her shoes. She must have kicked them off in her sleep, but she'd felt around as best she could in the limited light and hadn't been able to find them anywhere.

She shivered and pulled her sweatshirt tighter. What was taking Todd so long? Had the car broken down? Or was it something worse? She pictured the car at the bottom of a ravine, Todd's broken body tossed onto the rocky terrain. Tears pricked her eyes. He wouldn't leave her alone for all this time if he could help it. Something had to be terribly wrong.

She heard a coyote howl off in the distance and a rustling sound closer. She remembered Todd's story about bears and mountain lions. Her heart was pounding so hard and fast she thought it might explode. She stumbled through the dark cabin to the kitchen, where she found a match and lit it. The brief burst of light convinced her she needed to do something. She couldn't simply sit in the dark and freeze to death. She decided to brave a trip to the wood pile even if she had to do it in bare feet. The wood wasn't far from the house, and a fire would provide both light and heat.

Hands outstretched, she shuffled through the dark until she found the door. But when she turned the knob, the door wouldn't open. She turned it the other way and yanked. It still didn't budge.

She felt around for a deadbolt, but found nothing. Panic blossomed in her chest and spread like an electric current throughout her whole body. She turned the knob to the right and the left. She turned it hard and fast. Then gently and slowly. No matter what she did, the door wouldn't budge.

She was locked inside a cold, dark cabin. Alone.

What if there was a fire? What if Todd never returned?

She shook the door, banged on it with her fists, then stumbled to a window. Years of paint and dirt and neglect had taken their toll. She couldn't open it, either. She tried other windows, without success.

She tried to calm herself. She could break the glass. Granted, it wouldn't be easy climbing through with shards of glass encircling her escape, but she did have a means to get out. She'd simply lost track of time, she told herself. Todd had prob- ably only been gone a couple of hours. She was scaring herself for no reason.

She felt her way back to the couch and curled into a ball. The minutes passed slowly. She thought about her parents. About Alyssa and Oliver. About the life in Sterling she'd run from so eagerly. What had she been thinking? She missed them all with an ache so deep and agonizing it took her breath away. Her parents loved her. How could she have treated them so badly? The tears came again and this time they wouldn't stop. She wiped them away with her sleeve but they kept coming.

The night seemed to go on forever. Eventually she heard the rumble of an approaching car. She caught the glare of headlights on the dirt road leading to the cabin. Warm relief flooded her veins.

And then fear.

What if it wasn't Todd? What if it was a burglar who thought the house was empty? Or a rapist and murderer?

She heard the car door slam shut. Then footsteps approaching.

When the door opened and Todd appeared she burst into hysterical tears. "Where have you been? Why didn't you tell me you were going?" She knew she was screeching but she couldn't calm herself. Now that he was back, all the confusion and anger and fear erupted in a torrent of words and weeping.

Todd set the bags he was carrying on the floor and put his arms on her shoulders. "Take it easy, honey. Didn't you see my note?"

"Yes, but it was getting dark. It *is* dark. I didn't know when you'd be back."

"The cabin has lights."

"They're propane. I was afraid to light them."

"So you've been sitting here in the dark?" He stroked her cheek. "My poor baby."

"I was so scared."

"We'll have to give you some lessons in self-sufficiency, won't we?"

Jamie detected an edge of rebuke in Todd's remark, like she'd come up short by panicking the way she had. "Why didn't you wake me before you left?" she asked.

"You looked so peaceful lying there. I didn't want to disturb you."

"I don't know why I fell asleep. I never nap."

"You obviously needed it, and I didn't expect to be gone long. Still, it was only a couple of hours."

"It felt like longer." Now that Todd was back, Jamie felt foolish about giving in to panic so easily. "And I couldn't find my shoes."

He looked down at her bare feet. "Where'd you leave them?"

"I must have kicked them off when I was sleeping, but I felt around by the couch and they aren't there."

"Let me get some light in here and we'll take a look." Todd pulled a packet of matches from his pocket and began lighting the lamps.

"I couldn't get the door open, either," Jamie said.

Todd stopped. "Why were you trying to open the door? You weren't going to leave, were you?"

"No, of course not. I wanted to get some wood."

"Just as well. The fireplace is tricky. You'd probably have smoked up the whole place."

"But why wouldn't the door open?"

Todd shrugged. "It opened fine for me." He lit the three central fixtures, turning the handle on each to release the propane, then waiting for the flame from the match to ignite the mantle, which it did with a *whoosh*. The lamps scared Jamie even when Todd lit them.

He got down on hands and knees and felt around under the couch. "Here are your shoes," he said.

"How'd they get way under there?"

"They're your shoes, Jamie, not mine. You ought to keep track of where you leave them."

Jamie didn't remember removing them, but no way would she have pushed them back under the couch. It was creepy that they'd wound up there.

"Let me start a fire," Todd said, "and then we'll fix dinner. I bought steaks. And real potatoes. No more canned stuff for my little princess."

She followed Todd to the porch and watched him gather wood from the pile just beyond. When she turned back, the cabin looked warm and cozy, not dark and frightening.

She was silently chiding herself for acting like a child when she noticed the padlock near the top of the doorjamb.

She didn't recall seeing it before.

CHAPTER 47

Gordon tossed his coat onto the couch and headed straight upstairs to his desk. He'd gone to campus for his classes, but skipped office hours so that he could come home and continue his investigation into Travis Winslow. He had been up most of last night digging on the Internet, but had learned surprisingly little, although he'd found another photo that bolstered his belief that Travis Winslow and Todd Wilson were one and the same.

From what he'd been able to piece together, Travis was the youngest of three Winslow siblings. They had inherited Citizen's Choice, a small bank in Texas, when their parents were killed in a private plane crash twelve years ago. Travis's older brother, Frederick, was currently the CEO, and his sister, Stephanie, was listed as President. Gordon hadn't been able to find an article that laid out the family history in the sort of detail he would have liked, but he'd found other sources that talked about a deal between Citizen's Choice and AG National Bank.

He had phoned Detective Phillips first thing this morning, thinking it might be easier for the police to locate Todd now that they had his real name. But Phillips wasn't much interested. Wilson or Winslow—it was all the same to him. His response had been something along the lines of "Great, thanks for letting us know. We'll update our BOLO bulletin."

It had been too early at that hour to call the bank in Texas, but Gordon grabbed a few minutes between classes and tried to reach both of the older siblings. He'd gotten the corporate runaround and had left his name with little hope of hearing back.

Now, he settled at his desk and tried again, explaining first to the bank operator and then to the secretaries for each of the siblings that the matter was personal and extremely important.

"Mr. Winslow is unavailable at the moment," Frederick Winslow's secretary said, echoing the words of Stephanie Winslow's gatekeeper. "If you want to leave your name, I'll give him your message."

Gordon contacted Customer Service next, and from there was transferred to Human Resources. Everyone he spoke with was polite, but he never reached a single person who was able or willing to talk to him about Travis or the Winslow family.

He felt he'd cracked a big piece of an important puzzle—the man they were looking for was Travis Winslow. And he knew something, albeit only in general terms, about the man's background. But he was at a loss where to go with it from there. He made himself a cup of coffee and went back to Googling.

He'd pretty much exhausted his search for information about Travis Winslow last night, so today he focused on the brother and sister and the bank itself. Most of the recent business articles dealt with the structure and finances of a possible merger. Finally, he stumbled across a business-oriented blog by a guy named Simon Jennings, who seemed fairly knowledgeable about the inner workings of Citizen's Choice. Gordon tried to find a contact phone number, and when he couldn't, typed out an email asking Jennings to contact him.

Then he called Marta. He had hoped to have more detailed information to pass along, but knowing Todd's real name was still significant. He also wanted an update on her activities. He'd received a cryptic email from her that morning, saying she had a lead on a possible location where Jamie might be and she and Cassie were heading there. Annoyed at the vagueness of her message, he had tried calling. The phone rang directly to voice mail. He didn't know whether to be worried or angry.

"Finally," he said now when she answered. "I tried reaching you earlier."

"I must not have had reception."

"Where are you? And what's going on? Your email explained nothing."

"We're in Trout Creek," Marta told him. She sounded tired. "It's a very small town, more of a wide spot in the road really, in the way northern part of the state. Up near Shasta."

"What makes you think Jamie is there?"

"It's a long story. Too complicated to go into right now."

"What?" Gordon felt his anger returning. "You practically refused to let me come with you and now this is all I get? What the hell is going on?"

"The short of it is, Cassie may have met Todd—"

"Met him? When? How?" Anything involving Cassie spelled trouble. And fifty-fifty it would turn out not to be true.

"I told you, Gordon, I can't explain over the phone. But what's important is, he told her about a family cabin in the woods near Shasta."

"Why would he do that? Cassie's not the most reliable—"

"It fits perfectly with what Jamie told me about where she was."

"There must be hundreds of little towns up there."

"There are a lot of them. But Cassie thinks she recognized the name Trout Creek."

"She *thinks*?"

"It's our only lead."

Gordon was beside himself. "Finding Jamie is too important for your sister's games. I'm surprised at you, Marta. Don't you have more sense?"

"It's not a game," Marta snapped.

Gordon tried to rein in his irritation. Criticizing Cassie was never a good move. "I know you don't think it's a game. It's just seems—"

"Do you have a better idea?"

"No. But I'm worried you might be going off on some tangent."

"That's possible," Marta admitted. "But I think we might be on to something. We met a woman here in town who said she would hand out flyers to her customers. In a small area like this, somebody might recognize Todd."

"I have news that might help," Gordon offered, softening his tone. "I learned that Todd's real name is Travis Winslow. His family owns a small bank in Texas. His older siblings are the CEO and President. I don't know where Travis fits in."

"How did you come up with that?"

Gordon explained about the article Carol had printed out, and how he'd zeroed in on the Winslow family photo. "I've tried to reach both the brother and sister, but neither has returned my calls. I've scoured the Internet, without a lot of luck. But then I stumbled on a blogger, Simon Jennings, who specializes in mergers, or at least on business—"

"Talk about going off on tangents!"

"Don't you think knowing Todd's real identity is important?"

"How sure are you?"

"Reasonably sure."

"Reasonably?" Marta parroted. "Finding Jamie is too important for name games."

Gordon was stung. And furious. He heard his computer ping and saw he had a response from Jennings. "I've got to go," he said. "The blogger I told you about just sent me a message."

He hung up before Marta could insult him further.

CHAPTER 48

The Ponderosa Pines Lodge was an old, bungalow-style "resort" facing a parking lot. The front entrance was framed in half-round logs but the architecture was solidly early motel. Marta and Cassie were the only guests.

"Creepy," Cassie said when they checked in.

Marta didn't find it creepy, but it wouldn't have been her first choice if there'd been any alternative. "Dolores recommended it," she pointed out.

Their room wasn't elegant by any means and only marginally comfortable—twin beds, thin mattresses, one rickety bureau, and one low-watt bulb. But it was clean, cheap, and convenient. And, as Dolores had predicted, Harry, the manager, was more than happy to allow Marta to use his computer and printer as long as she reimbursed him for paper. He promised to take a flyer for himself and post it by the front desk.

"Maybe by July there'll be another customer here to see it," Cassie whispered as they left his office.

"He must get more business on the weekends. Besides, we need all the help we can get."

"Shouldn't we add the name Travis Winslow to the flyer?" Cassie asked after a moment.

Marta had already modified her original flyer to include Todd's photo, but Gordon's call hadn't come until after the flyer was printed, too late to add Todd's real name. "We'll have to write it in," she said.

"I know, but there's a chance one of the old-time locals will recognize the name and know where the cabin is."

Despite Gordon's enthusiasm for his discovery, Marta remained skeptical. Todd did not strike her as someone who was part of a Texas banking dynasty. But it couldn't hurt. "You're right, we'll add it."

The beds were narrow and cramped and creaked every time either of them moved. Cassie seemed to sleep just fine, while Marta lay awake for what seemed like most of the night. In the morning, she was up and showered before her sister opened her eyes.

"Time to get moving," she said once she was dressed.

"Okay, okay." Cassie rubbed her eyes and trudged to the tiny bathroom where she took a long and very steamy shower.

They drove into town for breakfast at the Whitefish Café, and Dolores greeted them like old friends. She immediately posted a flyer in the cafe's window and another by the register.

"What's your plan for the day?" she asked them as she poured more coffee.

"We're going to distribute flyers around town, if people will take them."

"Oh, they'll take them all right. People around here may be a bit eccentric but they've got good hearts."

"We've got some new information," Marta told her. "The man my daughter is with might use the name of Travis Winslow. Does that ring a bell with you?"

"Can't say it does."

After breakfast, Marta took the east side of the block, and Cassie the west. Dolores had been right, every single person they spoke with took a flyer and promised to post it. After their experience in San Francisco, the response was heartening. But it was a short block and the only commercial district in town, so it didn't amount to much.

"We could go door to door in the neighborhoods," Cassie suggested.

"We might, at some point." Marta felt antsy. "Let's touch base with the sheriff first. Then we'll check out some of the nearby towns. If the businesses there are as willing as they were in Trout Creek, that's probably a better use of our time than canvassing individual homes."

The deputy sheriff they met with was sympathetic and open to helping, but he readily admitted that without more to go on, there wasn't much he could do. He took several flyers and promised to spread the word among the other officers.

"If you get more information, give me a call," he said, handing Marta his card. "Both the office exchange and my cell number are on there."

Marta thanked him, then she and Cassie covered the main street of Yreka before continuing their drive through the smaller surrounding towns, although the word "town" was something of a misnomer. Many were smaller than Trout Creek.

They took their time, chatting up anyone who was willing to listen, not only spreading the word about Jamie but trying to learn what they could about the back roads and the rustic cabins along them.

The clerk at a gas station convenience stop thought Todd might look familiar, but he couldn't say for sure. He'd never seen Jamie, however. And the bearded, suspender-wearing bartender at Harry's Saloon and Bait Shop thought the name Winslow rang a bell, but couldn't tell them why.

As they were leaving Burnet, a town about thirty miles from Trout Creek, Marta slammed on the brakes.

"What's the matter?" Cassie asked.

"That trailer park."

"What about it?"

"Jamie told me she drove through a town with a mobile home community called Royal Gardens."

Cassie frowned. "That's not Royal Gardens. It's Royal Oasis. And it's not a mobile home anything, it's a trashy trailer park."

"It's close." Close enough that Marta felt a burst of optimism. "Jamie is somewhere nearby," she said. "I can feel it."

"I sure hope so." Cassie stretched her arms. "We did good today. But now I'm hungry. And tired. Can we call it quits?"

"I'm ready for a break, too."

Rather than head back into Trout Creek, they stopped at a small roadside bar closer to the motel called the Hungry Coyote Saloon. The blinking neon sign above the door advertised "Food," although Marta had no idea what sort of food.

As she suspected, the bar offered burgers and chicken wings, and, oddly, grilled scallops, along with three kinds of fries. They both ordered hamburgers.

"You going to call Gordon?" Cassie asked.

"Later."

Cassie gave her a quizzical look. "You haven't talked to him since yesterday."

"There's nothing new to report. And I'm sure he'd call me if he learned anything useful."

"You two are on the outs, aren't you?"

Marta no longer knew what they were. The man she'd married was not the man she was married to now, but until recently, she'd had faith that everything would work out. The tension in yesterday's phone call only added to her doubts.

"We're going through a rough patch," she agreed.

"All because of me."

"You talking about Todd?"

"Yeah. I feel so guilty."

"You should. But it's not just that. Losing his job changed Gordon. He's been withdrawn and detached and negative.

Besides, you told Todd I'd be in Minneapolis, you didn't force me to sleep with him. And you didn't tell him to seduce Jamie."

"God, no. Never." Cassie played with the salt and pepper shakers on the table. "You believe me, don't you?"

"Of course." It surprised Marta to find that she actually did.

"You know how Mom used to tell me, 'Why can't you be more like Marta'? It did make me resent you, but deep down I think I really wanted to be like you. I just never knew how."

"And now you know that was all a load of crap. I'm not a role model for anyone, not even my own daughter."

"You're being a bit hard on yourself, don't you think?"

"No. I screwed up and hurt everything and everyone I hold dear. It's my fault Jamie's in jeopardy."

"But we're close to finding her," said Cassie, playing cheerleader again. "Remember, we passed that trailer park Jamie saw?"

"As you pointed out, the name wasn't what Jamie remembered. It might mean nothing." Marta's earlier optimism had deserted her. She ate a pickle slice. "Let's not talk about this anymore, okay?"

"If that's what you want."

Marta looked toward the bar. There were a handful of people seated there—a couple of male construction workers and a young blond who kept giggling at everything they said. At the far end of the bar, an older woman in trousers and a flannel shirt sat by herself, drinking a beer.

"We should leave a flyer here, too," Marta said. "I'll go ask the bartender."

She angled into the empty spot next to the lone woman. The bartender came over right away. "What can I get you?"

"I have a favor to ask." She showed him the flyer and gave him the short explanation.

"Sure, I'll post it. Never had kids myself, but my sister's oldest is a real hellion so I can imagine what you're going through."

The older woman picked up the flyer and examined it. Marta began a second recitation of her explanation when the woman interrupted.

"I heard what you told Harlan." She nodded to the bartender.

"You recognize either of these two, Maggie?" he asked her.

She shook her head. "Nope. But there was an old guy named Winslow had a cabin here years ago. My father and him were fishing buddies. Funny guy. 'Course Winslow's not an unusual name so it don't mean much."

"Do you remember where the cabin was?" Marta asked.

"I was only there a couple of times, a long time ago." She turned back to her drink and Marta thought that was the end of it. A few moments later, the woman said, "Out by Porcupine Ridge, I think. Off a road that came right after a creek crossing."

"Porcupine Ridge, where's that?"

The woman called to the bartender. "Hey, Harlan, you got a pen I can use?"

Harlan pulled a pen from his pocket and handed it to her.

The woman took the paper napkin from under her beer, turned it over, and sketched out a crude map. "Wasn't but one road up that way back then. Not so sure about now."

"And there was a bridge?"

"More of a creek overpass."

Marta could barely contain her excitement. "Thank you. You've been a big help."

"Maybe. Maybe not."

Marta hurried back to their table and told Cassie what she'd learned. "Hurry up and finish your burger," she urged.

"What? We're going out there tonight?"

"I can't sit still and twiddle my thumbs."

"Shouldn't we wait for morning? We don't even have a flashlight."

"We'll see if there are any cabins that appear to be occupied. We'll go back in the morning, but taking a look tonight will save us time."

CHAPTER 49

Gordon had been playing phone tag with Simon Jennings, the business blogger, since yesterday afternoon. They finally connected as Gordon was finishing the tuna sandwich that passed for his dinner.

He had explained the situation in general terms in his email, which allowed him to get down to business early into the conversation.

"I was hoping you might be able to tell me about the family," he said. "Particularly Travis Winslow."

"Happy to try, but I'm not sure any of it will help find your daughter. You said she ran off with Travis?"

"Right. At least I'm fairly sure it's the same man. He told us his name was Todd Wilson."

"Interesting." Jennings seemed to think about that for a moment before continuing. "Travis is the youngest of three. Youngest by far. The product of a second marriage. His father, Eric Travis, divorced wife number one, mom of the two older kids, and married Jacqueline Henderson, who by all accounts was some bimbo he knocked up while still married to wife number one. The older kids were in their late teens by then. Understandably, they resented the hell out of her, and if I had to guess, their new half-brother."

"That marriage lasted?"

"Despite predictions to the contrary, it did. Right up until the happy couple was killed in a private plane crash some time in the late eighties. Travis would have been about fifteen or so at the time."

"And the bank?"

"The three siblings inherited equally. The older two kids were already being groomed to take over, so in terms of the business, the transition wasn't as jarring as one might expect. At first it was quite smooth, in fact. Citizen's Choice had four branches at the time of the senior Winslow's death, and it's grown to six at the present. But the bank is in trouble financially. The mortgage crisis took a toll, made worse by some bad business decisions."

"Where does Travis fit in? Is he involved with the bank?"

"Good question. He's a key player, at least on paper. Nominally he's got some title, but I get the impression his main job is laying low and staying out of trouble, something he's managed with limited success. In fact, his inheritance is controlled by the family attorney, a man named Conrad."

That explained the cell phone account.

"The bank is in talks with AG National," Jennings continued. "It's looking to expand into the Texas market. The brother and sister can't afford to retire, so they're hoping to structure a deal that gives them a continued role at the new, larger entity."

"Bigger pond and all that?" Gordon didn't understand the world of high finance, but he was all too familiar with the concept of getting ahead by moving on to bigger and better.

"Exactly. I think their biggest concern now is that Travis will screw up the deal. Seems he's a bit of a loose cannon. He's been in trouble pretty much his whole life."

"What kind of trouble?"

"That's not entirely clear. The family has tried to keep it all hush-hush. I do know he was kicked out of prep school as a teenager, but given that it was around the time his parents were killed, I'm not sure it means much. There are rumors that he broke a woman's arm in college, and he was involved in the death of another. No charges were filed in either case. There does appear to have been a restraining order filed against him by an ex-girlfriend but it has since expired."

"Serious stuff."

"If it's true. There were also some drug charges that led to a couple of stints of rehab."

"Sounds like a prince," Gordon noted with sarcasm.

"Probably not the kind of guy you want your daughter hanging around with, but I don't know any of this firsthand. Travis Winslow isn't the focus of my reporting. On a personal level I find the family story fascinating. I mean, here's this kid, part of a wealthy, prosperous family. Born with a silver spoon in his mouth. Except his father is an older man, probably not much involved in his young son's life. He has older siblings he doesn't really know, and they hate him. Then his parents are killed, and, boom, he's all alone."

"But still rich."

"Absolutely. Some people rise to the occasion and develop character. Others . . . Well, I get the sense that Travis is one of the others."

Gordon didn't share Jennings's empathy with Travis, but then his knowledge of the guy was personal. "One last question. Do you know anything about a family cabin in the woods of northern California?"

"Can't say I do. But the old man, not the father killed in the crash, but his father, Lincoln Winslow, who founded the bank, was a big outdoors guy . . . hunter, fisherman, all that stuff. And he grew up in California. So I wouldn't be surprised if he had a cabin there somewhere."

Gordon was practically vibrating with excitement. Although he wasn't sure what he'd accomplished in terms of finding Jamie, it had to be a step in the right direction. He tried calling

Marta, but the phone went directly to voice mail. He left a message asking her to call him as soon as possible.

Next he called the assessor's office for Siskiyou County where Trout Creek was located.

"Can you give me the location of a property?" Gordon asked.

"Do you have a parcel number?"

"Just a name."

"A name?" The clerk seem perplexed.

"I'm trying to get the address of a property owned by someone with the last name of Winslow," Gordon explained.

"Maybe you should try the phone book."

"I don't have a phone book." Gordon took a deep breath. "Don't you have a list of properties by owner's name?"

"Parcel number, address, and assessed valuation."

Gordon's phone pinged indicating an incoming call. "Thanks," he told the clerk, adding silently "for nothing." He clicked to the second call, hoping it was Marta.

Instead, it was Detective Phillips. "I got a call from the authorities in California," he said. "One of the interviews your wife gave there prompted a report from a woman who thinks she saw your daughter last week."

Gordon's heart skipped a beat. "Where?"

"In the East Bay. A town called Emeryville. She saw a girl who looked like Jamie in the condo building where she lives. What's more, the owner of a condo in that building reported that strangers were living in his unit while he was out of town. They were gone by the time the police did a security check."

"Right, they've moved on," Gordon reminded him. "Remember, Jamie called us from a cabin somewhere in northern California."

"I'm aware of that. But I thought you might like to know your efforts are generating some response."

If Jamie's photo had prompted one call, maybe there would

be others. "There's a chance my daughter is near a town called Trout Creek. At a cabin that was at one time owned by Lincoln Winslow, grandfather to the man who's holding her captive. Is there any way to get a location for the place?"

"Let me make a call to local officials out there."

"Thanks. You'll keep me posted?"

"Absolutely."

Gordon tried reaching Marta again, and when the call again went directly to voice mail, he tried Cassie. Her phone did likewise. They had to be in an area without cell coverage, but couldn't they find *someplace* to make a call?

Or was Marta intentionally ignoring him? Possibly, he thought, remembering the angry words they'd exchanged yesterday. But surely Marta would put finding Jamie before marital acrimony.

He was three thousand miles away. Cut off, out of touch, and hopelessly isolated.

To hell with it! Gordon went online and booked a flight to San Francisco. Then he cancelled his classes for the remainder of the week, left another message for Marta, and packed a bag. He was tired of feeling like a fifth wheel.

CHAPTER 50

Jamie was having trouble thinking about anything but the padlock on the outside of the front door. Todd had explained that it was to keep people from breaking in when the cabin was vacant. That seemed reasonable, but it didn't mean that he *hadn't* locked her in. Why wouldn't the door open yesterday?

She'd been playing the night over in her mind all today. On the surface, everything had been nice. The steaks were delicious, the fire warm and cozy, and Todd cheerful. He teased her about being panicked at finding herself alone, but it was a sweet sort of teasing. He was so loving and attentive, she suspected he probably felt guilty about leaving her, even though he wouldn't admit it.

She'd slept fitfully. Every time she woke, it was with an edge of fear. She wanted to trust Todd, but she couldn't stop the doubts from hovering in the back of her mind.

In the light of morning, she decided she was letting herself get worked up over nothing. When Todd suggested they take a drive, she'd flown into his arms with excitement. They had taken a ride through the countryside. Todd showed her a waterfall he'd loved as a child, a spot high in the hills were you could see almost forever in every direction, a berry patch thick with ripe berries, and he told her repeatedly how beautiful she was and how much she meant to him. They laughed a lot and she found it easy to remember why she loved him.

But when she again broached the possibility of calling home

to let her parents know she was okay, he'd grown quiet and sullen. She hadn't pushed it.

She wondered if they were looking for her. Did they miss her or were they angry with her? Would they even want her back?

It had been a wonderful day, but now, as she finished washing tonight's dinner dishes, she was again thinking about the lock. Was she being paranoid? Imagining the worst for no reason? It made total sense to padlock the door when the cabin was vacant. Up here with no one around, vandals and burglars could pretty much come and go as they pleased. But she couldn't remember Todd *unlocking* a padlock when they'd first arrived. In fact, she didn't recall seeing a lock at all. And it seemed newer and shinier than anything else on the cabin's exterior.

Todd patted the couch beside him. "Come sit with me."

Jamie put away the last of the dinner dishes and curled next to him, working to push the troubling questions from her mind.

"I'm thinking maybe it's time to move on," he said after a moment.

"Where to?"

"That's what I'm trying to decide. I mean it's nice here. I've always liked it. But we can't stay forever." He smiled at her. "Roughing it gets old after a while."

Jamie's heart leapt with joy. She didn't hate the cabin as much as she had at first, but she didn't like it, either. It was still dark, dingy, and isolated. The sooner they left, the better.

"We need someplace we can settle in and get on with our lives," he added.

A real life with Todd. That's what she'd wanted from the start. Jamie experienced a rush of excitement. Then felt it dim with the shadow of sadness. She thought of her parents. And her friends. She missed them all so much.

She longed to see her mother's smile, hear her dad's laugh.

She even missed their nagging, which she understood now showed they cared. She wanted to hang out with Alyssa and walk to English class with Oliver. She wanted to listen to music she liked and sleep in her own room.

"How about Hawaii?" Todd asked. "Have you ever been there?"

Jamie shook her head.

"Sunshine, beaches, warm weather. I could teach you to surf. And buy you a bikini." He winked at her. "We might think about getting a boat, too. What do you think? Sounds good, doesn't it?"

It did, and it didn't. "Isn't Hawaii more of a place to vacation than to live?"

Todd laughed. "For some folks, yeah. But lots of people live there, too." He ruffled her hair, teasing her like a child. "We're on the West Coast, halfway there already. We could get a condo near the beach and you could finish school."

The idea of starting over in a new school held no appeal at all. "What about your job?"

He laughed again. "That's my problem, not yours."

Todd wanted a life with her. That's what she wanted, too. So why did she feel herself resisting? "What about my parents?" she asked.

"What about them?"

"Could we tell them?"

"It's probably best to wait until after you turn eighteen."

"But—"

"You're acting like a child, Jamie." He pulled away and looked at her sharply. "People grow up and leave home. That's the natural order of things. You want to stay with Mommy and Daddy forever?"

Jamie swallowed hard. Tears stung her eyes. Why did he have to talk to her like that? Like she was some infantile idiot. Like what she wanted or felt didn't matter at all.

Suddenly, Todd stood and went to the window. "You hear that?"

"What?" And then she picked up the soft hum of a car in the distance.

"Someone's coming."

"Who do you think it is?"

"How should I know?" he snapped, turning down the light. "Out this way at night it probably means trouble."

A bolt of fear electrified Jamie. They were all alone with only spotty cell reception. There was no way to call for help.

"Stay away from the windows," he barked. "I'll get my gun."

"You have a gun?" She couldn't decide if that was good news or bad.

He scurried up to the loft and came charging down as the car drew closer. Jamie could see the headlights reflected in the trees outside.

"Can I count on you?" Todd asked.

"Count on me?"

He seemed to answer his own question. "Better that you hide." He opened a small door in the corner of the kitchen. "Get down there."

"Where?" Jamie hadn't even noticed the door before. It was flat and flush with the floor.

"It's a root cellar. Go on. You have to keep quiet. For your own protection."

"What do you mean?"

"You need to stay hidden and safe."

"What about you?"

"I'll deal with it."

She shook her head. "No, we'll deal with it together."

"I don't trust you, Jamie. You say the wrong thing and we're screwed." Todd dragged her toward the newly revealed hole in the floor. "Come on, get down there."

Jamie looked into the pit at her feet. A narrow ladder lead down into pitch blackness. "Please, Todd, I'll be good. I won't say a word."

"You brought this on yourself, honey. You've proven untrustworthy before."

"I didn't—"

"It's for your own protection. Don't make a sound. If anyone gets hurt it will be your fault." He shoved a flashlight into her hands. "Remember, not a peep." He pushed her down into the abyss and shut the door.

Clinging to the ladder, Jamie found the switch on the flashlight. It gave off a weak yellow beam that was only marginally better than nothing.

She bit her lip to keep from crying and slowly eased herself down the ladder to the ground.

CHAPTER 51

After half an hour of driving in the dark along poorly marked roads that supposedly lead to Porcupine Ridge, Marta was beginning to think Cassie had been right. They should have waited until morning.

She was on the verge of admitting defeat when Cassie pointed up ahead.

"I bet that's it," she said. "The bridge, I mean."

"How can you tell?"

"The fencing on the side of the road. The woman at the bar said the turn-off was after a creek overcrossing."

Marta slowed as they crossed over a creek, or what she assumed was a creek below.

"There," Cassie said. "Up ahead. I see a road off on the left."

Marta turned onto a narrow strip of pockmarked asphalt and they headed into the hills. The road morphed from asphalt to gravel, and continued to narrow as they wound further up. Eventually it ended where a rutted dirt road angled off to the right.

"This can't be right," Marta groaned.

Cassie turned on the dome light and examined the hand-drawn map. "No, I think it is. See, she made this part more of a dotted line." Cassie peered into the darkness ahead. "You think we should go on?"

Marta's instinct was to turn around and come back in daylight. Then she thought of Jamie, who might be close by and desperate for help. "Maybe just a little farther."

The driving was difficult and Marta worried she would pop a tire or get stuck in one of the large potholes that were practically impossible to see in the dark.

"I guess we should call it off for tonight," she said finally. "We can't help Jamie if we're stranded in the woods ourselves."

She was looking for a place to turn around when through the trees ahead, she thought she saw a faint light. Cassie saw it too.

"Could be a cabin," she said. "Looks like someone's there."

Marta inched forward. She stopped short of the light, which was coming from a small, rustic building that struck her as more shack than cabin, unsure what to do next.

"Maybe we should call the cops," Cassie suggested.

"We don't know that this is the right place. Or that Jamie's here."

"There's no way we're going to be able to find out tonight. We can't go knock on the door."

"Let's just take a look." Marta pushed on at a snail's pace.

Suddenly the lights in the cabin dimmed.

"Let's get out of here," Cassie cried. "It's creepy."

Marta spotted a dark-colored car parked to the side of the cabin. "Just a minute. I want to get the license number."

"I'm calling the cops." Cassie took her phone from her purse. "Damn. No signal."

Marta pulled to the side of the narrow road and turned off the engine.

"What are you doing?"

"There might be better reception outside this car and I want to check the parked car's plate."

They got out and circled behind the car. The night was pitch black and the ground was uneven. Staying close together, they inched toward the cabin. Cassie kept her eyes on the signal-strength icon. Every so often it would look like she'd found a good spot, but the signal faded again before she could complete a call.

"Let's get out of here," Cassie whispered. "We can come back tomorrow."

"I want to find out if Jamie's inside."

"You can't, not without maybe getting your head blown off."

Cassie was right. There wasn't any way to discreetly learn who was inside that cabin. Or to get near enough to the car to see its plate. But to be so close, to think Jamie was within hollering distance and simply walk away? Marta couldn't do it.

A crackling sound behind them startled her. Her heart jumped into her throat. She turned and was immediately blinded by a bright light. Cassie gasped and grabbed Marta's arm.

"Hello, Marta. And Cassie," Todd said.

"Where's Jamie?" Marta said. "Is she here?"

"Why would she be here?"

"Don't play stupid. She called me a couple of days ago, remember?" Just before you slapped her and wrenched the phone from her hands, Marta added silently.

He lowered the light so that it was no longer blinding them, and Marta saw the gun in his other hand. "She's gone," he said.

"Gone? Where?"

"How should I know?" He gestured with the flashlight. "Come on, let's go inside."

"Is she okay? When did she leave?" What did *gone* mean. Marta's stomach clenched. Was Jamie dead?

"Go on," Todd said. "I'll follow."

Staying close, Marta and Cassie moved toward the cabin. Despite the shadowy light from Todd's flashlight, Marta stumbled several times. Her legs felt like rubber.

"Why are you doing this?" Cassie whimpered. "We just want to know that Jamie is safe."

"I'm surprised you're part of this, Cassie. I thought you despised your sister."

"Not true," Cassie croaked to Marta. "I never said I despised you."

Todd chuckled.

Inside the cabin, he turned off the flashlight and motioned them to wooden chairs set around a small heavily marred table. The gun remained in his hand.

"How'd you find me here?" he asked.

"You told me about the cabin," Cassie said. "Near Trout Creek."

"What a memory!" He laughed.

Marta looked around. The cabin was sparsely furnished and not very clean. There was no sign of Jamie. "What's upstairs?" she asked.

"A sleeping loft. I'd give you a tour but this isn't a social call, is it?"

"I want to see Jamie. Where is she?"

"I told you, she's not here." He smiled. "But you are."

CHAPTER 52

Jamie was grateful for the flashlight, weak though it was. She stood at the bottom of the ladder and circled the light around her, taking stock. The cellar appeared to be smaller than the cabin, and the ceiling was so low a taller person would have had trouble standing. No skeletons or dead animals that she could see. No live animals, either. That was a relief. But the beams were layered with dust-laden spider webs and the air smelled musty. She shivered and crossed her arms protectively. How long would she need to stay here?

She heard the cabin door creak and Todd's footsteps descending the outside steps. Then quiet, broken only by an occasional snap of branches. She thought she saw a sweep of light through the cracks in the siding, and she heard the sound of a car door.

She lowered her flashlight beam and held her breath.

A short time later she heard footsteps above in the cabin and muffled voices. Someone was inside. Todd or intruders? Or both?

At first, she'd been upset about being pushed into the cellar, but she was scared enough now to think that Todd had been right. He was only trying to protect her, after all.

Someone was definitely here. What if Todd was in trouble?

Jamie's mind raced with possibilities, none of them good. Her heart pounded and her stomach churned. He had a gun, she reminded herself. He wasn't defenseless. And she hadn't heard shouting or sounds of a fight. But whoever it was hadn't left yet. She was pretty sure she'd have heard if they had.

She was afraid to move lest she make a noise. Afraid, almost, to breathe. But she couldn't stop shivering.

In the dark cellar, she lost track of time. She was surprised when the cellar door opened and Todd called down to her. "You can come up now, honey."

Was this a trick? Had he been forced to admit she was hiding below? Would he use her as bait?

No, Todd wouldn't let anything bad happen to her.

Slowly and cautiously, Jamie climbed the ladder into the shaft of light from above. Todd was waiting and she fell into his arms.

"Who was it?" she whispered. "What did they want?"

Keeping an arm tightly around her shoulders, he turned her toward the table. When her eyes adjusted to the light, she was able to make out two figures sitting upright in the kitchen chairs.

She blinked and looked again. Her heart leapt to her throat. "Mom? Aunt Cassie?"

"Jamie!" They called her name in unison.

"How did you know . . ." Her words caught in her throat when she saw they were bound to the chairs with rope.

She started to run to them, then remembered Todd's warning. If anything bad happened, it would be her fault. She looked at him. "What's going on?"

"Your phone call the other day," he said. "I warned you. Now look what you've done."

What she'd done? Jamie took a tentative step forward. "Are you guys okay?"

Her mom stopped crying long enough to say, "More importantly, are you okay?"

"I'm fine," Jamie said, and at the same time realized it wasn't true.

"You still want to come home?"

Yes, she did. With all her heart. But her mom was in no position right now to make that happen.

"I miss you," Jamie said, feeling her own rush of tears. "I didn't want to cause you trouble. I just wanted to talk to you."

"We miss you, too. We've been so worried. That's why we had to find you."

Her mom wasn't angry. She'd flown all this way because Jamie needed her!

"Why did you have to tie them up?" she asked Todd, her throat aching with choked-back tears.

He laughed without humor and waved the gun. "Jamie, you're as dumb as shit sometimes."

She flinched. Heat rose to her face. "What do you plan to do?"

"Not sure yet."

"Let Jamie go," her mom begged. "Cassie, too. I'll stay with you. We'll go away. I'll do whatever you want."

"You had your chance, Marta. You blew it."

Her mom's face was etched with desperation. "What do you want?"

"I have it." Todd grinned. "You're begging me. Tit for tat."

"It's not the same at all."

"You were cruel to me, now it's my turn."

"I'm married. I wasn't trying to be cruel. I wanted to make you see things for what they were."

Jamie sucked in a breath. It was true then? Her mother hadn't lied about Todd pursuing her. The memory of their argument reached out and grabbed Jamie by the throat. Why hadn't she listened? If only she hadn't been so stupid. So determined to prove her mother wrong.

Todd stroked Jamie's cheek. "As it turns out, I prefer your daughter. She's more woman than you could ever be." His hand slid lower, brushing her breasts and belly. "And I didn't have to

325

beg. She offered it all."

A sour taste rose in Jamie's throat. Todd didn't prefer her. He'd been using her all along, just as her mother warned.

He stretched and yawned, making an elaborate show of both. "Bedtime, ladies. Jamie, you go on up, I'll be there in a moment or two."

Jamie's legs felt wobbly. He couldn't possibly think this was a normal night, could he?

"What about my mom and aunt?"

"They're going to enjoy the charm of the cellar tonight."

"No, Todd. Don't make them—"

"Shut up, Jamie. Remember, I'm calling the shots here. Now scoot."

She looked toward her mom and Cassie, silently begging them to understand. She didn't want to abandon them, but what could she do? Todd was bigger and stronger, and he had a gun.

He put his hand on her neck, pressing so hard she had trouble breathing. "I told you to go upstairs," he said. "Now do it!"

"Go on," her mother said in a voice that was thin and tightly strung. "Do what he says. We'll be fine."

Jamie moved toward the loft ladder. If only she could figure out what to do.

CHAPTER 53

The sun was coming up when Gordon saw the first road sign for Trout Creek, thirty miles ahead. He'd raced to make his flight last night, dozed fitfully on the plane, and arrived in San Francisco a little after midnight. He'd gone straight to the rental car agency and had been driving for nearly five hours. Although exhausted, he hadn't wanted to waste a minute's time.

He was drained physically and his mind felt worn thin with worry. Why wasn't Marta answering her phone? She wouldn't ignore his calls, no matter how angry she might be. And Cassie wasn't answering her phone, either. He could think of no explanation that wasn't troubling as hell.

And what about Jamie? Had they managed to find her? If they had, Marta would have called. But what if Todd had found Marta first?

Gordon felt as though his heart was being squeezed by an iron claw. He couldn't lose them. His wife and his daughter were his whole world. He made deals with God. *I promise never to take them for granted. I promise to cherish them forever, to devote the rest of my life to being a good husband and father. I promise anything you ask, just let them be safe. Please.*

He saw a gas station and pulled in. He needed coffee and the use of the restroom as much as he needed gas.

When he got back in the car with his large cup of sweetened coffee, his phone rang. His heart leapt. Marta?

But it was Scott Jennings. "I have more information on

327

Winslow, if you're interested."

"Yes, I'm interested. Did you find out where the family cabin is? I'm in California right now."

"Sorry, nothing about the cabin. I did some more digging on Travis and his siblings."

"And?"

"Do you remember I told you Travis was suspected in the murder of a woman?"

"Right." Gordon felt goose bumps rise along his arms.

"Well, he was also questioned in conjunction with a different missing woman."

"But not arrested?"

"No. Same story. Lack of evidence and pressure from the family."

"So he's maybe gotten away with murder twice. And his family covers for him?"

"That's one way of looking at it. Doesn't mean that's what happened, though. Maybe he's innocent.

"It's troubling stuff, but I figured you deserved to know. I'd want to in your shoes."

"Thanks, I appreciate your following up."

"The siblings know about your call to their attorney. For what it's worth, I get the feeling they're fed up with Travis and the trouble he attracts. I think they might be as eager to find him as you are. They don't want a scandal to interrupt their latest business deal, no matter who gets hurt. I thought you should know what you're dealing with."

"I appreciate it."

Gordon's coffee had grown cold. He took a couple of last swallows, dumped the rest, and drove on to Trout Creek. His conversation with Jennings circled through his mind in an endless loop. He needed a plan but couldn't think past finding his wife and daughter, and keeping them safe.

When he reached the turnoff for Trout Creek, Gordon pulled to the side of the road. Marta had mentioned the hotel where she and Cassie were staying. Ponderosa something. He tapped the name into the browser on his cell phone and was rewarded with the full name—Ponderosa Pines—and a detailed map.

The hotel was a long, low building of mountain rustic design with a manager's office in front. The office was empty so he rang the bell on the counter.

A man with thick gray hair and a ruddy face appeared from the back room, pulling on a sweater as he approached.

"Check-in time isn't until three," he said, somewhat irritably.

"I'm looking for my wife. She and her sister were staying here. Marta Crawford and Cassie Reynolds. I can't reach them and I'm worried."

"Your daughter is missing, right?" His tone softened. "I can understand why you're worried."

Gordon saw the flyer with Jamie's photo on the wall. "I see you've got one of my wife's flyers. I've been calling her, but she doesn't answer."

"We got spotty reception around here, but let's take a look at her room." He rooted around in a drawer, then looked up. "I suppose I should ask for some I.D. first."

Gordon pulled out his driver's license and credit card.

Harry took a cursory look, then led the way to the second floor and knocked on the door.

Gordon pulled out his phone and called. Nothing rang from inside the room. "Can you open the door?"

Inside, the beds were made up, suitcases laid out open. He checked the towels. "I don't think they slept here last night," he said. "When did you last see them?"

"Yesterday morning. They were heading out."

Yesterday morning. *Twenty-four hours ago!* "Do you recognize the name Winslow?"

329

"No. Your wife asked me that, too."

"Any idea who would?"

"Best bet is to ask around town. I think that's what your wife was going to do."

As Gordon returned to his car, he remembered showing Harry his credit card. Why hadn't he thought of that earlier? He pulled out his phone, logged into the bank, and checked the credit card statement. Marta's last charge was The Hungry Coyote Saloon. He typed the name into his browser and was again rewarded with an address and a map. Gordon had never had much use for cell phones, but now he was a true believer.

The Hungry Coyote Saloon was open, even though it wasn't yet ten in the morning. There were already two patrons seated at the bar, enjoying scrambled eggs, bacon, and beer.

"I'm looking for my wife and her sister," Gordon told the man behind the bar. "They were here last night."

The man raised an eyebrow. "I try to stay clear of domestic spats."

Gordon pointed to the flyer of Jamie near the cash register. "We're looking for my missing daughter. That's her. Now I can't find my wife and her sister."

The man's face softened. "Yeah, they were here asking about a cabin owned by the Winslow family."

"Do you know where it is?"

"I don't. But Maggie Hendrix thought she might. Said it was out by Porcupine Ridge."

Chapter 54

Jamie tugged at the covers, pulling them up to her chin. Todd was still asleep, but she hadn't slept at all. There were no windows in the loft, so she had trouble judging the time, but it was clearly morning. The birds were chirping, and she could see the far wall below.

All she could think about was her mom and Cassie in the cellar. Jamie knew how dark and dank it was, and they didn't even have a flashlight. Or a blanket. She'd gotten up once during the night when she thought Todd was sound asleep, but he'd heard her before she'd moved half a dozen steps from the bed.

"Don't even think about it, Jamie," he said. "Come back to bed where you belong."

Again, she pleaded with him to let them go. "They love me," she said. "They just wanted to know I'm okay."

"It was your phone call that caused this. It's your fault that they are where they are."

Thank God he hadn't touched her last night. How had she ever thought she loved him? It made her sick remembering the way she'd acted, the things they'd done.

If she could play along, pretend she didn't hate him, pretend nothing had changed, maybe she'd find a way to make things right.

Finally, she couldn't lie still another minute. Todd was breathing evenly, not moving. It was light enough to see. If she was careful, she might be able to make it downstairs before he woke.

She eased away from him toward the edge of the bed, careful not to disturb the part of the sheet and blanket covering him. The bed squeaked and she held her breath, but Todd didn't stir. She got one leg over the side and was slowly lowering the other when he rolled to face her and grabbed her wrist.

"Where do you think you're going?"

"It's morning," she said. "I was going to start breakfast." She'd never risen first. It was Todd who got up early, not her.

"Don't lie to me, Jamie. I don't like that."

"I'm not lying."

"I need to know that you're with me, not fighting me. Is that understood?"

She nodded.

"Good. Now get back into bed."

She lay there, eyes on the ceiling, still as stone, willing him not to reach for her.

"My little Jamie," he murmured. He rolled onto his side and began running his fingers through her hair, smoothing the loose strands on the pillow. "What am I going to do with you?"

"I don't understand what it is you want," she whimpered, thinking how she'd once craved his caresses. Now she found them repugnant.

"No, you wouldn't."

He continued petting her until she thought she might scream. Then he got out of bed as if nothing had changed.

"Let's get the day started," he said in a cheerful voice.

"What are you going to do?"

"Not sure yet. I'm working on a plan."

Todd made coffee while Jamie scrambled eggs. Her stomach turned at the thought of food, but until she could think what to do, she was going to play along. Her gaze drifted to the hatch door that led to the cellar.

"Shouldn't we give them something to eat?"

Todd laughed. "Why?"

"They must be hungry, and cold. We should at least give them some water."

"I'm sorry if I seem harsh," Todd said, "but this is serious. You understand, don't you?"

She didn't, but nothing good would come of saying so. She nodded.

"They shouldn't have come here," he said. "They should have known better."

"Please, Todd, please check on them. It's been all night."

He set the kettle down so hard the water spilled. He stomped to the hatch, opened it, and called, "Come on up. One at a time. Marta, you first."

Jamie was relieved to hear movement. At least they hadn't frozen to death.

Her mom emerged through the hatch first, and Jamie had to bite her lip to keep from crying out. Her mom looked limp and broken. Her arms were scratched and dirty, her skin almost blue with cold. She glanced at Jamie and tried to smile.

Jamie wanted to wrap her arms around her mother but Todd stood in the way.

He yanked her mom into the room and tied her hands together. "You next, Cassie."

Her aunt, too, looked bedraggled and frightened as Todd tied her hands. Anguish tore at Jamie's heart. It was all her fault. How could she have been so blind?

"Morning, ladies," he said. "Jamie here was worried you might not be enjoying yourselves. I'm afraid we don't have enough breakfast to go around, but she thought you might like a little water."

Jamie locked eyes with her shivering mom. *I'm so sorry. I'm trying to help, I just don't know how.* She hoped her mom could read her mind.

CHAPTER 55

Marta was frozen to the core. Her muscles were tight, her feet and fingers numb. Last night had been the worst experience of her life. Frigid temperature, a sour stench, the night so thick and dark that she and Cassie had held onto each other to keep from getting separated. But worse than the impenetrable blackness and the freezing cold was the endless reel of images running through her head. She'd shaken with fear as much as from lack of warmth.

Now, looking into her daughter's eyes, she tried to hide her despair. Tried to sense what Jamie was thinking. She wanted to protect her, but how?

All through the sleepless night, she and Cassie had tried to come up with a plan. Or rather Marta had tried while Cassie sobbed and apologized and cursed her own foolishness.

"I'm so sorry, Marta. If we get out of this alive, I'm going to be the best sister you can imagine. I'm going to make it up to you, I promise."

"If we're going to get free, we have to think," Marta told her. "We aren't exactly playing from a position of power."

But Marta's mind was as empty of ideas now as it had been last night.

Todd nodded to Jamie. "Get them a glass of water. One glass. They can take turns drinking from it. No point dirtying more dishes than necessary."

Jamie filled the glass from the faucet and handed it to Marta.

The soft warmth of her daughter's hand on her own brought tears to Marta's eyes. She blinked them away, took a few sips, then handed the glass back, again brushing Jamie's hand, desperate for more contact.

Jamie offered the glass to Cassie.

Marta looked Todd in the eye. "Let's stop this," she pleaded. "You've made your point. You wanted to hurt me, and you have. There's no need to hurt the others, too. Let them go."

"You're so cute when you're being earnest, Marta. You ought to try it more often."

Marta wanted to spit in his face.

Cassie stood tall and raised her voice. "What the hell are you up to, *Travis*?"

Jamie frowned. "Travis?"

"That's his real name," Cassie said. "He told me it was Ted. He was Todd to you and your mom. Tim, to her business partner, Carol. He's a liar and a phony. He gets off on manipulating people."

"That's like the kettle calling the pot black," Todd shot back. "Does your sister know you set her up?"

Marta stepped closer to Cassie. "She told me. I know all about it."

Jamie looked confused. "Set her up? How?"

"Your aunt bet me I couldn't get in your mom's pants." Todd grinned. "I won."

Marta cringed with humiliation and looked away.

"You told me it was the other way around," Jamie exclaimed. "That she seduced you."

Todd chuckled. "Relationships are complicated, sweetheart."

Marta pulled at her wrists, twisting to free her hands. The twine was tight, the knots secure. She wanted to claw his eyes out.

"None of that matters now," he said, pulling Jamie to his

side. "Your mom was a game, yes. But when I met you, my heart was lost. I've never fallen for anyone like I fell for you. You're my little princess."

"Don't listen to his lies!" Marta shouted. "He's using you."

"And he's dangerous," Cassie added. "He killed Carol."

"What? Carol's dead?" Pulling away, Jamie looked at Marta in horror. "Is she really?"

"I'm afraid so. A hit and run." Marta had worried Jamie was complicit in Carol's death, but seeing her daughter's surprised reaction reassured her.

Todd looked amused. "Why would I want to hurt Carol?"

"She knew about you," Marta said. "She called me that night before she died and left me a message."

"You can't prove it was me."

"The cops might be able to."

"I was with Jamie that night."

"How do you know what night she was killed?"

"Just guessing," he said with a smirk. "I've been spending a lot of time with your daughter."

"It was the night you left home," Marta told Jamie.

Jamie shook her head. "He wasn't with me very long. He picked me up and then dropped me off at a motel. Left me there all night. Alone." Turning to Todd, she said, "Is that where you went? You left me to go kill Carol?"

Todd spread his hands. "Enough! I didn't mean for her to die. I just wanted to shut her up."

"Shut her up about what?"

"Everything. She was pissed that the partnership wasn't going to get some hotshot new client I'd told her about. She went crazy." Todd was pacing around the small kitchen area. He kicked the counter with his foot, picked up the water glass, and tossed it across the room. "She threatened to go to my saintly stepbrother and stepsister, the anointed ones. And to AG

National. She would have killed the deal. So I told her to meet me, and we'd talk."

So Gordon had been right, Marta thought. She hated herself for doubting him, and was sick with the thought that their testy conversation might be the last he heard from her.

Jamie had moved toward the stove, out of Todd's immediate reach. "What deal?"

"The bank deal," Todd explained. "My family owns a bank. My stepbrother and stepsister run it and I get treated like shit. They're always on my case, constantly criticizing me. The bank is in trouble, though. There's a deal in the works to merge with a bigger bank. Without the deal, we'll go under."

"So you killed her?"

Todd's eyes blazed, his face flush with indignation. "I told you, it was a goddamn accident. I insisted she meet me in the parking lot of a mall and we'd work something out. We argued and she fell. I just wanted out of there. She ran in front of my car trying to stop me."

Marta's stomach knotted. She didn't trust Todd's version of events. Abruptly, Todd stopped pacing. He opened the cupboard under the sink and pulled out a gas can. Then he turned to Jamie.

"If the deal goes through, I'm set for life, Jamie. We'll live like kings. We can go to Hawaii like we planned. I have to keep things from blowing up until then."

Marta eyed the gas can with a growing sense of horror.

Todd smiled at Jamie. "You still love me, don't you?"

Jamie gave her a pleading look, and Marta thought her heart might break. Jamie didn't love Todd. But she was scared.

"She must be overwhelmed and confused," Marta offered by way of cover. "She's had a lot to take in."

"You better decide fast," Todd said, uncapping the can. "Your choice. You can come with me or you can stay and burn."

Jamie looked stricken. "What are you going to do?"

He moved toward the cellar door. "Have you made up your mind?"

In one swift movement, Jamie picked up the skillet and swung at him, sending scrambled eggs flying. Marta could see mid-swing that she'd miss her mark. She'd hit Todd's arm, but not hard enough to do any real damage. The veins in his neck stood out in livid ridges. He grabbed her wrist and twisted her arm behind her back, forcing her to her knees.

"That was a foolish move, Jamie."

"You can't do this!" She struggled to stand. "Please!"

He yanked Jamie to her feet, then pulled a handgun from his pocket and nodded at the cellar door. "Okay, all of you, over there."

Cassie rushed toward Todd, swinging her bound arms wildly and screaming at the top of her lungs.

"Run!" she yelled. "Go!"

Marta pushed Jamie toward the door. "Get going. Make a run for it."

Cassie tackled Todd, knocking him off his feet. The gun went off and they fell together, landing in a heap on the floor.

Todd rolled away and slowly got to his feet. Blood began to pool around Cassie's motionless body.

Marta nudged Jamie. "Come on, we have to get out of here."

"We can't leave her there!" Jamie cried.

"Just go. We have to find help."

They barely made it through the doorway before Todd caught up with them. The gun was in his hand again. "Back inside," he ordered.

"How can you do this?" Jamie wailed. "You said you loved me."

"Don't believe everything you hear." Todd's voice was like ice. "You're nothing but a dumb, fat kid." He slammed Jamie in the head with the butt of his gun. She crumpled to the floor and didn't move.

"Jamie!" Marta moved toward her, but Todd stepped forward and touched her chin.

"Well, Marta, it's you and me again."

CHAPTER 56

Gordon drove in a race against time. He pushed the rental car as fast as he dared, weighing speed against the likelihood of a broken axle or bent rim. His heart pounded, fueled by caffeine, sugar, lack of sleep, and especially fear.

He had no illusions. He wasn't an action hero or trained warrior. He was an unassuming, middle-aged academic, and he was in way over his head.

He'd spoken with Maggie Hendrix, who'd given him the same hazy directions she'd given Marta.

"It's been a long time since I was there," she cautioned. "I told your wife the same thing. Might not even be the right cabin."

Gordon understood, but he didn't know where else to look.

He'd called the sheriff, too.

"Hostages, you say?" the dispatcher asked.

"My daughter. Maybe my wife and her sister, as well."

"Your daughter is the runaway from Georgia, right? Someone was here yesterday asking about her. Probably your wife."

That was good to hear. "Can you get someone out there to check on them?" he asked.

"What's the address?"

"I don't have an address. I've got some directions though." He started rattling off what Maggie had told him.

"Sir, we need a more precise location."

"I don't have one." Gordon had thought his head might

explode. "If something happens to my family, do you want to be known as the department that allowed it to happen? I'll make damn sure every news station in the country knows."

There was a beat of silence. "Tell you what, why don't you meet us in front of the general store in Trout Creek? We should have someone there in about an hour."

"An hour? That's too long. I'm heading out to find the cabin right now."

"That's not a good idea. Wait for a deputy to accompany you."

"I can't wait," Gordon had told her. "I'm going. Send someone as soon as you can."

Now, as he bumped along the rutted road, he wondered if he'd been rash. What in God's name was he going to accomplish by himself? Assuming he even managed to locate the cabin.

Then, ahead on the right, he saw the glare of something silver. On closer look, he recognized the bumper of a car. Two cars. Parked near a cabin.

He pulled his car in behind a clump of trees about fifty yards away. How long would it take for a deputy to arrive? Would they even send someone out?

Gordon called again. "I think I found the cabin," he told the dispatcher. "Please, send someone out soon."

"Don't try . . ." A burst of static. ". . . area," she said. The call cut out.

Gordon cursed and hit redial. No coverage.

Area. Did they have someone already in the area? Or maybe they didn't cover this area. He had no idea.

Frustrated, he looked back the way he'd come, hoping to see a sheriff's car approaching. Nothing. No cars, no people, no sounds but the rustle of wind and the chirping of birds.

He couldn't just sit here. What if the sheriff never showed up? He got out of the car for a closer look at the cabin.

Suddenly, two sharp cracks that sounded like gunshots shattered the surrounding stillness. A blue jay squawked and flew into the air with a great rush of wings. A chipmunk, chattering loudly, darted up a tree.

Gordon's heart leapt to his throat. Had the shots come from the cabin?

He ran back to the car for the jack crank. It wasn't much of a weapon and he hoped he wouldn't need it. Then he raced toward the cabin and peered through the dusty window.

Inside, Todd and Marta were facing one another, and Todd was pointing a gun at her. Two bodies lay crumpled on the floor. His insides twisted in a knot when he recognized Cassie's blond head and Jamie's darker one.

God. No.

Gordon's mind froze. What could he do? The iron crank was heavy but it would be useless against a gun.

In a burst of crazed inspiration, an idea came to him. He reached for the key fob in his pocket and hit the alarm. The rental car's horn began blaring loud, staccato blasts.

Breathing hard and fast, he stood near the cabin door, out of sight, and raised the jack crank. Would Todd ignore the sound or come outside to look?

The door squeaked open and Todd emerged, gun in his hand. Gordon swung the crank, catching Todd across the chest and knocking the gun from his grip. Then he swung again and slammed the iron down hard on Todd's skull, knocking him to the ground. He kicked the gun away.

Marta ran outside. "Gordon!" Her expression was a mix of surprise and anguish. "Come quick. Jamie's hurt and Cassie's been shot."

Gordon picked up the gun, holding it gingerly. Todd wasn't moving, but he was breathing. Shoot the bastard like he deserved? Maybe. But he wasn't going anywhere in the next few minutes. Gordon dashed into the cabin with Marta at his heels.

She ripped her sweater off, dropped to her knees and pressed it against Cassie's shoulder. Jamie was holding her head and struggling to sit up.

"Daddy! Oh, Daddy."

Gordon helped her to her feet. "Are you okay? How's your head?" He didn't see any blood but he worried about internal bleeding and a concussion.

"It hurts bad." Jamie clung to him. "Is Cassie alive?"

"She appears to be," Marta said. "But she needs medical attention fast."

Through the window, Gordon saw a sheriff's van approaching.

CHAPTER 57

Two Weeks Later

Seated in the middle of the couch in her own living room, Marta reached for a handful of popcorn, then passed the bowl to Jamie, who was curled up next to her. Gordon was nestled close on her other side. Marta sighed contentedly.

"You need more?" she asked Cassie, who was sprawled out in the recliner with her own bowl of popcorn.

"I'm good."

Marta smiled. "Yes, you are. You're wonderful, in fact."

"Not hardly. But I'm working on it."

"Don't sell yourself short," Gordon said. He'd been coddling all three of them since the rescue. Cassie's self-sacrificing courage in facing down Todd had earned her Gordon's boundless gratitude.

Jamie shushed them. "I want to hear how the movie ends."

Life was slowly returning to normal. They were a family again. A remarkably strong family, Marta thought. Gordon appeared on his way to forgiving her, something she was unable to do, herself. But she was learning to accept what she couldn't change. And Jamie, whom Marta had worried might carry the emotional scars of her ordeal for many years, had slipped into her old life with impressive tenacity. The first few days had been rocky for all of them, Jamie especially. But now, two weeks later, the volcanic swings of emotion were largely in the past.

Cassie was staying with them while she recuperated. She'd

345

been lucky. The bullet missed vital organs, and while it damaged her shoulder, the doctors said that with time and physical therapy, she'd probably come close to regaining full use of it.

The movie ended and Cassie unfurled herself from the recliner. "I'm off to bed," she announced. "I know it's early, but I'm beat."

Jamie gave her a hug. "Goodnight, Aunt Cassie."

"Sleep well," Marta added.

Jamie's cell phone rang—Oliver's special ring. He called almost daily, even though they saw each other at school. He wasn't a boyfriend, Jamie insisted. They were just friends. And that was fine with Marta.

Jamie grabbed the empty bowls and headed for the kitchen.

"I heard from Scott Jennings today," Gordon announced. "It looks like the bank merger will happen, but our friend will get nothing."

"I thought he was one of the principals."

"He was, of Citizen's Choice. But the deal with AG National was structured in a way that shares of Citizen's Choice are valued at almost nothing. Todd's step-siblings will get well-paying jobs and large bonuses, which leaves him out in the cold."

"Not to mention facing time in prison," Marta noted with glee.

"And hefty attorney's fees if he doesn't cut a deal or settle for a public defender."

Todd was currently in Siskiyou County jail, charged with attempted murder for shooting Cassie, and facing extradition to Georgia for Carol's murder. He also faced possible charges for unauthorized entry into the condo in Emeryville, which he'd finagled with a key from one of his many low-life contacts.

"I hope he goes away for a long time," Marta said.

"Me too." Gordon shifted in his seat and cleared his throat.

"I have a confession," he said.

Marta felt a prickle of fear. "I'm not sure I want to hear it."

"Todd had me fooled, too. I didn't listen when you told me to stay away from him. We continued to get together for lunches and stuff. In fact, I was at dinner with him the night Jamie ran away."

"You were there? You knew he was meeting Jamie?"

"Good God, no. He never talked about her at all. But he did get a call as we were finishing our dinner. I now realize it was Jamie's call."

"Why are you telling me this?"

"Because I know you're beating yourself up over what happened. You aren't the only one at fault, Marta. Todd played us all."

"I started it."

"The important thing is that we won and he lost. We scored gold because we care about one another. Todd doesn't care about anyone but himself."

Jamie, with her phone still to her ear, blew them a kiss on her way upstairs. "Love you," she mouthed to them.

"Love you, too," Marta and Gordon replied in unison.

Marta felt a glow. How many parents got that kind of affirmation each night? She knew it wouldn't last, but she was going to savor it as long as she could.

She recognized, too, that there were challenges ahead. She had returned to work but had yet to decide whether to keep the business going without Carol. Although Gordon's paper had been accepted for presentation at the History and Humanities conference, a tenure decision wouldn't come for another year. She knew she'd find reason to be annoyed with Gordon down the road, and he with her, but these were all surmountable bumps in the road of life.

She laid her head on Gordon's shoulder. "I'm the luckiest

woman in the world," she said.

He kissed her cheek. "And I'm the luckiest guy."

ABOUT THE AUTHOR

Jonnie Jacobs is the bestselling author of fourteen mystery and suspense novels. A former practicing attorney and the mother of two grown sons, she lives in northern California with her husband. Email her at jonnie@jonniejacobs.com or visit her on the Web at www.jonniejacobs.com.